"Eliot, I want you to
take over the investigation,"

Mayor Burton said. "I want you to turn your desk over to your executive assistant and make the Mad Butcher of Kingsbury Run your top personal priority."

Ness grinned. "I have no problem with that."

"Eliot—it's not that simple. We would put you and your reputation on the line. The man who got Capone sets out to become the man who gets the Butcher. That sort of thing. If you'd like to decline, I'll understand. . . ."

"I'll tell you what I'd like," Ness said, and his grin was gone. "I'd like to stop the killing. I'd like to stop fishing arms and legs out of rivers, to stop finding the remains of human beings scattered like so many cuts of beef across the godforsaken landscape of the Run. I'd like to put that evil bastard, whoever he is, in the electric chair."

Burton laughed shortly. "When would you like to start trying?"

"I already have," Ness said.

BUTCHER'S DOZEN

an Eliot Ness novel

Max Allan Collins

BANTAM BOOKS

TORONTO • NEW YORK • LONDON • SYDNEY • AUCKLAND

This is a novel based upon events in the life of Eliot Ness. Although the historical incidents in this novel are portrayed more or less accurately (as much as the passage of time, and contradictory source material, will allow), fact, speculation, and fiction are freely mixed here; historical personages exist side by side with composite characters and wholly fictional ones—all of whom act and speak at the author's whim.

BUTCHER'S DOZEN

A Bantam Book / November 1988

ISBN 0-553-26151-7

Published simultaneously in the United States and Canada

Bantam Books are published by Bantam Books, a division of Bantam Doubleday Dell Publishing Group, Inc. Its trademark, consisting of the words "Bantam Books" and the portrayal of a rooster, is Registered in U.S. Patent and Trademark Office and in other countries. Marca Registrada, Bantam Books, 666 Fifth Avenue, New York, New York 10103.

PRINTED IN THE UNITED STATES OF AMERICA

KR   0 9 8 7 6 5 4 3 2 1

*This is for my friend
Michael Seidman,
who had nothing to do with it*

*"Just a jackknife has Macheath, dear—
and he keeps it out of sight."*

Marc Blitzstein translating Bertolt
The Threepenny Opera

PROLOGUE
September 23, 1935

1

If the face of Cleveland had been cut by a knife, Kingsbury Run would have been the scar. A rank, sooty gulley just southeast of downtown, the Run was barren but for brown patches of weeds and brush and the occasional rusting tin can or broken bottle. And, of course, rails and switches and motionless freight cars, as here was where the city's trains made their escape to the suburbs and beyond, to Youngstown and Pittsburg and points east.

While commuters were carried home by rapid transit lines to the comfort of tree-shaded streets and landscaped lawns and ritzy residences, less affluent, nonpaying passengers also traveled by rail to and from this dirty, desolate ravine, bordered by the prisonlike walls of factories and warehouses. Whether hobos by choice or circumstance, the men in tattered clothing who walked through this vale of tears were constantly reminded of who they were (and weren't) and what they had (and had not) by the industry that surrounded the Run, the same industry that had created wealth for some and livelihoods for others and ugliness for everyone.

The air in the bone-dry creek bed that was the Run was an affront to eyes and nose alike; beneath the dried-up bed, water still flowed, diverted underneath into sewers, surfacing as a foul, stagnant pool atop the channel flowing into the Cuyahoga River. Nearby, near the train tracks, scattered about the hillside, was the shantytown where so many of the nameless, out-of-work men had made a pathetic home on a stench-fouled stretch of real estate no one could begrudge them.

On this chilly fall afternoon, darting through brownish-gray weeds and scrub brush that clung to the craggy earth like clumps of hair stubbornly gripping a balding scalp, two boys from a nearby low-income neighborhood were using the Run as a playground. Prospecting for treasure amongst the refuse, running back and forth across the railroad tracks, plucking the occasional incongruous sunflower, the boys in their aimless adventuring led themselves to the rubble-strewn sixty-foot promontory known as Jackass Hill.

Jimmy, laughing, charged down the steep, weedy hill, knowing the younger boy couldn't catch him. The boys were not brothers, but each was wearing his own brother's threadbare clothes. They'd been playing tag, fifteen-year-old James Waggner and thirteen-year-old Peter Kester, and Jimmy, small for his age, was enjoying the natural superiority of being the oldest. Scrambling, stumbling, Jimmy careened into a bush at the foot of the hill and, twisting as he fell, found himself suddenly sitting down. The bush had cushioned him, but his pride was wounded. Above him, hands on hips, atop Jackass Hill, Petey was laughing.

"Nice play, Shakespeare!" the kid called. Jimmy felt his face burn and he began to push himself up.

But his hand settled on something cold; at first he thought it was a tree limb, but his eyes told him it was another sort of limb altogether.

Jimmy shot to his feet; his heart was pounding; he tried to swallow.

Two legs extended from under the thicket. Their flesh was white, very white, above black shoes. The brush overtook the legs just above the knees, but everything you could see of this guy (and it seemed to Jimmy to be a man) was bare.

"Petey, get down here!"

"What is it? Ya tear your trousers or somethin'?"

"Get *down* here, I said!"

The younger boy made a face, then came scuffing down the hillside.

"What's the big deal, anyway?"

"That," Jimmy said, and pointed.

"What is it?" The boy was backing up; he stood somewhat behind Jimmy, peeking around.

"I think it's a dead guy," Jimmy said. "I'm takin' a closer look."

"Yeah. Good idea." But Petey stayed put, while Jimmy moved forward.

"Maybe he's just sleeping," Petey offered.

"Mister!" Jimmy said as he began brushing the branches of the bush aside. "Mister, wake—"

But he didn't bother finishing his suggestion.

He was looking at the rest of the man with the black socks—or anyway, as much of him as there was to look at.

Stepping back as if he'd been burned, the branches snapping back, Jimmy swallowed thickly, his mouth dry, eyes popping.

"What's *wrong*, Jimmy?"

"He ain't got no head," Jimmy said.

"What?"

Jimmy swallowed again. "And that ain't all."

"Huh?"

"He ain't got no thing, either."

"No thing?"

"No dick."

"No dick?"

"No dick."

The younger boy touched his groin and grimaced. "I'm not gonna look."

"You better not," Jimmy agreed. "You might puke or something."

"Y-you didn't."

"I'm older."

"Maybe . . . maybe I will look."

"Don't."

Petey thought about it. Still planted in the same spot, he said, "You think somebody cut the guy's head off?"

Jimmy nodded. "And his dick."

"Is there blood all over?"

"I don't see any."

"I—I wonder where they are."

"Who?"

"Not *who*, stupid . . . where *they* are—his head and his thing."

"Well, *I'm* not looking for 'em."

"Me either," Petey said, shivering. "We oughta do something. We oughta get help."

"I don't think anything's gonna help that guy."

"We better find somebody and tell them."

Jimmy agreed, and skirting the hill, they trudged up the incline at the edge of the Run, which was as steep as Jackass Hill itself, glancing behind them as they went, as if the corpse might get up and follow.

Panting, they stopped at the run-down frame building on the corner of Forty-ninth and Praha; a man was sitting on the wooden steps in front of the sagging gray rooming house. He was a big almost-handsome blond man in a red and black plaid shirt and gray pants, clothing that was not at all fancy, but neither did it have the frayed, ill-fitting look of what the two boys were wearing. The man seemed to Jimmy to be almost as pale as the headless, thingless corpse.

"Where's the fire, fellas?" the man asked pleasantly; his teeth were very white in a wide smile; his light blue eyes seemed to smile, too.

"There's a guy down there," Jimmy said.

"And he doesn't have no thing," Petey said.

"Really," the man said. He rose, smiled, stretched, as if awaking from a nap. "Well, why don't I call somebody for you, then?"

"Would you, mister?" Jimmy asked. He looked toward the ramshackle house. "They got a phone in there?"

"Sure," the man said. He patted the boy on the shoulder. "I'll call the railroad dicks."

Petey winced at the word "dicks."

"Now," the man said, smiling back at them as he climbed the rickety steps, "why don't you go on back and stand guard, till help comes?"

Jimmy looked at Petey.

Petey looked at Jimmy.

"Do we got to, mister?" Jimmy asked.

"Yes," the man said. He smiled like something was funny, but his voice was somber: "It's your civic duty."

And the boys went back to the Run. They stood at the edge of Jackass Hill, looking mutely toward the black socks extending from the brown bushes.

Hardly fifteen minutes had gone by when two railroad detectives arrived, and within half an hour sirens announced the arrival of Cleveland city cops—several uniformed men and a pair of detectives.

The uniformed men stayed up at the top of the incline, keeping sightseers away. The pair of detectives descended; neither man wore a topcoat, but it was cold enough for their breaths to smoke.

One of the detectives looked so young he might have been the other detective's son; his name was Albert Curry, and he was a pasty-faced, cherubic man of twenty-seven who looked twenty. The man he was following down the step incline into the ravine was Martin Merlo, a tall, thin, serious-looking individual with glasses. He might have been a school teacher. He was, instead, one of the best homicide detectives in the bureau—partnered, at his own request, with Curry, the city's youngest detective.

Curry, whose first assignment was to partner with Merlo, and who this late Monday afternoon was going out on a murder case for the first time, had no idea why the older, well-respected cop had requested him. But he was not complaining; he felt lucky to be here.

Lucky, that is, until he saw the man with no head and black socks.

"Judas priest," Curry said, and he turned away and threw up in a nearby bush.

Merlo came over and put his hand on Curry's shoulder as the younger cop bent forward, hands on his knees, staring whitely at what had been in his stomach.

"I'm okay, Detective Merlo," Curry said.

"Try not to puke on any body parts," Merlo said, not unkindly, slapping him on the back.

Merlo, notepad in hand, pearl-gray fedora tilted back on his head exposing his professorial brow, began questioning the two boys. The two railroad dicks, a middle-aged stocky guy and a slim guy about thirty, both in rumpled brown suits, got them dirty by kneeling in sandy earth perhaps twenty feet from the bush under which the corpse lay. They began digging with their hands, as if rooting for truffles.

Curry, feeling dizzy but better, approached them. "What are you men doing?" he asked.

"Looked disturbed here," the stocky one said. He had a face as rumpled as his suit.

"Looked disturbed?" Curry asked.

"The ground," said the slim one. "I think something's buried here . . . hell-oh!"

And he withdrew from the ground his harvest: a human head, which he grasped by its long dark hair. The eyes were half-lidded, staring at Curry blankly, out of a round, jug-eared face.

Curry didn't feel so good.

But he'd be all right; Christ knew there was nothing left in his stomach to puke up.

"Bingo," the stocky one said, and withdrew his hand from the sand and held up his palm; in it was what might have been a turnip but was in fact a severed human penis.

And Curry stumbled back to his bush and found that something had remained in his stomach, after all.

Merlo was in the process of dismissing the young boys; they had been helpful, but (Merlo told Curry, as the latter stumbled over, wiping his mouth) rounding up these body parts was nothing a kid should see. Curry couldn't have agreed more.

Meanwhile, back at the corpse, the railroad dicks were trying to put the puzzle together.

"I tell you it ain't his," the stocky one was saying.

"The dick?" the other dick asked.

"No, you moron. The head. The head belongs to a guy in his late forties, early fifties maybe. Looks like he'd be kinda heavyset. That body is a young guy's body."

Merlo joined them. The head had been placed on the ground above the neck of the corpse. The penis had been placed in the correct general area as well.

"The genitals don't match, either," Merlo said dispassionately. "Torso is white as snow, head and penis have a peculiar discoloration."

"So would yours," said the slim one skeptically, "if somebody hadda whacked 'em off without so much as a howdy-do."

"Yeah, and where's the goddamn blood?" asked the stocky one.

"Not here," Merlo admitted.

Curry approached, tentatively. "Detective Merlo . . . if that head doesn't match the body, doesn't that mean we have two homicides?"

Merlo nodded. He gestured toward nothing in particular. "Scout the area, why don't you. Maybe you'll turn something up."

Curry nodded back and began a reluctant search. Not thirty feet away, under more brush, was the other headless corpse. This oak-colored, stocky, emasculated body seemed a match for the items the railroad dicks had dug up in the sand.

Also under the brush was a dark blue suit coat with a B.R. Baker Company label, and a white shirt and underwear. All three garments were stiff as cardboard in places where they were stained a reddish brown.

"Finally found some blood," Curry told Merlo, handing him the pile of clothes.

"They weren't killed here, then," Merlo said, eyes narrowing. "These look like they belong to the older, heavier guy's clothes; he was killed wearing them, but not here. Both bodies were drained of blood, somewhere else, and in the case of the older man possibly treated with some chemical, God knows why."

"Preservation?"

"Good guess, but why? A murderer should *want* his victim to decompose. Why preserve evidence?"

"Decay attracts attention; preservation might delay the bodies being found."

"Maybe," Merlo shrugged, his expression like that of a math teacher pondering a problem. "But in Kingsbury Run, who'd notice the smell?"

"Sir, how could somebody haul these bodies here without being seen?"

"He may have done it after dark; or maybe he *was* seen. Only who could see him, but some 'bo?"

"Is that who these men are? Were? Hobos?"

Merlo looked in the direction of the shantytown. "It's our job to find out, isn't it?"

About seventy-five feet from the second body was more earth that looked "disturbed." Curry (now wearing gloves) found the second head and the second penis buried there. He had nothing left in his stomach, by this point, and was getting numb to the horror of the afternoon. Dusk was settling in, threatening evening, and the dimness gave less reality to the round head he cupped in his palm. It had a young, curiously innocent face, male but with feminine lips.

"Who's that you have there?" Merlo asked with a thin smile. "Yorick?"

"Who?"

"Never mind. Let's put the puzzle together."

The body parts all matched up now, but at this hour it took flashlights to prove it.

"I'd say the older one was about forty-five," Merlo said to Curry as they stared down at the reconstructed corpse. "About five six. Dark hair. Some decomposition. Killed before the other, I'd say. Coroner will fix that, soon enough."

They walked to the other, younger corpse. Night had overtaken dusk, but the black sky was lit somewhat by the glow of the open-hearth furnaces of the steel mills.

"This poor bastard," said Merlo, flashing the light on the white body, "looks younger than you, Curry."

Curry said, "Flash that on his hands."

Merlo did, one hand at a time.

"See that?" Curry asked, kneeling, pointing to the dead man's wrists.

Merlo nodded. "Rope burns."

Soon the boys from the county morgue were placing the torsos on stretchers and the body parts in separate wicker baskets and began hauling them away. Curry and Merlo watched from a distance, atop the incline of Kingsbury Run, near their parked unmarked car.

"How do you read this, Detective Curry?"

"A madman did this."

"Could be a crime of passion," Merlo suggested. "Love triangle gone awry."

"What, a woman did this?"

Merlo smiled patiently. "No. I think this is a man's work, all right."

Curry thought about that.

Then he asked, "Why am I here, sir?"

"Call me Martin, or Marty. All right, Al?"

"Okay," Curry said, smiling a little. "But why me?"

"Don't you know?" Merlo asked with his own wry smile. "You're a hero."

That embarrassed Curry. He knew what Merlo was referring to: traffic cop Curry had pulled several people, including a small child, from a burning car; he got good press in a city where the cops seldom got good press and was promoted to detective.

"You didn't buy your badge," Merlo said. "That's a rarity in Cleveland, these days. I wanted an honest cop to work with—that meant a new cop, a fresh, young one. An apple that hadn't got spoiled yet."

"Oh," said Curry. He didn't know whether to feel complimented or insulted. "The force is in a bad way, isn't it?"

"There are good people," Merlo said, looking down into the darkness of the Run, "and bad ones, and those in between. We start out good, most of us, and drift into that in-between place. With you at my side, my boy, perhaps I can help us both from drifting all the way to that other place."

They stood silently for a while.

Then Curry blurted: "I believe there *are* evil people in the world."

"Do tell," Merlo said, watching the morgue boys climb the incline with wicker baskets in hand. They might have been carrying their laundry.

"We'll have a new mayor soon," said Curry. "Things may change."

"Don't hold your breath," Merlo said, "unless it's just to keep the smell of the Run out of your nostrils."

In less than three months, the new mayor would appoint Eliot Ness safety director of the city of Cleveland, and the young former T-man would indeed begin cleaning up Cleveland's corrupt department. And both Curry and Merlo would benefit.

But right now, detectives Curry and Merlo were wrapped in the darkness of the night and the Run and the evil that man was so obviously capable of; and the only light in this night was from the steel mills.

Not far away, standing in the darkness of the backyard of a run-down rooming house, a big almost-handsome blond man in a red and black plaid shirt was watching the two detectives and smiling.

ONE
July 1–26, 1937

Searchlights stroked the night sky in alternating shades of red, white, and blue; a blimp glided into their cross fire, hovering above modernistic buildings poised along the lakefront, like the set of some fantastic science-fiction film. Moving beams of light rose from behind the lagoon theater and fanned out, painting the dark clouds with an aurora borealis.

On this cool if humid Saturday evening, wide-eyed visitors wandered a world that seemed quite apart from both Cleveland and the depression that racked it. Just two blocks from Public Square, citizens fleeing reality were greeted by seven seventy-foot pylons whose flat surfaces were rendered red, white, and blue by lighting. Beyond, for fifty cents admission, one could stroll, or take an open-air bus or grab a rickshaw to ride upon, freshly paved lanes through the immaculately landscaped gardens of the sprawling one hundred and fifty acres of the Great Lakes Exposition. Divided by its terrain into an upper and lower level, the expo's gifts to Clevelanders on the occasion of the city's hundredth birthday included starkly modern exhibition halls, where one might experience, via dioramas, models, and wall-size photographs, "The Romance of Iron and Steel"; an "International Village," where sidewalk cafés and shops sold authentic foods, drinks, and curios from forty countries; and a vast midway, where Spook Street, the "Strange as It Seems" museum, and the Midget Circus vied for attention.

It all seemed overly familiar to one patron this muggy evening, and not just because this was the expo's second year. Eliot Ness was a Chicago boy, and the Great Lakes Exposition was, he knew all too well, a rehashing of the even larger Century of Progress back home, in '33 and '34.

Many of the exhibits were the same, and even those that were new to the expo shared the severe, futuristic building designs that marked the World's Fair, though the pastel lighting effects there were replaced by brighter colors here. The Firestone Building again had its "Singing Fountains," colorful cascades of illuminated water with continuous classical music. Even Sally Rand was booked in—at the Streets of the World, a pale imitation of the Chicago fair's Streets of Paris where the famed fan dancer had first feathered her nest.

Not that Ness looked down upon this project. He was a city official, after all—safety director, in charge of both the police and fire departments—and as such, considered the expo a fine idea. It brought in much-needed jobs, even if only for a limited time, pumped in plenty of cash from expo-goers, and provided good publicity for a city too often dismissed as dull.

He had found Cleveland anything but dull. As a prohibition agent in Chicago, first as a Justice Department man and then moving over to Treasury, he'd waged a successful war against the likes of Al Capone and Frank Nitti. Later he'd battled moonshiners as a "revenooer" in the mountains of Kentucky, Tennessee, and Ohio. Cleveland should have been restful by comparison, but what he found in this "dull" city were enough crooked cops, corrupt politicians, and prevailing gangsters to make a Chicago boy feel right at home.

Which was how the World's Fair-like expo should have made him feel, as well, but it didn't. It seemed a ghost town version of the Century of Progress—perhaps because tonight's attendance was so meager. Way down from last year's huge crowds. Well, the Fourth of July was around the corner, he thought; that should be a record-breaking day.

Ness walked the paved midway, passing the "Panthéon de la Guerre," a war exhibit that had been at the fair, heading for "The Front Page," a concession that was new to this expo. Most expo-goers were dressed in casual summer clothes, but Ness wore a gray and black tie and a slash of white handkerchief in the breast pocket of his expensively tailored gray lightweight suit. He was a six-footer and slim, his features boyish, his expression shy, his gray eyes calm.

You would not guess, looking at him, that he was physically powerful, but he was. Despite a certain collegiate look, he had not earned his physique on a playing field, but in the Pullman plant on Chicago's South Side where he worked as a young man. Daily workouts on a handball court and jujitsu training kept him fit now. He didn't smoke. He did drink. Too much, at times, he knew.

He had gone hatless tonight—his only nod to the balmy evening—and as he hesitated before the tent of "The Front Page," he brushed a comma of brown hair back to its temporary place while he studied several sandwich board signs that bore mock newspaper front pages. MAN DIES IN ELECTRIC CHAIR! one headline said; WOMAN HANGED TILL DEAD! said another. The largest of all said: TORSO KILLER DEATH MASKS INSIDE! He bought a ticket at the booth and went in.

Attendance at the expo in general might have been off tonight, but the benches inside this tent were jammed. Ness found a place to sit at the end of one bench and got a funny, "Why the suit, mister?" look from the straw-hatted apparent farmer he sat next to before the lights dimmed.

A velvet curtain parted and revealed, centerstage, an electric chair much like ones Ness had seen in use in prisons. A pale, heavyset man in black, wearing a black string tie, looking like a parson, led a pale, thin fellow in a gray-and-white-striped prison uniform to the chair. The "prisoner" sat in the chair and allowed the parson to place the electrical cap upon his head. The parson then walked to one side of the stage, to an apparatus that included three large switches. Then he threw each switch, to much electrical sparking, much convulsing by the thin fellow in the chair, and much noise from the startled audience. An acrid smell filled the tent. The prisoner slumped in the chair. The velvet curtain closed.

The audience were talking amongst themselves, screams and shouts having given way to nervous laughter, and soon the curtain opened again. An attractive blond woman in a white evening gown stood with an expression as blank as death and a noose dangling nearby, the rope disappearing upward. Her hands were tied before her.

The audience, transfixed, stared at her. The only sound in the room was that of breathing.

The parson walked out on stage slowly, deliberately. He carried a hood. He placed it over her head, her shoulder-length blond hair hanging out from around the bottom of the hood. He placed the noose around her neck. Cinched it tight, behind her left ear.

The pastor stepped to one side. He raised his hand in a signaling fashion; when he brought it down, the blonde plunged suddenly down and out of sight, through a trapdoor. The rope pulled tight. Then it swayed.

The audience was still gasping as the curtains closed.

When they opened again, the pastor was on stage, smiling and gesturing to the thin young prisoner, who smiled and bowed, and the blond woman, who did the same. The audience applauded wildly; some whistled. Some people even stood up.

The lights came on, and the pastor, speaking for the first time, directed the audience into a section of the tent declared to be "The Front Page Museum of Crime." Several display cases held guns and clothing labeled as having belonged to John Dillinger and his associates. A shot-up car, roped off, was labeled the Bonnie and Clyde "Death Car." Another glass case bore three death masks, three male faces, painted rather garishly, as if wearing feminine makeup. Their expressions were placid, strangely innocent, almost angelic. A large sign within the case, behind the frozen faces, said in large black block letters: "Do You Know Us? Any One of Us?" In smaller print, information was given about whom to contact at the Cleveland police department, making mention of the $5,000 reward posted by the city council. Ness smiled to himself as people paused at the display, studying the plaster faces. A uniformed cop—the real thing, not a security guard—was posted near the display case. His eyes narrowed when he saw Ness, and the two men nodded, imperceptibly, at each other.

Behind the display case was a large poster that bore the words "Do You Know This Man?" The poster showed the outline of a body, and superimposed over the chest was a photo of a handsome young man whose eyes were shut and whose longish dark hair seemed unruly. The poster, drawn with a cartoonist's flair, mapped the location of various tattoos—right shoulder: butterfly; outer right arm: heart with piercing arrow; inner right forearm: crossed flags with the initials W.C.G.; inner side of left forearm: names "Helen and Paul" beneath the image of a dove; calf of right leg: anchor and cupid; calf of left leg: "Jiggs" comic strip character. A dotted line at right indicated height: "5 ft. 10 in." The poster was further labeled: "Age—22 to 25 years, dark or olive complexion, very dark brown hair, weight about 150 lbs."

"Hope this does some good, Mr. Ness," a female voice said.

Ness looked over his shoulder. A handsome if somewhat hard-looking brunette woman of about forty, wearing a red blouse and black skirt, was lighting up a cigarette. No one, other than Ness, recognized her as the "blond" hanged on stage.

"I appreciate the effort you're making, Mrs. Castle," Ness said.

She nodded, pulling on the cigarette. "Our biggest draw," she said. "I owe you a vote of thanks, even if I don't end up with a piece of that reward."

"If any of your patrons identify any of the victims, you'll get some reward money, that I guarantee you." Ness glanced at the death mask display, where people lingered in fear and fascination. "A lot of people are filing past those faces. Maybe somebody will recognize one of them."

"I don't know what I'd have done, without you and this 'Mad Butcher' character," Mrs. Castle said, smiling wearily. "You know, I had to fire Dillinger's father last week," she added, pronouncing "Dillinger" with the correct, hard g.

Ness nodded sympathetically. "I noticed you weren't listing him out front anymore."

"Yeah, pasted the Butcher come-on right over his. It's too bad. He's such a nice old gentleman. But people around here just don't seem to be interested, especially not in a town that's got a crazy 'torso killer.' Who wants to hear a nice old guy tell about how he ran a store while his boy John ran around loose and got in with bad company? Mr. Dillinger used to draw just dandy for me, but I guess his public-enemy-number-one son is yesterday's news. Anyway, thank you, Mr. Ness."

"You can thank Sam Wild of the *Plain Dealer*," Ness said. "It was his idea."

He smiled and shook hands with Mrs. Castle, nodded again to the cop on duty by the display, and slipped back out on the midway.

It seemed breezy suddenly, and he tucked his hands in his pockets, checking his watch before he did so. Nearly ten. Time to meet Vivian.

He walked briskly from the midway into the area dominated by the Hall of Progress and other massive modern structures, skirting illuminated fountains and decorative pools and the occasional sculpture of a ship or boat. Much of the expo had a nautical theme—even the lampposts were made to resemble masts; from where he stood, he could see Admiral Byrd's ship, *The City of New York*, moored and lit up like a Christmas tree. Otherwise, Lake Erie, getting choppy, was free of craft.

Just to the west of the lagoon theater, where Vivian had been attending a fashion show, the three-story Horticultural Building rose, a red, blue, and mostly white affair fashioned after the streamlined forward deck of an ocean liner. Ness entered the massive boat of a building at the top of a twenty-five foot incline where two giant pylons framed the entrance.

From the top deck of this landlocked *Titanic*, Ness paused to enjoy the cooling crisp air and the bracing scent of the lake and the panoramic view to the west: a hillside replete with rock gardens, waterfalls, and rare plants, a five-hundred-foot slope of landscaped grass falling to a giant fountain and reflecting pool, and a promenade winding beneath the trees at the edge of Lake Erie. The deck, sparsely populated for a Saturday night, and the impressive view gave Ness a feeling of solitude and calm that he drank in like a thirsty man.

Vivian was sitting at one of the small tables beneath a red umbrella, drinking in the view herself—that, and a Bacardi. She was a slender blond—even seated, she appeared tall, which she was, nearly as tall as Ness. She wore, with casual grace, a light blue blouse and dark blue slacks with a white sweater about her shoulders, the arms tied about her neck, reminding him of the other blond and the noose. He touched her shoulder and she smiled without looking up at him, recognizing his touch.

"How was the fashion show?" he asked.

"Fashionable," she allowed. A smile tickled the corner of an attractive if wide and thin-lipped mouth lipsticked bright red; her teeth were as white as porcelain, her eyes green as jade, her suntan brown as amber.

Vivian Chalmers was a divorcée of thirty with no children and plenty of social pull. Her father was a banker—a solvent one—and she was, as the society pages liked to say, "an all-around sportswoman"—expert trapshooter, golfer, tennis player. She had also been, for well over a year, an active agent of Ness's—unpaid, other than satisfying her sense of adventure—in his ongoing war against the Mayfield Road mob, the gangsters who controlled gambling, prostitution, and the policy racket in these environs.

Ness would call upon her to case various gambling joints he planned to raid; she, as a socialite, could take a fling in any joint she chose without raising any suspicion. He had proposed this alliance in bed, having met her hours before at a country club dance where the both of them got a little drunk. She had accepted the offer of being an undercover agent for him as readily as she had accepted being undercover with him.

"I'm surprised we never got out here last year," she said, meaning the expo. Her voice had an edge to it, a mannishness that somehow took nothing away from the woman she was.

"Well," he said softly, "we weren't being seen together much, were we?"

She looped her arm in his, cuddled, grinned widely. "No. Not you and your undercover agent."

He smiled gently and looked away.

Still, he caught the tightening around her eyes as she said, "It's getting chilly."

"It may rain," he allowed.

"I wasn't talking about the weather."

He looked at her. Jade eyes that were hard and soft at once. Like her.

"It can't go on, Vivian."

"They've *made* me, you mean."

He sighed. "Yes. I'm afraid Patton and Miller and their people do have you made. Your presence in those clubs has been too often followed by my presence. Besides," he said with a shrug, "we have the gambling situation pretty well under control now."

She withdrew her arm. Looked out at the lake. "But we're not just talking about police work, are we?"

He licked his lips. Measured the words. Said, "We can't live together, Viv. Sooner or later it'll catch up with us."

She'd been staying for several months at the Clifton Lagoon boathouse, where Ness lived, though it wasn't his official address. The boathouse was a perquisite of his job.

"Because you're a public figure," she said. "With enemies. Political and otherwise."

"Exactly."

"Bullshit."

He winced. He couldn't get used to a woman talking like that. Her sailor's mouth was something that both excited and repelled him. Like her adventurousness in the bedroom.

"There already have been mentions in the columns," he said, "about moonlight swims and dawn boat rides."

"Hell, you have the press in your pocket," she said bitterly, dismissively. "Sometimes I think you and Sam Wild are sleeping together behind my back."

He glanced to see if anyone else was within earshot. "For God's sake, Viv—"

"I embarrass you. I was fun for a while, but I'm not exactly the prospective next Mrs. Eliot Ness, am I? You don't think I'm up to the job."

Was there a quaver in that strong voice? he wondered.

"I asked you to marry me," he said gently. "You said no."

"Why . . . why don't you ask me again?"

"Would the answer change?"

"It might."

He took some of the gentleness out of his tone. "I want children, Viv. I want a very conventional wife, a very conventional life. I'm not very imaginative, I'm not very adventurous, when it comes to my private life."

"I know." She smiled a little, shaking her head, looking out at the choppy lake. "You save your imagination and your goddamn adventurousness for your job. You save almost everything you have for your job."

"That's who I am," he said unapologetically.

She leaned forward, touched his hand, which was resting on the white metal table, and said, "Don't you see it, you sap? I'm right for you. You're going places, and I can help you get there. You love the social life, don't try to kid me. And with me at your side, you're going to climb all the faster. You can fly right to the top of the social register."

"That's something you can give me, Viv. And that's fine, far as it goes. But it's not as important to me as you think."

"What *is*?"

He spelled it out for her: "Making my next marriage work. Making sure . . . nobody get hurts this time."

A waiter dressed like a ship steward came and took Ness's order and departed. Ness studied the reflection of the overcast sky on the restless lake surface while Vivian studied him with sympathetic eyes.

"Eliot," she said finally, tentatively. "I know the divorce hurt you, but these things happen. And I don't mean to be unkind, but don't you see that Eva was exactly the kind of conventional wife you say you need?"

He shook his head. "It wasn't Eva's fault it didn't work out. She just . . . couldn't take the pressure."

"That's just it—the little woman in the little house behind the white picket fence . . . that kind of woman isn't cut out for being married to somebody who lives as recklessly as you."

The ship's-steward waiter arrived with Ness's drink, a double Scotch, straight up. Ness sipped it. Then he spoke without looking at her.

"I want kids, Viv."

She squeezed his hand. "We could have that. Someday. I . . . I don't rule it out . . ."

Now he looked at her. "We're in our thirties. And I

have no desire to be Grandpa Daddy to my sons and daughters. I want to live long enough to see them graduate college."

"You sure as hell have it all planned out," she said, thin upper lip curling, eyes wide in wary contemplation of these as yet unborn sons and daughters. "Like another raid on another goddamn nightclub."

"I just don't want us to live together, Viv. It doesn't feel right."

"You mean it doesn't look right."

He ignored that. "We can still see each other. I'd like that."

"That's swell of ya."

"We could take it a little slower, pursue a different tack than the one we've taken . . ."

"Our fling is flung, is that it?"

"Viv . . . I still love you. And on the right terms . . ."

"Your terms."

"They'd have to be *our* terms. We'd both have to agree to them."

Her nostrils flared as she withdrew her hand from his. "What is this, a salary negotiation? Don't pull your executive horseshit on me. What's *really* bothering you, anyway? You haven't been sleeping worth a damn, not for weeks."

He shrugged that off and looked out at the lake. Choppier. Even choppier.

"It's that fucking Butcher, isn't it?" she said through her teeth, her lips as thin and red as a razor's stroke.

"Please don't talk that way. It bothers me."

"Like those sick photos you been studying bother you. You don't like to admit it, do you, Eliot? That something can get to you. You like to think of yourself as an executive . . . a young go-getter who fresh out of college chose law enforcement because it seemed a good career opportunity. A wide-open field for somebody ambitious. Which is you all over."

"What's wrong with that?" he snapped.

"Well, you're only fooling yourself. If professionalism and career is everything to you, why don't you stay behind your desk and *be* an executive? Why do you insist on going out in the field to investigate, to kick doors down, to play cops and robbers?"

"You tell me."

"Because, first of all, you really do care. You really do believe in right and wrong, good and evil, you poor silly bastard."

"And what's second?"

"That's easy: you *like* it. You get your kicks that way. Literally, when it comes to doors."

He lowered his head, smiled a little. She had a knack, didn't she? A knack for seeing through him. A knack for knowing him better than he knew himself. A knack for being right.

She sat up, looked at him sharply. "Wait a minute. I *know* why you want me to move out."

He began shaking his head no, even before she continued.

"You've been studying those files—studying those sick pictures—reading all that horrible 'Mad Butcher' material . . . you're going to ask the mayor to give you the goddamned case!"

How did she do it?

Carefully he said, "Maybe I am going to be involved in something that . . . might make it dangerous for you to be around. Something that's going to require all my concentration . . . no distractions—"

"I'm a distraction now! It is the Butcher, isn't it?"

He sat forward, found himself almost pleading with her. "Viv, look. These killings have been going on for *years*. Just a month ago we had number nine, for God's sake. Somebody's got to do something."

"You."

"It's ultimately my responsibility, after all. I'm in charge of the police department."

"You're in charge of the fire department, too, but that doesn't mean you ought to go around pissing out every fire in town."

"Viv, please . . ."

"I don't know whether to kiss you or toss you into the lake. You're protecting me, aren't you? You don't want me endangered, isn't that it?"

That was part of it. Part of it, too, however, was that he really was intimidated by her. By her strength of character, by the sexual dynamo she became between the sheets.

And after weeks of studying the Butcher files—with their descriptions of emasculation and sexual assaults upon dead, headless bodies—sex, particularly sex that in any way deviated from the missionary-position norm, made him feel . . . funny.

But he didn't say that to her. He said only: "I have to do this. And I can't have you living with me while I'm taking an active role."

"You dumb sap. It's the most dangerous case in the history of the goddamn world."

"No, it isn't. He kills transients, this madman. He won't kill me."

She shook her head, smiling tragically. "A man who wants a conventional life with a wife and kiddies. Who wants to play it safe, he says, as he prepares to go toe-to-toe with the Mad Butcher of Kingsbury Run."

He shrugged. "It's my job."

"Oh, please! Spare me the Gary Cooper baloney! What does Matowitz say?"

"I haven't discussed it with the chief."

"What about Burton?"

"I haven't discussed it with His Honor, either."

"Do you really think he'll approve?"

"I don't know," he said honestly. He was thinking about threatening to resign if Burton vetoed his wish to tackle the Butcher case personally; but he was afraid he valued his job too much to risk it.

"Shit!" she said.

He was about to scold her once more for her language when he realized fat raindrops were plopping down just beyond their umbrella, splashing on them.

"We better get inside," he said, and took her arm and they rushed into the building. They watched the storm on the lake from a glass wall within the landlocked ship, waiting for it to subside so they could make their way to the car. But it finally became apparent the rain would not let up. They had to go out in it. They got very wet.

Rain beat on the roof of the boathouse as they made

love through the night, not talking at all. It was still raining in the morning as Vivian packed her bags.

And in the coming days the rains continued, providing a damp Fourth of July for Cleveland and terrible attendance at the expo. The storms seemed as unrelenting as the Butcher himself. The heavy rains washed foliage and garbage and various other objects from the land into the Cuyahoga, and on the morning of the following Friday, the tender on the Third Street Bridge saw something floating on the oily river surface. The tender, John Haggerty, thought at first it was a dressmaker's form, or a corset dummy like he'd seen in stores.

Then whatever it was took a roll in the current and Haggerty could see that it was a section of a human body—the lower half of a man's torso.

Pretty soon a leg floated by, and Haggerety called the cops.

3

The ride from City Hall began on Lakeside Avenue, then moved quickly to West Third, which jogged through the respectable heart of the city, turned into a hill, and fell to the Flats, where West Third leveled out, as did the respectability. The sleek black limo glided like an apparition of affluence through the shabby assembly of warehouses and saloons in the Flats, the bottomland area that was home to the crazily winding Cuyahoga River and the steel mills and factories that crouched there.

Faded brick buildings gave way to an open, overgrown field, alongside of which the limo pulled up. The uniformed police driver got out and was about to open the door for his passenger, but, as usual, that passenger beat him to it.

Mayor Harold Burton did things for himself.

He was a powerfully built, fifty-year-old, wedge-shaped man of medium height whose broad brow, this sunny Monday morning, was creased in concern, his gray eyes half-circled with sleeplessness as he stood and contemplated the gray shimmer of the Cuyahoga, visible beyond the field. Beyond the river, beyond the industrial valley, fifty-two-story Terminal Tower loomed like a reminder of pre-Depression optimism. With a tight smile and a hand gesture, he indicated to his police driver to stay with the car. Then he started toward the river.

Burton wore a light brown suit, rather rumpled, and a battered gray hat; his wardrobe looked not remotely mayoral, with the possible exception of his dark brown tie and the gold stickpin, the latter presented him by the American Legion. He crossed the field quickly, the earth giving under his feet, still damp from the several days of rain that had let up just before dawn. The land here managed to look predominantly brown, despite patches of green weeds and wildflowers. The sun beat down harshly, though Burton—who had once done both farm work and lumberjacking—did not mind it, in fact barely noticed it. His feet crunched the gravel and glass around the railroad tracks, which he stepped over, beginning down the very gentle incline toward the river's edge, where four men stood around a wicker basket.

One of the men was a middle-aged fellow in overalls and an engineer's cap; another was a young uniformed police officer. The other two, wearing suits and ties, might have been businessmen. Burton recognized one of them as Detective Albert Curry, who despite his youthful looks was ranked among the best investigators on the department and had for almost a year now been attached to the safety director's office.

The other man, a deceptively mild-looking individual in a smartly cut, dark gray suit and a blue and gray tie, was the director of public safety himself, Eliot Ness. Burton owed this man much—which, at the moment, made the mayor feel uneasy, even guilty, about the job ahead.

Working his way through the brush and the garbage-littered shore, Burton approached Ness, and the two men exchanged tight smiles and shook hands with a certain ceremony. Curry, nervous in the mayor's presence, smiled a little when Burton offered a hand to shake.

"Sorry I had to cancel our appointment," Ness said to the mayor. "But this came up . . ."

"Think nothing of it," Burton said, waving it off.

In the midst of the small gathering of men, like a fire they might warm their hands at, was a wicker basket; in the basket was a human arm, obviously male, gray and somewhat decomposed, cut cleanly just above the elbow. The hand rested at the edge of the basket, as if about to grip it.

"Beautiful morning for such a grim task," Burton said.

Ness glanced at the sky as if the beauty of the day hadn't occurred to him, nodded, and introduced the man in overalls to Burton.

"This is John Haggerty," Ness said, gesturing to the man. "He's the bridge tender who spotted the torso and the leg Friday morning."

"Pleased to meet you, Your Honor," the man said as he and Burton shook hands. Haggerty's face held a haunted look; the circles under his eyes made Burton look well-rested.

"Your alertness is appreciated," Burton said, not exactly knowing how to commend an individual for spotting body parts floating down the river.

"It's been horrible," Haggerty admitted, clearly shaken, "just horrible. Yesterday some more of him floated by—rest of his torso, they said—stuck in a burlap bag. Then another leg. Then today an arm . . . it's enough to make a man call in sick."

"I can understand that," Burton said, patting the fellow on the shoulder.

"What's it gonna be tomorrow?" Haggerty asked, his eyes a window on the horror he'd seen. "The damn *head*?"

"I wouldn't worry about that," Ness said coolly. "The head almost never turns up."

This seemed scant consolation for Haggerty, who touched his own head with a trembling hand. "If you gents don't need me . . . I . . . I better be getting back to work."

Burton glanced at Ness, who shrugged a little.

"Go right ahead," Ness said.

Haggerty walked along the pilings at the river's edge, where the gray Cuyahoga gently lapped, and moved quickly toward the low-slung drawbridge off to the left, retreating to the safety of his watchtower.

"This is a pretty lucky catch," Ness said, smiling, referring to the "fish" in the wicker basket. "The Butcher usually keeps the head and hands, you know. With fingerprints to work with, we may identify this one."

"That would be helpful," Burton said.

Out on the river a Coast Guard launch cruised; against the gray surface of the river with its oily yellow splotches, the white launch trimmed red and blue was an incongruously cheerful and colorful presence. Two sailors in crisp Coast Guard whites were aboard, one guiding the launch, the other watching the water; also on board was a thin man in shirtsleeves.

"That's Merlo," Ness explained.

"He's been on this case from the beginning," Burton said.

"Yes he has. He's a top-notch investigator."

"But he hasn't got the job done," Burton added.

"I believe in Merlo. No way I want him off the case. He knows more about the Butcher than anyone outside of the Butcher himself. But he needs support." Ness lifted an eyebrow, put it back down. "And the investigation could stand some fresh blood, if you'll forgive the expression."

"I agree," Burton said.

The sun went under a cloud and turned the Flats even grayer. It was cooler here, by the river. Oddly peaceful. Birds chirped and cawed; insects buzzed lazily; taller weeds, violet wildflowers, swayed. The wind in the weeds made a shimmering sound, like the soft riffle of playing cards.

"There's the other one!"

It was Merlo, standing in the motorboat, pointing.

Burton looked out toward the reflecting surface of the river, didn't see anything.

Ness said, "There." He pointed.

Now Burton saw it, something floating like white-gray

driftwood. The launch cut its speed even further and eased over to it. One of the sailors, his sleeve rolled up, eased out beyond the edge of the boat and reached.

Then he pulled back into the boat and stood and held the severed limb in his hand and yelled, "Got it!"

The sailor was young and even at a distance you could see he was grinning. He lifted his prize in the air and waved with it. From here it looked like an extension of his own arm, as if a hand at the end of a grotesquely long limb was waving a greeting.

Ness was not pleased. "Put that thing *down!*" he called. "Be *careful* with it!"

Within the boat, Merlo was apparently making similar admonitions.

The young safety director seemed quietly outraged. "Doesn't anybody have a clue as to how evidence is handled or preseved?" He gestured to the wicker basket and its grisly contents. "That should be in a rubber evidence bag, zipped tight, kept away from the elements."

Curry and the uniformed cop exchanged glances, wondering if this question/accusation applied to them.

Burton said, "I've heard similar complaints from the coroner."

"We have little enough meaningful evidence in this case as it is," Ness said, "let alone handle it carelessly."

"Something definitely has to be done," Burton said.

"I agree."

"Let's talk," Burton said, and gestured toward the gentle slope of land behind them.

Ness followed the mayor to the edge of the train tracks. "About our appointment . . ." Ness began.

"No apologies necessary," Burton said. "I admit, though, that I was glad to find you'd made an appointment for this morning. I needed to talk to you. But when you canceled . . . well, let me say I was relieved to hear where you were."

"Relieved?"

Burton had to turn away from the frank, even naive gaze of his younger associate. Ness was perhaps the most intelligent, tirelessly hardworking, and cold-bloodedly fearless man Burton had ever encountered in his many

years of public service; but the man would never understand politics. Ness would, Burton feared, always be
unaware of the forces that shaped things; would, for all his
experience in criminal justice, remain in this one way an
innocent.

"I have to ask you to take a risk," Burton said.

"That's what I'm paid for."

"Eliot. Keep your enthusiasm in check for a moment.
My conscience requires that I spell this out to you. I can't
let you commit to this blindly, rashly."

"Commit to what?"

Burton sighed. "When you came aboard, I had to ask
you to take a career risk that few men would have put up
with."

Ness nodded matter-of-factly, as if to say, "So?"

Burton laughed, shook his head. How could he hope to
get through to Ness on this subject?

When Burton had asked Ness to become his director of
public safety, in December of '35, it had been with the
condition that Ness would enter the office to much fanfare
about his background as "the man who got Capone," the
former G-man whose squad of "untouchables" had brought
Chicago's mob to its financial knees. Burton, an independent who had been elected on a law-and-order platform,
had faced a factionalized city council, much of which
opposed him. In order to get his police and fire department
budgets passed by this hostile group, he needed glowing
press and had accordingly played upon Ness's reputation—
and put that reputation on the line—by promising an
immediate cleanup of the rackets, particularly of Cleveland's impossibly corrupt police force. Ness would have
only a matter of months to accomplish the job.

If Ness had failed, after coming in to such fanfare, it
would have been career suicide; but he had taken on the
job eagerly.

And he got the headlines, putting dents in the local
gambling and policy rackets while exposing a network of
corrupt cops, specifically nailing the "outside chief," the
high-ranking officer who oversaw this venal "department
within the department." A score of other corrupt officers,

exposed in a graft report personally assembled by Ness, were successfully prosecuted shortly after.

And Mayor Burton got his budgets passed.

"I swore to myself," Burton told Ness, "that I would never put you in that sort of spot again."

Ness said nothing; his head was moved forward, however, eyes slitted.

"Now I have to ask you to do much the same thing again, and I have no right to. You can say no. I won't hold it against you. Not in the least."

"Say no to *what*?" There was more than a hint of impatience in Ness's voice.

Burton gestured in a conciliatory manner. "You have to understand, Eliot, that while we've accomplished much, there is much yet to accomplish."

"I know," Ness nodded with a sour smile. "There's still corruption on the force. We still have gambling, policy . . . labor racketeering. None of it is gone."

"Strides have been made," Burton said. "Remarkable strides. And your deams of modernizing the force, of putting a patrol car within a half-minute of any home in the city, of reorganization of the traffic bureau, of instituting a juvenile delinquency unit . . . we need to make them come true. I have a great belief in your theories, and their practical application, Eliot."

"I appreciate that, sir."

"But the sad truth is, we have an election coming up."

Ness smiled. "You'll take that in a walk."

"It's not that simple. I'm running on the Republican ticket, but I'm perceived, correctly, as an independent. I'm going to be up against four challengers in the primary race, Eliot."

"Well, if there's anything I can do . . ."

"We'll get to that. You have to understand that for me to win I need more than just the support of the people. I need the support of the business community."

"You've had that in the past," Ness said. "I probably know that better than anybody."

"Yes, you do. The industrialists, the merchants, who came through with private funding for so much of the work you've accomplished, who've kept our slush fund full, have to be convinced that we're still worth backing. That we're not going to embarrass them and the community."

Ness frowned. "I don't understand . . . our successes have gotten us attention all over the country. The world! I've got clippings in my scrapbook from as far away as . . ."

Burton lifted a hand, gently. "Yesterday's news, as your friend Mr. Wild might say."

Ness thought about that, darkly.

"The Butcher," Ness said.

"The Butcher," Burton agreed, sighing. "What the world knows about Cleveland right now is that we have America's answer to Jack the Ripper stalking our streets. And our police department can't seem to do a thing about it."

"We're being made to look ineffectual by this maniac."

"You haven't been tarnished by it, personally. Everyone knows you have your own staff of investigators, that you've hired outside investigators"—that was one of the major reasons for seeking slush-funding from the business community—"that from time to time you do your own investigating. You've managed to stay aloof from the . . . embarrassment."

Ness said nothing, his expression an understated scowl.

"I know you care deeply about this case," Burton said. "I'm well aware that you, personally, arranged to have those 'death masks' shown at the expo. At a midway attraction, no less. . . ."

Ness bristled. "Hundreds of thousands of people—maybe millions of people—will walk by those dead faces. And maybe one of those people will make an identification."

"But Eliot—a carnival tent?"

"I tried eleswhere," Ness said tightly. "Don't think I didn't. I was blocked at every turn—even the U.S. government building, with their crime prevention section, where I thought I had connections, turned me away. The display was found too . . . unpleasant. Bad for the image of the expo, of the city. Well, having that son of a bitch at large is bad for the image of the city, too."

Burton smiled gently, touched the shoulder of the younger man. "Son of a bitch" was about as rough as the safety director's language got; the expression was a gage of how deep his concern really ran.

"I've taken some heat," Burton admitted, "for the damage you've done the city's 'image.' The movers and shakers in our community hardly find a display of death masks of the victims of the Mad Butcher of Kingsbury Run a positive contribution to the public's perception of our fair city. On the other hand, I agree with your decision to have the masks shown."

"You do?"

"I do. I only wish you had spoken to me—I might have been able to arrange a more . . . dignified exhibition hall."

"I'm sorry, I—"

"Never mind. But you have to understand the displeasure of our financial 'angels.' Attendance at the expo this year has fallen off drastically. Shopping downtown is similarly well below last year's mark. This new discovery of yet another Butcher casualty, just a month after the last such discovery, is hardly going to help pull people our way, either."

A twitch of irritation tugged Ness's cheek. "It's silly," he said. "The Butcher strikes exclusively at the poor homeless bastards of the Run, of the worst sections of the Flats. The average expo attendee hardly has any—"

"Eliot, you're looking at it like a policeman. Look at it as if you were still living in Chicago. Let's say you're in the insurance business. You're looking for someplace to take mom and the kids for a summer holiday. You start thumbing through the Sunday paper, to look for travel ideas, and you come across a story about the discovery of victim number nine of the mad headhunter who is stalking Cleveland's streets."

Ness smirked humorlessly, shrugged. "I guess I wouldn't be taking the next bus here, at that."

"Exactly. That's why I have to ask—propose—that you consider taking this risk."

"Whatever it is, ask."

"I want you to take over."

"Take over?"

"The investigation. I want you to turn your desk over to your executive assistant and make the Butcher your top personal priority."

Ness grinned. "Hot damn! Is *that* what this is about? Why do you think I made the appointment with you? I wanted to request this goddamn case!"

Ness was laughing and shaking his head, but Burton smiled uneasily and patted the air with his palms.

"Eliot—it's not that simple. We would enter this arena with the same fanfare as before. We would put you and your reputation on the line. The man who got Capone sets out to become the man who gets the Butcher. That sort of thing."

Ness, still smiling, nodded. "I see no problem with that."

"You don't? What if you fail?"

"Fail?" he said. As if the possibility had never occurred to him.

Burton shook his head woefully. "If I lose the primary—or if I win but then lose the election that follows—there's very little chance my successor would hold you over. Not if you go on the line by making the Butcher your personal meat, as it were, only to have the killings continue."

Ness nodded matter-of-factly.

"And frankly," Burton said, "even if I do win, I might be pressured to get a new safety director. If you've been made to look . . . well . . ."

"Stupid?" Ness was grinning. "Ineffective?"

"Well, yes. Pick your own disparaging adjective, if you like."

"I'll tell you what I'd like," Ness said, and his grin was gone. "I'd like to stop the killing. I'd like to stop fishing arms and legs out of rivers, to stop finding the remains of human beings scattered like so many cuts of beef across the godforsaken landscape of the Run. I'd like to put that evil bastard, whoever he is, in the electric chair."

Burton laughed shortly. "When would you like to start trying?"

"I already have," Ness said, and began walking down the gentle slope to the edge of the river where Merlo, Curry, and the uniformed cop, and two dismembered arms awaited.

4

The Torso Clinic, as the press came to call it, met at seven the next evening in the ballistics lab on the second floor of the Central Police Station. Shortly before seven, grave-looking men began filing into the stark, high-ceilinged room. Work desks with comparison microscopes had been moved to one side, as had various file and card cabinets, to make room for rows of folding chairs; an aisle had been left to allow the slide projector its path to the screen set up before them. Few of the men were taking their seats as yet; they were studying in churchlike silence the wall of torso-murder photos the coroner had arranged for his guests. Coroner Samuel Gerber had also set a table, just in front of the large bulletin board where the photos were thumb-tacked, a table covered by a white cloth as if a meal were about to be served; but rather than china and silverware, the coroner provided an arrangement of human bones, including several skulls. The photos, and bones as well, were clearly labeled as to which victim or victims were represented.

Ness had stood in the hallway greeting the clinic attendees, shaking hands, thanking them for coming at such short notice. Among them were Dr. G. Clifford Watterson, professor of anatomy at Western Reserve University medical school; Dr. Louis A. Williamson, superintendent of the Newburg state hospital for the insane; Police Chief George Matowitz; County Prosecutor Frank T. Cullitan; Sergeant Hogan, head of the homicide squad; several other doctors, including a psychiatrist in the probation department of criminal courts; and various detectives, including Merlo and Curry, all of whom had worked one or more of the individual killings.

A brace of reporters had also been invited, to give evenhanded coverage to all the papers. The representative of the *Plain Dealer* was the last to show.

"You sure you know what you're doing?" Sam Wild, lighting up a Lucky Strike, asked Ness.

"Yes."

Wild was a tall, pale, bony-looking man in his mid-thirties. His hair was dark blond and curly and his features were pointed, giving him a pleasantly satanic look. He wore a white seersucker suit and a blue bow tie and a straw fedora with a blue band.

"Your self-confidence is an example to us all," Wild said, exhaling smoke, smiling, looking like a happy cadaver. "But you're putting more on the line than just your good name, you know. Like your ass, for instance."

"Sam, I'm just doing my job here."

"Bullshit. Your job is to be an administrator. Your *hobby* is chasing crooks down. But I'm not complaining. You always do right by me where the headlines are concerned, and this is sure as hell no exception."

Wild had been exclusively attached to City Hall, specifically to cover the activities of the safety director, for well over a year now.

"I'll get you your headlines," Ness said.

Wild laughed. "Christ, you're a smug son of a bitch! Well, I'm with you, pal. Only, you lead the way. I'll be right behind you—*watching* behind you."

"With my 'ass' on the line like it is," Ness said with a quiet smile, "that'll come in handy."

Wild's smirk dissolved and he stared at Ness with a curious blankness. "Aren't you afraid?"

"Not really."

"Don't shit me, Eliot. Don't you realize what you've done?"

"Sure. I'm risking embarrassment . . . maybe a career setback . . . if I don't pull this one off."

"Embarrassment? Career setback? You've come out and publicly made the Mad Butcher of Kingsbury Run your personal public enemy number one! That sick fucking son of a bitch is into wholesale human slaughter."

"I noticed," Ness said, taking Wild's arm, leading him into the lab, where the men were settling into their chairs, to one of which Ness led Wild. "Now sit down and get out your notepad. You ain't seen nothing yet."

"I haven't been covering this ghoulish damn story—"

"Well, you are now," Ness said, and sat him down.

He walked down the aisle and turned and faced the assemblage of men, many of whom were trusted colleagues, such as Cullitan and Matowitz, while others—such as the various doctors who'd been asked in as experts—he knew only by reputation.

"Again, my thanks to all of you for rallying at such short notice," he said. "This is an emergency measure, as with the recent discovery of Butcher victim number nine, it's clear that these inhuman killings have reached epidemic proportions. It's my hope that this conference will channel various expert opinions—pointing the way toward a solution to this mystery. I'd like to turn the proceedings over to Coroner Gerber."

There was polite applause as Coroner Gerber, a small, sallow man, rose from the front row and began by taking off his suit coat. Most others in the room followed the coroner's lead, as the several wall-mounted fans weren't nearly up to combating the warmth of this summer night. Ness, who left his coat on, sat in the front row.

Gerber, eyes large and dark and mournful behind wire-frame glasses, was a man of forty who looked older, white beginning to overtake his dark hair, including his mustache, lines creasing his face.

Nonetheless, he had great energy as he spoke, moving restlessly before his audience.

"This mass-murder mystery is the equal of any of the famous mass-murder cases known in history," Gerber said with a strange combination of enthusiasm and dread. "Equal in interest, gruesomeness, and—most important, gentlemen—ingenuity on the part of the murderer." He glanced toward the back of the room and said, "Lights."

And the lights went out and the projector came on. In photos sometimes larger than life, the sorry parade of dismembered bodies began.

Of the victims whose bodies were found by the two boys at the bottom of Jackass Hill on September 23, 1935, one had been identified, through fingerprints: the younger man, Edward Andrassy, twenty-eight years old, a minor street tough in the so-called Roaring Third precinct, the seedy, crime-ridden area adjacent to Kingsbury Run. Possibly a homosexual, Andrassy had once been employed at Cleveland City Hospital as an orderly. The older, stocky victim had not been identified.

On January 26, 1936, in the Roaring Third itself, the next victim emerged, in several installments. First, a local butcher, attracted by the insistent barking of a dog behind a nearby factory, found various body parts of a white woman—lower torso, right arm, both thighs—wrapped in newspaper, left in two burlap bags and a half-bushel basket. Thirteen days later, the left arm and lower legs turned up behind an empty building on Orange Avenue, SE, near East Fourteenth Street. Though the head had not yet turned up, identification was made by fingerprints, an identification confirmed by the woman's ex-husband, who recognized an abdominal scar. The woman was Florence Polillo, a forty-one-year-old, heavyset, heavy-drinking prostitute.

On June 5, 1936, two colored youngsters playing hooky from school were wandering Kingsbury Run much as had those two other boys in 1935. Just half a mile from Jackass Hill, the boys noticed a pair of trousers balled up and stuck under a tree on the embankment. One of the boys grabbed a stick and poked at the pants, and a head rolled out and tumbled to their feet.

This was the head of the handsome young man, thought to be a sailor, whose heavily tattooed body had turned up intact in bushes nearby; the elaborate body markings seemed to insure prompt identification. While the sailor's fingerprints were not on file, a poster detailing his tattoos and including a photo of his handsome, almost pretty, dead face had been widely circulated to the press (and was still on display at the expo). To date, he remained unidentified.

On July 22, 1936, a man's head had been found separated from his body; the two lay fifteen feet apart in the weeds near railroad tracks and a hobo camp, in the dismal, desolate Big Creek region on the West Side of town. This victim—like the tattooed apparent sailor—had not been emasculated. He remained unidentified, his death mask on display at the expo.

On September 10, 1936, a hobo hopping a freight spotted two halves of a male torso bobbing in the fetid, stagnant pool where the sewers flowed out from under Kingsbury Run into the Cuyahoga. Police fished out the torso halves, then with grappling hooks brought up the lower legs and thighs. Then they provided a diver with the thankless job of the decade: to go exploring for the arms and head in the pool of excrement. When this task proved as fruitless as it had been unpleasant, the pool was drained, flushed with a fire hose. No head. No arms. No identification. Also no genitals: the Butcher had, with this victim, reverted to his emasculating ways.

February 23rd of this year, the upper torso of a young woman washed up on Euclid beach from the icy waters of Lake Erie, where it had apparently drifted from the Cuyahoga. The woman was not identified, but the discovery caused police to recall another similar incident.

Two and a half years before, on September 5, 1934, a man gathering driftwood on that same beach had discovered the lower torso of a woman; a few days later, a suitcase containing the headless upper torso was fished out of the same waters. Prior to the February 23rd discovery, Gerber conceded, this slaying had not been connected to the Mad Butcher. It had not yet been officially added to the roster.

On June 5th, a fourteen-year-old boy walking under the Lorain-Carnegie Bridge, kicking stones, kicked a skull. The rest of the skeleton was nearby. The body had probably been under the bridge for nearly a year, Gerber said; the victim had been decapitated, but the skeleton was otherwise intact—including bridgework with three gold teeth. From the formation of the jawbone and the skull, Dr. Watterson, professor of anatomy at Western Reserve University School of Medicine, had deduced the victim was a colored woman.

"Which brings us to the most recent victim," Gerber

said as slides of the Third Street Bridge discovery began filling the screen, "who has yet to be identified. What we know about this deceased gentleman is that he was approximately six feet tall, weighed one hundred and eighty-to-ninety pounds . . . and his heart, liver, and various other vital organs were removed. Lights."

As the lights came up, the men on the folding chairs winced as their eyes got used to the light. Ness glanced around at them; this was a somber group, sickened and perhaps numbed by the shocking, dismaying material they'd viewed in Gerber's wall display and his slide presentation. Overkill on Gerber's part, perhaps; but overkill on the part of the Butcher, most certainly.

Ness rose, turned, and spoke to his audience. "Seeing this panoply of the Butcher's handiwork should bring home to us just what it is we're facing—just what it is we have to put an end to. Now, I've asked Dr. Strauss, our county pathologist, to say a few words."

Strauss, a dignified, heavyset man, displayed on an easel a large chart of the crimes, comparing them as to dismemberments, condition of bodies, clothing, and other factors. He mentioned that the decapitations were invariably made between the third and fourth vertebrae of the neck.

"The muscles in the neck had retracted," Strauss said, "which indicates that the heads of these victims were cut off while they were still alive . . . or at least immediately after death, while their reflexes were still operating. Ah, but the woman found at Euclid beach . . . that's the second woman found there, I should say . . . evidence indicates she was decaptiated *after* death. Otherwise— cause of death could well be decapitation."

Silence hung in the room like a dark, heavy curtain.

Strauss smiled pleasantly, said, "Thank you, gentlemen," took his chart off the easel, and sat down. The wall-mounted fans churned the air.

Ness stood, thanked Strauss, and said, "While in a few instances we've recovered the heads of the victims, I think it's significant that the heads and hands are usually *missing*."

Chief Matowitz, a friendly-looking bear of a man whose crisp blue uniform bore its customary red lapel flower, spoke from his front-row seat.

"By 'significant,'" Matowitz said, "you mean these are the items by which we'd most likely be able to identify the victims."

"That's right."

"But those items *have* turned up from time to time," Matowitz said.

"Yes," Ness admitted. "I think in those instances, the murders may have been more spontaneous than others. My feeling is that, for the most part, the killer has stalked his prey, possibly getting to know them, associating with them for several weeks or even months before the kill."

Dr. Williamson, the psychiatrist, spoke from the second row; he was a small bald man in a tan suit. "On what do you base this conclusion, Mr. Ness?"

Ness smiled. "It's less than a conclusion, Doctor. It's part instinct, maybe a little bit common sense. The victims here seem to be of the lower strata of life—little or no family ties, vagrants, drifters, perverts, prostitutes—living on the fringes of society. Specifically, in the vicinity of Kingsbury Run."

"What does that tell you, Mr. Ness?" Williamson asked.

Ness could detect no skepticism in the psychiatrist's voice; it seemed an honest question. He gave an honest answer: "To associate with such a group—without arousing suspicion—the murderer must have been of the same physical makeup . . . that is, a white male, probably a known frequenter of the area."

"Why a male?"

"Well, let's say probably a male. At any rate, well developed and strong enough to do the heavy . . . let's call it, *disposal* work required. Hauling bodies in the dead of night, that sort of thing. Probably, if he does indeed associate with his victims, he is in their same general age range—twenty-five to forty."

Dr. Gerber, who'd been standing patiently to one side, said, "Let me say that I concur wholeheartedly with Director Ness. It seems to me that the slayer has gained the confidence and possibly the friendship of his victims before beheading them. What we have here, I believe, is that rarest of criminals—the killer who kills for the sheer love of it—a man who sees himself as God, with the power of life or death."

Silence again draped the room.

"I'd like your thoughts, Doctor," Ness said to the psychiatrist.

"I don't have many worth sharing at this point, I'm afraid," Williamson said with good-natured chagrin. "I can tell you only that this murderer does not fit into any recognized form of insanity."

Prosecutor Cullitan, a big man in his late fifties with salt-and-pepper hair and wire-frame glasses, turned and looked at the psychiatrist, startled. "Are you saying this killer is *not* insane?"

"Hardly," Williamson said. "I'm saying this is not a variety of insanity readily diagnosed and treated. I have done some reading about mass murderers of this general type . . . and I have encountered nothing in my research that closely parallels this. There seems to be a sexual basis to at least some of the crimes—the emasculation of the men, in particular—and it is my understanding that there was sexual attack in several of the cases . . ."

Up at the front of the room, both Ness and Gerber were nodding. This fact had not been made public, and it sobered—shocked—the already sober and generally shockproof audience of men.

". . . and that the sexual assault was performed on both male and female victims."

"That's right," Ness said.

"Jesus," somebody in the audience said.

"I would propose," Williamson said, "that there may be a reason, other than clouding identifications, where . . . shall we say, collecting certain body parts is concerned. For one thing, keeping certain parts might be viewed as, well, putting together a trophy collection. For another, we may have a case of genuine necrophilia here."

"What the hell is that?" somebody in back said.

Sam Wild.

Ness repressed a smile; he could not remember seeing the generally unflappable reporter look so . . . flapped.

"Sexual interest in the dead," the psychiatrist said, looking back at Wild.

"What do you mean . . . 'interest'?"

"He means sex *with* the dead," Ness said.

"Oh, Christ," Wild said wearily. "How do you expect me to put *that* in the paper?"

"I can spell 'necrophilia' if you like," Williamson offered ingenuously, and uneasy laughter rocked the room.

"You may have a point, Doctor," Ness said. "There is some evidence of attempts at body preservation—chemicals applied to the corpses, refrigeration, that sort of thing. What is confusing here is that there are enough elements, enough of a-consistent modus operandi, to identify all of these victims as genuinely 'belonging' to the Butcher. But nonetheless, the Butcher is all over the map—men, women, studiously planned killings, impromptu killings, this victim emasculated, this one not, this one sexually assaulted, this one not . . . even organs missing, in the most recent case."

"May I have a word?"

In response to the deep, distinctive voice from the third row, Ness said, "Most certainly, Dr. Watterson."

Dr. Watterson stood, a distinguished-looking, darkly handsome man in his mid-fifties; a surgeon of some renown, professor of anatomy of Western Reserve, Watterson's manner was one of complete, confident authority.

"All of these cases," he began, "indicate dissection by someone showing keen intelligence in recognizing anatomical landmarks as they were approached. As you know, I was called in on several of these cases to give an expert opinion; so I have examined some of the physical evidence itself. The word 'butcher' has been bandied about, and I think it is inappropriate—the technique here is not that of the slaughterhouse—although the subject may indeed have used a butcher knife. We are dealing, I believe, with a doctor or a medical student or possibly a veterinarian. Someone with definite knowledge of anatomy, and at least rudimentary surgical skills. No layman could have attempted such meticulous incisions. We are dealing with an intelligent human being—most likely *not* a denizen of the lower strata."

Watterson sat down.

Ness said, "Thank you, Doctor. Your views make a lot of sense—and they don't, incidentally, contradict my own. I agree with you that our killer is probably well educated and from the 'right side of the tracks.' But he's going slumming—with a butcher knife."

Watterson nodded from the audience.

Ness said, "Detective Merlo—a few words about your efforts?"

Merlo stood, but Ness motioned him to come forward. The thin, serious-looking detective said, almost shyly, "I wish I had more to report. Obviously our man is still at large. I've been on this case, with a variety of partners, since the beginning . . . well, at least since the first Kingsbury Run killings. At any rate, we've questioned more than fifteen hundred persons, mostly unsavory types in various hobo shantytowns and in the Flats and Kingsbury Run. Every butcher-shop employee in the city has been brought here to the Central station to be questioned. Every doctor in Cleveland and the surrounding area has been subjected to the most thorough scrutiny. We've interrogated medical students, hospital employees, parolees from all state mental institutions, keeping up surveillance on the latter. We've investigated hundreds of letters from almost everywhere—'hot tips' that never led us anywhere. We've crawled through rat-infested sewers, sorted through city dumps, fished body parts out of water . . . you name it. And I admit, without shame but without pride either, except for the pieces of the victims in question, we've come up empty-handed so far."

"Not quite," Ness said. "Of the suspects Detective Merlo has brought in for questioning, we've held on to forty-some who were found guilty of offenses ranging from misdemeanors to robbery, burglary, and assault."

The audience began to applaud, but Merlo waved them to stop.

"I appreciate the sentiment," Merlo said, "but I'd prefer we postpone the congratulations until this sick bastard is either dead, or in jail waiting to die."

There were nods of approval in the audience, and Ness put a hand on Merlo's shoulder, saying, "There's been some play in the press about the safety director's office taking charge of this investigation. And that happens to be true. I plan to be personally involved—but Detective Merlo remains on the job. I'm partnering him with one of my own top investigators, Detective Albert Curry, who with Detective Merlo was at the scene of the first Kingsbury Run find."

Ness gestured to Curry, who stood and turned and smiled tightly to the assemblage and sat down.

For the next hour the group discussed and probed the slayings, and finally Ness said, "Gentlemen, I appreciate your attention and welcome these comments, insights, and ideas. But let us keep in mind—tonight we're right where we were the day the first body was found."

The group, many of them nodding solemnly, rose and began threading their way out of the room.

Wild approached Ness and said, "So, you think because you're not a vagrant, you're safe from this guy."

Ness shrugged.

"If that's what you think," Wild said, "you're as nutty as he is. Nuttier. You've declared war on a mass murderer, you fruitcake."

'Well," Ness said pleasantly, "he knows where he can find me. Buy you a drink?"

5

Kingsbury Run was a good place to live.

That's how Ben saw it. Right in the middle of the city, here was a wide-open place where a man could fend for himself—and keep to himself. There was game to hunt—squirrels, wild dogs, pigeons, Hoover hogs (jackrabbits)—and if a man wanted to make his own fire and cook his own food, he would be left alone. At least Ben usually was. Folks in the jungle, the shantytown near the Thirty-fifth Street Bridge, knew about Ben, and Ben's knife.

Even without his king-size jackknife, Ben was nobody anybody in his right mind would mess with. That knowledge gave Ben a certain amount of satisfaction, if not exactly pride.

Only five six, Ben was broad-shouldered, a barrel-chested, threatening-looking mole of a man whose dark blond hair was whitening; his clothes were old, even tattered, but he kept them clean. Unlike some, he had underwear; unlike some, he had shoes (boots, actually). He even had an extra pair, hid, in his cave, that he'd excavated high above the creek bed, away from shantytown, covering the opening with boards and tar paper. It was warm in winter, unlike the paper tents and cardboard hovels some of his neighbors endured. And when it got too damn cold, he could always flop at the Salvation Army—though a little bit of that pious Sally crap went a long way with Ben.

It wasn't like Ben was a hermit. He had friends in his world; he even made new ones from time to time. He was liked. He could sing songs from an Appalachian childhood, songs that were about all that was worth remembering from that childhood. Folks liked Ben's singing. Hobos (Ben didn't consider himself a hobo, but he put up with them, just as he did tramps—but he held no truck with bums) put a lot of stock in storytellers, joke tellers, and singers. There was a lot of time to kill in shantytown.

Nights when up the hill drifted the scent of a fine gump stew stewing—stolen chicken mixed with vegetables from the rubbish bins at Central Market—Ben would wander down, and get sociable. It would mean spending some time with folks—singing, putting up with the socialist talk that he'd once put so much stock in—but that was the price. Even in shantytown, nothing was free.

Ben liked being close to the city: there was something reassuring, comforting, about being in a wilderness bordered by city skyline. Best of both worlds, and both were at his fingertips.

With town so near, he could go scrounging for food at Central Market, mooch two-day-old bread from bakeries, or hit the soup kitchens or missions, and pick up the odd job here and there, when need be. Even a man like Ben needed *some* money. Coffee and sugar and cigarettes couldn't be scrounged. And drinking canned heat and moonshine got old—sometimes a man needed to sit in a saloon and put away some real honest-to-God beer and, praise the Lord and pass the ammunition, hard liquor. That took money. Sometimes a man needed to get his ashes hauled, too—and most of the women riding the rails were either hooked up with some 'bo, or queer. So that took money, too.

He'd never had a wife. He almost did once, when he was working regular, at the slaughterhouse. That was after the war. His brothers told him he was crazy to quit, but they were younger than him, they hadn't been where he'd been. They hadn't got gassed at the Argonne. They hadn't seen waves of young men with guns go charging across no-man's-land to the sound of bombs and bullets and the cries of the wounded and dying. They hadn't put a knife into a wounded comrade to put him out of his misery and stop his screaming.

His family had come from the backwoods to Cleveland around the time he was born (Ben was forty-seven, although he didn't know it, having long since lost track) to get pie-in-the-sky factory jobs like they'd heard so much about. His father worked in a steel mill for about year and then took off forever one day; his mother worked as a seamer in a knitting factory, a sweatshop job that killed her in her twenties. His brothers and sister wandered to other cities and found jobs; Ben had answered the call of the road, just another penniless, unattached drifter hopping freights in search of nothing in particular. Adventure, maybe. Seeing America.

Seeing the world was what he had in mind when he enlisted. And he had indeed seen things in the "great" war, things that had quenched his desire for seeing much more of anything else.

But back home, the public had been protected from the horrors soldiers like Ben had endured; like the song said, "Half a million boots went sloggin' through hell," but you had to have been there to understand. You had to wake up screaming, thinking you were still racing across no-man's-land through bombs and bullets and the cries of . . .

His brother Ed was in Chicago, working at Armour in the smokehouse. He helped Ben get a job there; Ben started as a common laborer on the killing floor and made a good impression. He had decided he'd best learn a trade, so he tried real hard, worked real hard; soon the foreman saw that Ben had a way with a knife. Before long Ben was given a better-paying position.

He became a hog killer.

Hogs chained by one rear leg to an overhead conveyer were brought in, squealing, upside down. Ben, standing in one spot as the hogs came helplessly to him, would grip each pig by its throat and dig his knife into its jugular, in a thrust and turn motion. Blood ran off his leather apron; his boots got painted red.

He lasted a week. He didn't ask for any other position at the slaughterhouse; he just hopped a freight and reentered the world of the hobo.

A hobo, which is what Ben was in those days, traveled around looking for work. Whereas tramps were those looking for the open road, for thrills; that described the prewar Ben. But he never was a bum, which was how Ben classified those who never worked at all, beggars who slept in doorways, drunks and junkies, the sort of vagrant that gave folks like Ben a bad name.

In those days after the war, after the slaughterhouse, Ben always thought he'd find work somewhere and settle down. Maybe get back in touch with Ida, the girl in "dry casings" at Armour who he'd been going with when he up and quit the slaughterhouse.

But instead he'd found himself on the hobo circuit, hitting the same towns year after year, seeking out jails to winter in, getting used to a life where lack of material belongings was a blessing, not a curse. He heard a lot of talk about socialism and communism; there was a sort of hobo underground, with organizations and such, hobo "colleges" and coffee houses, mostly under the wing of the I.W.W., the radical labor party.

And the Depression had swelled the ranks of the wandering homeless, with free-spirited adventurers being outnumbered by the evicted and the desperate. Still, these folks fell right in with the kind of life Ben and others were living. After all, a lot of the men were war vets, like Ben, and had endured much worse. They had lived out of backpacks before.

The last time Ben believed in anything but his animal needs had been back in '32, when he got swept up in the Bonus Army. Ben was pretty radical back then, took it real serious, and that June, Ben and twenty thousand or so other war veterans and their families poured into Washington, D.C.. They were demanding the government cough up the war bonus the vets were not due to receive till 1945. President Hoover liked to say there weren't any hungry people in America, but Ben and thousands of other vets and their thousands of stomachs knew better; starving, jobless, they knew they needed their bonus dough, now.

They put up a Hooverville on Anacostia Flats in the southwest of the nation's capital. This army camp had no tents or barracks; just lean-tos cobbled together out of cardboard boxes and packing crates and scrap metal and tarpaper roofing. Desperation and hope mingled in the air, as communists, socialists, Wobblies, and the just plain hungry climbed on the Bughouse Square-type platform, preaching to the converted about the bonus they had coming. Congress wasn't sold, but did vote to pay passage home for the ex-soldiers.

Hardcore radical leaders urged the Bonus Army to stay on, and only a few thousand took Congress's bribe; the leadership assured those who remained that this battle, this war, would be won. Hoover was already campaigning for reelection—he could hardly afford to oust the Bonus Army by force. Use bayonets against unarmed war veterans, many of whom had their families with them, an army whose only weaponry was petitions? It would never happen.

General Douglas MacArthur, astride a white horse, led four troops of cavalry, four companies of infantry, a mounted machine-gun squadron, half a dozen tanks, several hundred city cops, and a phalanx of Secret Service and Treasury agents against the Bonus Army. Ben saw one veteran shot to death, heard of another; saw veterans slashed and stabbed by bayonets and sabers—saw a man's ear cut off. The shanties were torched; smoke clouds hovered over the capital city. Countless men, women, and children were teargassed, Ben among them.

Gassed at the Argonne; gassed at Anacostia.

It had soured Ben on just about everything. He didn't blame the soldiers—they were just kids, like he'd been a kid when he was in the army, taking orders and doing what they were told, like he had.

To him the radicals were little better than goddamn Hoover. Here it was, four years later, and the revolution that they promised wasn't here yet. Ben's revolution had been an internal one. He would no longer answer to any authority but that of his belly, presidents and radicals be damned.

He had gotten off a freight at Cleveland—home—and had been part of the landscape of Kingsbury Run ever since. He and his knife had carved out a place for themselves. He cut a few 'bos who got tough or tried to steal from him, carved a homo or two who got cute, and the word spread. Feared and respected, he was. Just how he wanted it.

Today was Wednesday, but Ben was unaware of that; the only time he became aware of what day it was, was Sunday, because of the church bells. He would then know it was time for his weekly bath, which he'd accomplish in the lake usually, or at the Sally in winter; he kept himself and his clothes clean. Then, his weekly hygienics accomplished, time would turn into the vague, meaningless thing that it was in his life.

Yesterday and today, the newspapers had been filled with the story of the Torso Clinic, with much being made of Safety Director Ness taking on the Mad Butcher case personally. Ben was unaware of this, too: newspapers were of no interest to him in the summer. In the winter, newspapers had value: they kept you warm.

What was on Ben's mind this early evening was getting drunk and getting laid, in no particular order. He had spent the long, hot day at the Central Market, unloading boxes, and now had two dollars to help him fulfill both those needs. He knew just the place to get the job done, too. A nameless, seedy little saloon near Central and Twentieth; it had been a speakeasy during Prohibition and had never gotten around to making itself look legal.

If getting drunk had been all he had in mind, Ben could have just bought a bottle and retreated to his cave. But this saloon—in a neighborhood of rooming houses, secondhand-store fencing operations, and bookie joints, on the edge of an industrial area—was a hangout for professional beggars, one of whom, Blister Betsy, was a sort of sweetie of Ben's.

Ben entered the room and inhaled, with satisfaction, the aroma of stale smoke mixed with beer-soaked sawdust. An exhaust fan churned noisily, fighting with the sound of *Amos and Andy* on the radio. Half a dozen men dressed in sweaty work clothes stood at the bar, a foot on the rail, putting away beers; some were talking, several were listening to what the Kingfish was up to.

The pasty-faced fat bartender nodded at Ben noncommittally, drawing a beer from the tap.

Ben put fifteen cents on the counter and said, "Boilermaker, Pete. Betsy been in?"

"Nope."

"Well, it's early yet."

"Yeah."

Ben took his glass of beer and his shot of whiskey and sat in a booth and drank them slowly, savoringly. More patrons began wandering in, and they were a shabby-looking lot, but they had money to spend. They were professional beggars who gathered every evening at this nameless saloon after a day of shamming downtown, leaving their phony afflictions behind.

A few of the beggars had genuine handicaps—the wingies, who had one or no arms, and the peggies, who had one or no legs. There were also the blinkies (the fake blind ones), deafies, dummies, D and D's (a combination of the latter two categories), and fitzies (epileptics). Blister Betsy put acid on her arms to make it look like she had ugly sores that needed a doctor's care.

Ben didn't as a rule have much respect for beggars or panhandlers, but he thought people like Blister Betsy gave value for the dollar. It was a job; it was show business. The person paying got to feel good about himself, for helping out a poor needy soul.

Betsy herself was a skinny thing, with mousy brown

hair and a face as plain as a plank; but she laughed real pretty when she drank, and Ben liked the way her hips moved when he was in her.

A skinny character called Sightless Red spotted Ben and, after getting himself a beer, came over and joined him.

"It's been a while, pard," Red said, smiling, showing very decayed teeth, where teeth remained. Ben had all his teeth; he took care of himself.

"Yes it has," Ben said.

"Betsy was asking for you, while back."

Ben felt warm inside, and it wasn't just the boiler-maker. "That's good. Betsy and me get along fine."

Every month or so, Ben would show up at the nameless saloon, spend a buck or so of odd-job money on Betsy, getting her well-oiled, then go to her room at the boarding house nearby and do the time-honored lying-down dance.

"Hope she'll be along pretty soon," Ben said.

"I don't know," Red said, shrugging. "Ain't seen her in a week at least."

Ben tried not to let his sinking feeling show. "Oh?"

"She was talking about visiting her sister in Akron."

"Oh."

"Anyways, she hasn't been around for a couple weeks."

"Oh."

"But hell, you never know. She might show. I don't stop in here every night, you know—and Betsy and me don't work the same district. Maybe she'll be in."

Ben shrugged like it was no matter.

"You still hiding out in that hole on the Run, pard?"

"Sure."

"Beats paying the landlords," Red said. "Thought you might be flopping at the Sally."

"Why? It's summer."

"Yeah, but at the Sally you can sleep and eat and be safe and sound."

Ben frowned. "Hunting's good on the Run, this time of year."

"Yeah, but it ain't just jackrabbits bein' hunted."

"What else is?"

"People! Heads! I'd think shantytown woulda emptied out by now, with this here Mad Butcher on the loose."

Ben snorted a laugh. "I killed more people than that piker."

"What, with your jackknife?" Red grinned greenly. "Don't tell me *you're* the Butcher, Ben!"

"In the war," he said quietly.

"What?"

"I killed more than that bastard did."

"Maybe so, but you can still get killed out there."

"I can take of myself."

"I know. But I'd be sleeping inside, if I was you."

Ben shrugged, and so did Red, who grinned his green-and-yellow grin and went back to the bar for another beer. Pretty soon Ben shambled up after another boilermaker and went back to his booth and sat and got morosely drunk, wondering whether he should wait for Betsy to show or try to make Peggy Peg. She was kind of fat, but that didn't bother Ben. Fucking a one-legged woman didn't, either. He just had his heart, and hard, set on little Betsy.

"How you doing tonight, Ben?"

Ben looked up from the whiskey half of his fourth boilermaker and saw Andy, a husky, pleasant worker who frequented the saloon from time to time. They'd spoken before.

"Doing okay, Andy. Have a seat."

Andy sat; he was a good-looking man about thirty with sandy blond hair and a ready smile.

"Where's your honeybun?" Andy asked.

"I ain't got a honeybun."

"You know who I mean. That little girl with the blisters on her arm that you're always walking out of here with."

Ben smiled, but he felt sad. "I think she's seeing her sister. I don't think she's gonna be in tonight."

Andy sighed. "Yeah. I bet you been looking forward to seein' her, too."

"Yeah."

"I got stood up, too." .

Ben bristled. "I wasn't stood up—"

"Hey, same thing. Neither one of us is getting laid tonight."

Ben nodded. Gulped some whiskey. His belly felt warm. That much, at least, was going right.

They had another round, Ben his fifth boilermaker, Andy a beer.

"That's what I get for trying to date a girl in the front office," Andy said, bitter but accepting it.

"Snobby?"

"Yeah. Sometimes I think a guy's better off paying for it."

Ben nodded agreement, but said, "I like it better when they like you. Buy 'em some drinks and they like you. That's how I see it."

"Not a bad philosophy."

Ben stared into his whiskey. "I used to have a girl. Back in Chicago. At the slaughterhouse."

"You worked at a slaughterhouse?"

"Sure."

"God." Andy shivered. "Didn't that give you the willies?"

"No."

By eleven it was clear that Betsy wasn't going to show. Ben was feeling drunk, but not enjoying the feeling. Hell of a thing, working all day and getting screwed out of screwing.

He was digging in his pocket for his second buck when Andy shook his head and said, "Hey, save your dough. I got a bottle back at my place."

"Yeah?"

"Hell, I got two bottles. One for you and one for me."

Ben looked through bleary eyes at Andy. Andy seemed like a nice enough guy, but Ben didn't trust guys who looked as good as Andy. Andy's mouth was soft, like a girl's.

"That's white of you, but—"

"Hey. If you'd prefer to wait around for Betsy . . . maybe she'll show."

"She ain't gonna fuckin' show. But look, I got to say something and I don't want you to take it wrong."

Andy shrugged, smiled. "Okay."

"I don't cotton up to queers."

"Neither do I," Andy said matter-of-factly.

"Okay. I don't know you all that good, so I just wanted

to make it plain. Sharing a bottle is white of you. But I gotta warn you. I got a knife."

"Ben . . ."

"I ain't no wolf. And I killed punks before."

A "punk," in Ben's parlance, was a young homosexual. And a "wolf" was an older homosexual man who craved punks.

"Ben, I know there's a lot of that kind of thing down in shantytown," Andy said, "but I always knew you weren't a part of that. I hate that unnatural shit. Queers should all be killed."

Ben nodded. "Them that touches me is going to be."

"No argument from me. What do you say we blow this joint? If you'll excuse the expression."

Andy grinned at his own joke, but Ben was too drunk to get it.

In fact, Andy had to help Ben out of the saloon; as they walked down the dimly lit street, Andy supported Ben's arm, as if the man were a cripple like the beggars they were leaving behind pretended to be.

Andy lived a few blocks off the Run, on Central. Drunk as he was, Ben was impressed, even surprised by the place. Not that it was nice—it was a small, paint-peeling clapboard bungalow—but the single-story, single-dwelling frame structure, which even had something of a lawn about it, differed from the crowded-together, two- and three-story rooming houses that were its neighbors. The front windows were blotted out by dark drapes; a basement window in front was boarded up; at left, rickety stairs and a rusted iron rail rose to an entrance.

Unlocking the door, Andy led Ben into a small foyer. A connecting hall led to the whiteness of a kitchen, and straight ahead, to the right, was a living room. At left, on the wall, were a dozen screwed-on coat hooks. Andy motioned Ben into the living room, which was also small but seemed expensively furnished to Ben. The sofa and chairs were overstuffed and plush; oriental tapestries and pictures decorated the walls.

"How's a bottle of beer sound?" Andy said.

"Fine," Ben said, wobbling, not knowing if he should sit down on such an elegant sofa.

"Why don't you help yourself?"

"What?"

"Cold beer in the Frigidaire. Help yourself. I'll get us some whiskey and we'll put our own boilermakers together."

Ben nodded, smiled. "Sounds good."

He wandered on shaky legs down the hallway, past several closed doors, into the small, very clean, very white kitchen; the grayish-white linoleum floor glistened. This guy had money. Trusting soul, too, Ben thought, sliding a hand into this pocket, fingers on his jackknife. It would be easy to take this joe for everything he had. There was money in this place. There just about had to be.

But, drunk or sober, Ben just wasn't that kind, and he knew it.

He snorted a laugh and opened the refrigerator door, and Betsy looked right at him.

Betsy's head, that is.

Her eyes were open, and so was her mouth. Bottles of Hamm's beer sat on the shelf on either side of her.

He was frozen there, for a moment, mouth dropped open as wide as Betsy's, and just as his drink-clouded mind was forming the thought that he must get the hell out of here, he felt fingers grip the hair atop his head and something thin and cold and sharp pressed against the back of his neck.

The last thing Ben saw was Betsy's gray face.

Just as Andy's words were the last thing he heard: "Ben . . . I have a knife, too."

6

By midmorning Thursday, Ness had tied up the loose administrative ends, which would allow him to go out in the field, and was explaining to his executive assistant, Robert Chamberlin, what the setup would be over the coming weeks.

"I'll be in every Monday morning," Ness said, sitting with his back to his scarred rolltop desk that was against one wall of his roomy wood-and-pebbled-glass office at City Hall. "I'll sign whatever I have to sign from the week before, make a few phone calls to people we've had to put off, and then we'll go over whatever needs going over for the week ahead."

Chamberlin, who sat nearby with his back to one of the several conference tables that filled the central area of the room, nodded and said, "Other than that you'll be unavailable?"

"I may be in and out," Ness said, and shrugged, "but I'd say probably your best bet would be trying me at the boathouse, evenings. And even then it will be catch-as-catch-can."

"Understood," Chamberlin said with a confident twitch of a smile that made his small black mustache curl up at the ends. He was a tall, rangy man of thirty-seven with an oblong, sharp-featured face set off by a strong round jaw, his dark hair slicked back off a high forehead. Like Ness, he was impeccably dressed, wearing a three-piece suit and snappy tie.

Ness was saying, "If I haven't come up with anything in a month, well . . ."

"We should both start looking for other work, I'd imagine," Chamberlin finished wryly.

"Not a bad idea," Ness said with a half-smile. "I guess if my job goes down in flames, I take you with me. Sorry."

"Don't give that a thought," Chamberlin said with another twitch of a smile. "I'll land on my feet. Lawyers always do."

Ness was grateful for his friend's attitude—and Chamberlin was more than just his assistant, was indeed a friend, who'd been handpicked by the safety director when his previous executive assistant had played politics. Oddly, the former holder of that position—John Flynt—physically resembled Chamberlin; they both had the look and manner of British military officers out of Kipling.

Chamberlin checked his watch. "I'd better be getting back to my own office—you have a meeting in a few minutes."

"I'd like you to stick around for that. I don't want you cut off from this investigation."

"Well, thanks. I'll just keep my mouth shut and listen."

"You do, and you're fired."

Before long, Ness's secretary, redheaded, bespectacled Wanda, an efficient, attractive young woman he'd stolen away from the Clerk of Public Service office, ushered in Curry and Merlo. Merlo's brown suit was typically rumpled, his face haggard, haunted. Boyish, bashful Curry seemed intimidated by the older man, staying behind him, deferring to his every breath.

"Sit down, gentlemen," Ness said, gesturing to one of the conference tables, and they did. Chamberlin joined them.

There was a discreet knock at the door, the one that opened on to the hall and said SAFETY DIRECTOR'S OFFICE backward on its pebbled-glass. This door was kept locked, and Ness used a key on his vest chain to open it.

Sam Wild, bow-tied and bright-eyed, shambled in, in his loose-limbed way. He grinned wolfishly at Ness, saying, "You usually don't wait on me hand and foot like this," as the safety director closed and locked the door behind him.

Ness turned to Merlo, Curry, and Chamberlin, their expressions reflecting displeasure at the intrusion, Merlo looking the most annoyed. "I asked Sam to stop by, and to slip in the side door, away from the office staff. I wanted him in on this."

Merlo thought for a moment, his professorly brow creasing, then said, "Director Ness, I don't think it's advisable to have the press present at what you've described as a 'key briefing.'"

Ness gestured for Wild to sit but remained standing himself. "As you all know, I've worked with Sam on several cases, and he's been very helpful. He practically cracked the cemetery-scam racket single-handedly. And he's covering the Safety Director's office full-time for the *Plain Dealer*—and now that this investigation is coming under the wing of this office, well, I think it's appropriate for him to be here."

"Don't worry, gents," Wild said as he propped a Lucky Strike between his lips, "I'm under strict orders from your chief here not to write anything up till you've got something solid."

"Eliot," Chamberlin said, eyes narrowing, "I really don't think we should be tipping our hand to the opposition."

"We won't be," Ness said. "But keep in mind that the 'opposition' is a homicidal maniac who has the city in a state of panic, under a reign of terror. Part of our function is public relations."

Merlo was wide-eyed. "Public relations?"

"Yes," Ness said calmly. "We need to assure our citizens that their police force is on top of the problem. Doing everything it can to remove this madman from their midst. Mr. Wild's function will be to be a part of the investigation—and his investigative skills are considerable—which will lend his eventual reporting an insider's depth and authority."

Chamberlin said, "You may alienate the other papers."

"I'm keeping that in mind," Ness said. "I'll be monitoring Sam's output, and we'll be holding periodic press conferences and issuing press releases."

Chamberlin shrugged and leaned back in his chair; Merlo had an expression of pained skepticism, while Curry—caught between Merlo and Ness, two men he respected—stayed blank.

"We have ten victims, gentlemen," Ness said. "Nine are white, all were apparently healthy, able-bodied individuals, in the prime of life—between twenty-five and forty-five years. Six are males. Six were found within two to eight days after death. One was not found for two months."

Ness sat on the edge of the conference table.

"There was, Coroner Gerber tells me, relatively little hacking of the tissues," Ness continued, "and relatively few hesitation marks—but the direction of what marks there were indicates we have a right-handed individual."

"Hey, that narrrows the field," Wild said cheerfully. Merlo glanced at him coldly.

"I have spent a good deal of time going over the files in this case," Ness said. "I feel the police have done good work—particularly you, Detective Merlo—but we need to explore new ways of going about this investigation. Any ideas?"

Curry cleared his throat and said, "I think we should assign shifts of men to guard the approaches to the Run and perhaps patrol it."

"Not a good use of manpower, I'm afraid," Ness said. "Of the last five corpses, only one has turned up at the Run."

"What new ideas do *you* have?" Merlo asked, doing his best to keep impatience out of his voice.

"Well," Ness said, smiling pleasantly, "let's look at the facts. We have most of the bodies turning up in a given area of the city; and we have dismemberments that experts agree show a certain surgical skill. I think somewhere within or very near the Kingsbury Run area there is a well-equipped 'surgery' or 'workshop' or 'laboratory.'"

"A laboratory, in Kingsbury Run?" Merlo said.

"Yes." Ness gestured openhandedly. "It has to be soundproofed, easily cleaned, and there must be storage facilities of some sort—probably refrigeration."

Chamberlin lifted an eyebrow. "There couldn't be many places like that in the Kingsbury Run area."

"If such a workshop exists," Curry said thoughtfully, "we should be able to find and identify it."

"How do we do that, exactly?" Merlo said. "You can't see this lab or workshop or whatever from the outside—and there are hundreds upon hundreds of buildings in that area. Homes, shacks, industrial buildings, warehouses, butcher shops . . ."

"You go inside," Ness said.

"Without search warrants?" Merlo asked.

Ness smiled smugly. "Have you forgotten I'm in charge of the fire department, as well as the police? That's a run-down ratty section of town—I think it would be prudent to send fire wardens down there to check for building violations. Don't you?"

Merlo began to smile, too. "Yes. Yes. Very good, Mr. Ness."

"Something simple that we can do," Ness said, "is place advertisements and posters around the city asking for information—particularly the discovery of any large quantity of blood."

"That's been done to death," Wild said disgustedly.

"Not in forty-four languages it hasn't, which is what I'm having worked up. We're a city of just under a million people, Mr. Wild, of which seventy percent are foreign born or the sons and daughters of at least one foreign-born parent."

Chamberlin smiled, and so, finally, did Merlo. Curry looked intense. Wild just smirked, sitting in a cloud of Lucky smoke.

Merlo said, "These are good ideas, Director Ness. But I keep coming back to a basic limitation. Take our most recent victim—the fellow who floated by that bridge the other day, like a human jigsaw puzzle we had to try and put together. Even with his hands turning up, we haven't been able to I.D. him. In a murder case, you talk to the friends, you talk to the relatives. But how can you get a lead when you don't know who the hell's murder it is you're trying to solve?"

Ness pointed a finger at the rumpled detective, as if accusing him. "You've hit it on the head. We have to go back to square one. We have to concentrate on the victims we've identified."

"Andrassy and Polillo," Merlo said. Then he sighed. "But we've been over and over that."

"Not lately," Ness said. "Subsequent murders have a

way of taking precedence. Let's start back at Jackass Hill. What do we know about Edward Andrassy?"

Merlo said, without checking any notes, "Well, he lived with his parents on the near West Side. Rooming-house neighborhood. Police record as a drunk, petty brawler, jailed once for carrying a gun. He worked at several hospitals as an orderly, had medical books on gynecology and some of those nudist magazines in his room. He was seen in various saloons with various women, but was known to pick up men, too. He was a minor-league con man—sold toilet articles, peddled aphrodisiacs. The oddest incident we came across was when Andrassy told a friend of his, who'd complained that he and his wife hadn't been able to have a child, that he, Andrassy, was a 'female' doctor. Andrassy offered to examine the wife, and the friend agreed. During the 'exam,' Andrassy committed sodomy on her, with the husband in the room."

"It's like something out of Krafft-Ebing," Ness said, filling the room's shocked silence, shaking his head.

"Who?" Wild asked.

Ness said to Merlo, "You've talked to Andrassy's various girlfriends and boyfriends, obviously?"

"They all check out," Merlo said glumly. "Though we got the runaround from time to time—not all of them are nuts about cooperating with cops."

"That's the problem that runs throughout this case," Ness said with a tight, humorless smile. "We're dealing with vagrants and perverts and petty criminals—none of whom are terribly civic-minded."

Curry said, "But it's their own kind who are being struck down."

"They're individualists," Ness said. "They all think they can take care of themselves. We're the enemy."

Ness buzzed for Wanda, who brought the men coffee; Ness joined them at the conference table and they probed various aspects of the Andrassy killing.

"If Andrassy was an orderly," Chamberlin said, "he may well have met his eventual murderer at one of those hospitals—a doctor or an intern."

"We've checked," Merlo said, wearily matter-of-fact. "And double-checked."

"Tell us about the second victim to be I.D.'ed," Ness said. "Tell us what we know about Florence Polillo."

"Well," Merlo said, again without checking notes of any kind, "she lived in a rooming house at Thirty-two oh five Carnegie Avenue. She paid her rent by relief checks; her landlady reported she was no trouble, other than getting pesky when she drank, which was often. She'd apparently been sterilized in a botched abortion years ago and was all sentimental about children—she played with her landlady's kids and let them use her dolls. She had a big collection of dolls."

Curry said, "She sounds a little nicer than Andrassy."

"Who doesn't?" Merlo said. "But she was, to put it bluntly, a fat, drunken whore. Frequent arrests for street soliciting. She left behind a notebook of addresses, mostly relatives. We talked to taxi drivers, tavern pals, and so on, but got nowhere."

"You had one good suspect, though," Ness prompted.

"Well, yes," Merlo said. "'One-Armed Willie.' A bogus beggar. She lived with him for a while—not long before she got it. They used to hang around together at a seedy saloon near Central and Twentieth. They fought, over *what* we couldn't ascertain, and he's supposed to have threatened to 'cut her up in little pieces.' Thought we had a live one, but when we looked into it, Willie seemed innocent—of murder that is."

"Those are the two killings we're going to work," Ness said. "Andrassy and Polillo."

Merlo looked frustrated.

"And I want specifically to explore the angle that Andrassy and Polillo may have been acquainted. If we can prove that, if we can show that the Butcher is working the same 'social circle,' if you will, gaining their confidence and slaying them, one by one, we may be on our way to nailing him."

Merlo's eyes narrowed; grudgingly, he nodded his head.

"What I want you to do," Ness said to Merlo, "is work with the fire wardens in the search for the lab, as well as do follow-up interviews on all the upstanding citizens involved in the Andrassy and Polillo cases. Relatives and such."

"What about those citizens who aren't so upstanding?" Merlo asked. "Hobos and barflies?"

"That's not your department." Ness walked over to Curry and said, "Find yourself some smelly, dirty old clothes and lose your razor. You're going undercover."

Curry's eyes were wide. "In shantytown?"

"Exactly. Cops grilling the denizens of that community does no good at all."

"Like pissing in the wind," Wild said.

"Who's going with him?" Merlo asked.

"Nobody," Ness said.

Chamberlin spoke up. "But isn't it standard procedure for detectives to work in pairs?"

"Yes." Ness looked at Curry. "And that's why you're going in alone. Or almost alone—you'll wear a thirty-eight in an ankle holster. You'll work both settlements—the one at Commerce and Canal, and the one near the Thirty-seventh Street Bridge."

Curry raised his eyebrows, let out some air, and put the eyebrows back down. "Whatever you say, Chief."

"I want you to take a blackjack and a sharp jackknife, as well."

"No argument," Curry said.

Ness sipped his coffee. "I'll be going undercover myself," he said matter-of-factly. "I'm going to canvass the saloons around Kingsbury Run, and in the Flats."

"You'll risk being recognized," Merlo said. "You've had a lot of press."

"Thanks to me," Wild said.

"I'm a very ordinary-looking fella," Ness said with a wicked little smile. "And with some stubble on my face, and in some ratty old overalls, I'll just be another guy bellying up to the bar."

"Are you going alone, too?" Wild said.

"No," Ness said. "You're going with me."

"Oh," said Wild, flatly. Then with his usual archness: "Whatever you say . . . just don't expect me to call you 'Chief.'"

Ness turned back to Merlo. "Do we have a shot at identifying any of the other victims?"

"I *thought* we had a shot at the colored woman," Merlo

said, "whose bones were found under the Lorain-Carnegie Bridge."

"Her bones, including her bridgework," Ness said, nodding. "You've been checking with dentists?"

"Yes. Every one in the city."

"How many colored dentists are there in Cleveland?"

"Two. We've checked them both."

"She should be there. She should be in their records."

"I know," Merlo said, shrugging, frustrated. "She isn't."

Again Ness pointed at Merlo, his finger a gun. "Get a list of all the colored dentists in the state. There can't be too many. Approach them all. If that doesn't work, go national."

"It's a thought," Merlo granted him. "You know, there *was* a third colored dentist in town, but he died two years ago."

"Do his records exist?"

"Listings of patients, yes. X-rays and dental charts, no. They were transferred to other dentists."

Ness thought. "Tell you what. Take those patient listings and check them against any colored women whose names turn up on the local Missing Persons Bureau sheets. If you get a match, you may have our girl."

"That's a damned good idea," Merlo admitted. "But without dental records . . ."

"A relative may be able to identify the bridgework. I could identify my mother's bridgework at fifty paces."

Merlo shrugged, smiled humorlessly, said, "I'll give it a try. If we dead-end there?"

"We try something else." Ness turned back to Curry. "I want to be frank with you, Albert. I'm not sending you into shantytown just because you're a good investigator, which you are. And I certainly want you to worm your way into that sorry community and ingratiate yourself into some information. But I've also chosen you for this because, well . . . you may make a good Butcher bait."

"Butcher bait?" Curry said.

"Our man is homosexual, or bisexual, or . . . something. You may look good to him."

"Swell," Curry said.

"You'll need to be very careful. Trust no one, except your gun, blackjack, and knife. We have here, remember, a murderer who emasculated three of his male victims, while dismembering two of the female victims in such a way that the pelvic region remained attached to the upper thighs—fairly framing the victim's vulva. He has sex with both sexes, possibly after killing them."

Curry's face was white. "Mr. Ness, how can you discuss this so calmly?"

"Because it's the only way such things can be discussed."

Curry looked very white. "I . . . I don't know how we go about this, finding a madman. You're dealing with this like it's . . . a normal case. But he's a fiend . . . he's inhuman . . ."

"No," Ness said. "That's the awful part. He's as human as any of us. If he were a monster, we could pick him right out of the crowd. But we have an intelligent, possibly charming murderer who fits right in. Who may lead a perfectly normal life, except in this one little area."

"Having sex with the dead, you mean," Wild said with a sick smirk.

"What happens to the dead doesn't concern me," Ness said. "What I'm interested in, what we all are interested in, is the living—and keeping them that way."

"He should be killed," Curry said.

"He should be stopped," Ness said. "He's the Butcher, remember—we're the police."

7

Sheriff's deputy Bob McFarlin, though on duty, was out of uniform. His clothing—a light blue workshirt and baggy brown pants—wasn't frayed, nor (other than sweat circles) did it look worked in; this alone separated him from the rest of the clientele in the nameless tavern near Central and Twentieth. Bob was having a beer because he figured he deserved one; it wasn't the first beer of a long day, either, and probably not the last. He had, in fact, been deserving—and rewarding himself—beers right along.

A big man with a doughy face in which small, sleepy sky-blue eyes hid, he slouched bearlike against the bar, a foot on the rail, looking nothing at all like a representative of the law. Which perhaps made sense, as Deputy McFarlin—despite his title and position—had very little to do with the law, other than frequently breaking it.

He sipped his beer, lost in the bitter daze that he carried around with him much of the time; because as he slipped into his late fifties, he was definitely a man who felt life had given him the shaft.

Just a year ago he had been a city cop, desk sergeant in the Fifteenth precinct, where business had been good. Plenty of gambling and girls, which meant plenty of graft for all the boys. But then that lousy fucking reform mayor came along, with his lousy fucking G-man safety director, and holy shit, if cops didn't start going to jail! *Captains*, no less. And suddenly Bob McFarlin figured taking his pension was better than waking up to an indictment one sunny day.

Now he was reduced to this: just another bagman for the county sheriff.

Who was a decent enough guy, O'Connell, was, and being one of O'Connell's deputies would have been okay, back in the old days—a year and a half ago. But business these days was bad. The big gambling joints—the Harvard Club, the Thomas Club, and the rest—were shut down. That lousy fucking Ness wasn't content to play his goody two-shoes games inside the city limits—he had to go suck up to the county prosecutor, Cullitan, and line *him* up in this crime-busting shit!

And Cullitan, goddamnit, was a Democrat! Mayor Burton ran a *Republican* administration. What was Cullitan *thinking* of? It made no sense to McFarlin. What was politics coming to? Fuck, it hardly paid being a cop anymore.

Today, Monday, was McFarlin's day to make the rounds of the joints in the old Roaring Third precinct—only the roar was down to a dull one, these days. At least, thank God, the police crackdown hadn't yet found its way to the Flats and the other seedier working-class areas where little bookie joints and backroom card and crap games still thrived. Too small potatoes, McFarlin figured, and anyway, such operations tended to float.

But the Mayfield Road mob saw to it that a piece of even the smallest action in the city—and the county—got into their pockets; and they managed this through the sheriff's office. So Deputy McFarlin was a bagman for the mob *and* the sheriff, though it was up to somebody else to see that the Mayfield Road gang got its share.

Even in a sleazy little joint like this nameless hole, fifty bucks got coughed up weekly. After all, the weekend backroom poker game, three tables' worth, stirred up some profitable dust. Today McFarlin had hauled in better than six hundred bucks from the various payoffs from other bars, and handbooks, along the unsavory circuit he'd been working.

He was not worried about being jackrolled. He had a shiv in his pocket, and a .38 in his car, in the glove box where he stashed the money after each pickup. He kept the car locked up, parked in front of each collection spot. Nobody bothered it, or him. He was known on the streets he worked. Known as muscle for the sheriff and the mob.

He looked sleepy-eyed and doughy-faced and beer-bellied, but he had killed men with his hands, and people around here knew it.

It wouldn't have been such a bad dodge if the money were his to keep. But he was just the lousy goddamn bagman. He sipped his beer. He was glad this was the last stop. Late afternoon, and if he didn't shake a leg, he'd be tripping over the fake cripples and real perverts who swarmed around this smelly barrelhouse come evening.

"One more, Bob?"

McFarlin shook his head no to bullet-headed, cigar-smoking Steve, back of the bar, and was about to step away from the rail when a guy in shirtsleeves and a bow tie came in.

Tall, rangy, with curly, dark-blond hair peeking out from under a straw fedora, the guy looked familiar to McFarlin. He had a sharp-featured, sarcastic face, his mouth sneering around the cigarette dangling there, jacket slung over his arm.

He did not belong here. He looked clean and wore a seersucker suit. Guys who worked in steel mills did not wear seersucker suits, McFarlin knew—shrewd detective that he was.

Even if he didn't belong here, the guy moved with an easy confidence. He ambled down toward McFarlin's end of the bar and filled the space between the deputy and a bored-looking, stubbly-faced, out-of-work working stiff who'd been nursing the same beer for half an hour.

Now McFarlin looked closer and saw that the tall man had a notebook and pencil in one hand.

McFarlin said, "Another," and Steve nodded, looking with narrow eyes at the stranger in seersucker.

When Steve brought the beer to McFarlin, the stranger spun a silver dollar on the bar. Everybody standing at the bar looked at it hungrily. When it stopped spinning and clattered to a standstill, the guy said, "Just a beer. Keep the change."

Steve took the silver dollar, eyes narrowing even more. "Keep the change" was not something heard much in a joint like this.

"My name is Sam Wild," the guy said when Steve

brought the beer, and McFarlin recognized the name, or anyway, the byline. This guy was a reporter, with the *Plain Dealer*.

"I'm a reporter," he said. "With the *Plain Dealer*."

Steve looked at him blankly; his mouth was slack—it seemed a trick that the cigar didn't tumble out.

"I wonder if you'd mind a few questions."

Steve shrugged. He leaned back against the counter behind him. Found a dirty rag with which to polish a glass.

"I understand Florence Polillo used to come in here."

"That's right," Steve said. His voice was husky, but a little high-pitched.

"What can you tell me about her?"

"She don't come in here no more."

The reporter grinned, drew on his cigarette. "I guess not. Getting hacked to pieces cuts down on a girl's social life."

Steve polished the glass, getting it dirtier.

"Was she hooking?"

Steve said, "This is a reputable place mister."

The reporter glanced around, smirking, taking in the sawdust and smoke. "What could I have been thinking of?" He dug for something in a pocket of the jacket folded over his arm.

It was a mug shot, side and front photographs of a pleasant if vacant-looking, jug-eared young man.

"Ever see this guy before?"

Steve, without moving closer to have a good look, glanced at the photo the reporter was thrusting forward. He said, "No."

"You sure?"

"No."

"No? You mean you aren't sure?"

"I mean no I ain't ever seen him. You spent your dollar, mister."

"I'll spend more, if you got the right answers." He spoke up, working his voice above the sound of the exhaust fan in the ceiling. "That's a standing offer, if any of you gents would care to take a look at the photo."

"Fuck you," the stubbly-faced guy next to the reporter said.

But the guy on the other side of him reached for the photo and it was passed down the bar. The half dozen men present all had a look, but passed it back, without a word.

"His name," the reporter said, slipping the mug shot back in the jacket pocket, "is Eddie Andrassy. If that name's familiar to you, it might be because you saw it in the papers."

McFarlin, who was pretending to be paying no attention, damn near laughed out loud at that. Most of these guys couldn't read, and those that could wouldn't be wasting a nickel on a newspaper.

"He was one of the Butcher's victims," the reporter said, his smirk gone. "He was one of the first ones found. He had his dick cut off, gents. Balls, too. Cheers." He lifted his beer to them and slurped at it.

Nobody said a word. Steve seemed to be getting irritated, his face settling into a nasty mask.

"It would behoove you gents," said the smart-ass reporter, "to help me out if you can. Not only is there a standing reward of some five grand in it for you, it's folks on these very streets of yours that are getting hunted by this monster."

Nobody said a word. The ceiling fan churned.

"Florence Polillo used to hang around this joint," the reporter continued, "and I think Eddie Andrassy did, too, whether this apron here remembers him or not." He smiled without sincerity at the bartender and said, "Maybe you weren't working here back then. It's been over a year."

Steve said nothing; he had stopped polishing the glass, which was shining and filthy.

"Flo used to hang out with a guy named 'One-Armed Willie,'" the reporter said, mostly to Steve. "Does Willie ever come in here anymore?"

"No," Steve said.

"Is he around?"

"I hear he hopped a freight," somebody down the bar offered.

The reporter looked at Steve for confirmation, and Steve, with some reluctance, nodded.

"I'm interested," the reporter said loudly, above the fan, stepping away from the bar, "in hearing about anybody who used to do business with Flo, or was friendly with Flo—man or woman."

A guy down the bar a ways laughed. "You think the Butcher is a woman?"

"Could be. Over in London, they figured Jack the Ripper was a midwife, you know. Why, take old Flo herself. She looked sort of like a fullback I know, only the fullback is cuter. Any of you gents want to earn a few bucks, I'm paying for info—and unlike that standing reward, I pay up whether the info leads to an arrest or conviction or not."

The reporter smiled pleasantly at the bartender and his patrons, downed the remainder of his beer, and swaggered out, swinging his coat over his shoulder.

"Cocky son of a bitch," the stubbly-faced guy said, still nursing that same goddamn beer.

"The fucker," Steve said, looking at the door where Wild had disappeared.

"He should mind his own goddamn business," the stubbly-faced guy said.

McFarlin gave the man a more careful look. Something was stirring in the recesses of his brain.

"Did she really used to come in here," the stubbly-faced guy was saying, "that butchered broad?"

"Yeah," Steve said. "She sure did. She was a sweet ol' hag."

"Pity she got hacked up."

"Yeah," Steve agreed. "But she caused me trouble, getting it like that."

"How so?"

McFarlin, without being obvious, just out of the corner of his eye, studied the stubbly-faced guy. *I know him*, he thought. *Where do I know him from?*

"Well," Steve was saying, "her buying it like that brought the cops in here like goddamn flies. We had to shut the game down in the backroom, for weeks."

"Fuck that shit," the stubbly-faced guy said sympathetically.

"And they messed with our patronage," Steve said with an oddly dignified formality. "Rousting 'em, hauling 'em downtown for questioning. Some of the people who come in here, they got reason to wanna steer clear of the cops."

"Whores like Flo, you mean?"

"Yeah," Steve said.

Somebody down the bar laughed and said, "This place is fairy heaven, after seven."

Steve scowled at the voice's owner, said, "Go to hell, Pete." He looked at the stubbly-faced guy and said, "We ain't a fag hangout, bud. We just don't figure what hole you wanna stick it in is any of our business, catch my drift?"

The stubbly-faced guy grinned. "Their money is as good as mine, huh?"

Steve tried to smile back; it was hard for him. "That's it. It ain't any of our business, in general, is the idea."

Ness!

McFarlin damn near spit out his beer. He hoped his face hadn't shown his surprise.

But he'd be damned if this scummy-looking near-derelict next to him wasn't goddamn fucking Ness himself.

"Well, that guy Andrassy," Ness was saying, "I hear he was a fag."

"He was a two-way ghee," Steve said matter-of-factly, nodding, drawing a beer for a customer and taking it to him down the bar. Then he came back and said to the director of public safety, "But Eddie was a good kid."

And Ness, cool as a cuke (McFarlin had to hand it to the son of a bitch), said, "So he did hang out here, huh?"

"Yeah. He knew Flo. They weren't thick or anything, but they knew each other. Had, you know . . . mutual friends."

"That guy 'One-Armed Willie' the reporter was mentioning, you mean."

"Yeah," Steve said. "Him and others. Like, you know—Abe Seleyman, the strong-arm guy. And Frankie Dolezal—he's a plasterer who's plastered most of the time."

Ness laughed, sipped his beer.

McFarlin was impressed. He hated Ness's guts on general principles, but this was a fine, sneaky piece of police work. Ness was wearing well-worn work clothes, his hair was a brown, dry mop, his face stubbly, his teeth looked scummy. To almost anybody down here, he would be unrecognizable.

It took a cop like McFarlin to make him, and it had

taken him a while. McFarlin had never met Ness, but he had seen him any number of times, and not just in the papers; Ness, on the other hand, would not know McFarlin from Adam. There were scores of cops driven from the force, and only those prosecuted, or the higher-up ones, would have come to Ness's attention individualy.

But it wasn't the role Ness was playing that impressed McFarlin, though he was playing it well; it was the scam of coming in, sitting at the bar, waiting for the reporter to come in and prime the pump, and then sitting back with a bucket and letting the bartender fill it up. Part of McFarlin wanted to shake Ness's hand, but at the same time another part would've like to put a bullet in him.

"I don't think I know either of those guys," Ness was saying.

"Well," Steve said, "Abe's a real bastard to a lot of people, but he's always been jake around here. He's been shaking down small merchants in East Cleveland. The cops shut the real protection racket down, so a small-timer like him can make a little chicken-feed racket play, for a while."

"Nice work if you can get it," Ness said enviously. "This Frankie guy, is he in the same racket?"

McFarlin continued to be impressed: obviously Ness had heard Steve describe Frankie Dolezal as a plasterer, but was playing dumb to keep the bucket filling up.

"Naw," Steve was saying, "Frankie's a nice guy. He's kind of a roughneck—I seen him go after somebody with a knife before."

"Maybe *he's* the Butcher," Ness said, conversationally.

"You don't know Frankie," Steve said, actually smiling. "He's a sweetheart. He's got a brother-in-law on the cops, for Christ's sake. Goes to church regular. Works regular, too."

Ness shrugged, as if he'd lost interest. Finished his beer. Then he had one more, which he drank more quickly.

Once Ness had gone, McFarlin sat staring at the door.

"What's with you, Bob?"

McFarlin looked at the bartender blankly. He wondered, for a moment, what do do. Should he tell Steve who he'd just been blabbing to?

"Nothing at all, Steve," he said, downed his beer, and headed out to his car.

Within an hour he was standing before the desk in the office of Sheriff William O'Connell on the fourth floor of the Cuyahoga County Criminal Courts Building, which also housed the jail. The jail, as the sheriff and his people referred to the Criminal Courts Building, was separated from the Central Police Station by a parking lot and a world of bitterness.

"That goddamn gloryhound!" the sheriff, on his feet, was sputtering, waving a fist. He was a big, fat man with a square head and small dark eyes and, at the moment, a bright red face; he was sweating through his khakis despite the building's air-conditioning. His office was a moderately-sized affair decorated with awards of civic merit from the various suburban police departments where he had served the public and various gangsters, not necessarily in that order.

McFarlin knew all too well that the sheriff feared and resented Ness, who the papers were always saying would make a good county sheriff, if he ever got tired of the safety director's post.

"It was slick, Sheriff," McFarlin said, gesturing, shrugging. "Guy's a detective. You got to hand it to him."

"I hand him *shit*! That son of a bitch has cost us more money than . . ." Suddenly the sheriff began to smile. He sat back down. His desk was tidy in the way that the desk of a man who does little actual work is tidy.

"Sit down, Bob," the sheriff said. "Sit down."

Bob pulled up a straight-back chair and sat.

"This little Boy Scout bastard," the sheriff said agreeably, "has put his dick on the chopping block. You seen the papers?"

"Sure," Bob said, not getting it.

"He's taken over the 'Mad Butcher' investigation personally. Staking his whole goddamn rep on it."

"Well," Bob said, shrugging again, "you can't deny he's getting in there himself and doing the job."

The sheriff's face reddened again. "He's a showboat! An arrogant little prick! Doing it himself, out in the field . . ."

"From what I overheard," Bob said, "he was doing

good—gathering new information, lining up new suspects. He was getting somewhere."

The sheriff smiled like an evil cherub. "Exactly. And so can we."

"What?"

"Get somewhere."

"I don't follow you."

"You're not going to follow *me* at all." He pointed at his deputy. "You're going to follow Ness."

"Oh," Bob said, smiling, getting it.

The sheriff rose and went to a wire-meshed window and looked out, looked across at the Central Police Station and smiled. His small dark eyes glittered.

"And, Bob—you're going to steal that arrogant little prick's case right out from under him."

8

A knock woke Ness.

In the darkness, for a moment, he didn't remember where he was; then the stale smell, and the heat, and the rough, scratchy blanket, brought it back to him. He slipped out of the cotlike bed and padded toward the door in his stocking feet—he was sleeping in his socks, despite the heat, because the wooden floor in this rooming-house room was nothing you'd want to lay bare soles upon.

He didn't know what time it was—he'd left his wristwatch behind, back in the real world—but he'd gone to bed around one A.M., and it was still dark outside.

So whatever time it was, it was a hell of a time for somebody to come calling.

Another knock.

He was standing to one side of the door, questioning

the wisdom of going on this mission unarmed, reaching for the chipped pitcher on the washstand nearby, when he heard a harsh whisper from the other side of the door: "For Christ's sake, it's me."

Wild.

Ness let some air out, unhooked the eye latch that locked the door, and let the reporter in. He shut and relatched the door, and his hand fumbled across frayed wallpaper and found the light button. A bare bulb above threw weak yellowish light on the small shabby room and its sparse, metallic, institutional-gray furniture.

"This is a fucking cell," Wild said, pushing his straw fedora back, his eyes wide.

"Not really." Ness, in his underwear, sat on the cot. "I'd offer you a chair, but there doesn't seem to be one."

Wild sat next to Ness. "Well, we probably aren't the only guys sharing a bed in this joint tonight. Mind if I smoke?"

"What, and have you stink up the place?" Ness asked, then smiled and waved his permission.

Wild lit up and sucked on a Lucky, threw smoke out restlessly, shook his head. "Four nights in this dump. How can you stand it?"

"I don't mind. Beats hell out of a flophouse crib with a chicken-wire ceiling." Ness paused, then said, "You shouldn't be here, Sam."

"Well, I'm delivering a message. Merlo wants to talk to you."

Ness sat up. "Developments?"

"Think so." Wild shrugged. "He didn't tell me. He doesn't like having a 'newshound' on the team. Anyway, he's sitting in an unmarked car a couple blocks from here, off the main stem."

He gave Ness directions.

Ness got up and got his pants and shirt out of a dented metal wardrobe. "You better go on," he told Wild, motioning toward the door with his head. "We shouldn't be seen on the street together."

Wild stood, smoked nervously, said, "Eliot, you're going to get yourself killed. Why didn't we stick to the original plan, anyway? It was working out fine."

Stepping into frayed brown pants, Ness said, "I didn't know we were going to hit pay dirt so soon."

He was referring to the nameless tavern near Central and Twentieth. They had known it was a prime possibility, since Florence Polillo was known to have frequented the place; however, it was to have been only one of many such hellholes that Ness and Wild would hit, using the system Ness had cooked up whereby Wild asked provocative questions, then departed, leaving the already-present, undercover Ness to listen to what was said in the aftermath of the reporter's departure, asking questions himself when he could get away with it.

But discovering that victims Andrassy and Polillo had known each other—a fact that had eluded investigators for over a year—prompted Ness to stick with the nameless bar; and he had taken this room in a nearby two-story brick rooming house to better become an inconspicuous part of the local landscape.

He and Wild had continued pursuing their routine at other taverns in the areas bordering the Run, particularly the Roaring Third, but only from late morning till around six. Evenings, Ness—alone—would spend leaning against the rail in the seedy joint near Central and Twentieth. The canvassing has slowed down accordingly.

"Look, Sam," Ness said, bending to tie the laces of his heavy work boots, "I have three good suspects in that bar—and I've struck up conversations with all of 'em. In fact one of them lives right here in this rooming house."

"Jesus!" Wild said.

Ness, standing back up, raised a finger to his lips.

Wild went to the window and sent his cigarette trailing sparks out into the night. Then he turned to Ness, now fully dressed in his threadbare apparel, and said, "You're going to get yourself fucking killed."

Ness smiled dismissively.

Wild went to him and stared him down. "You don't even have a goddamn gun."

"I don't need a gun."

"Oh, yeah, you know all about that jujitsu stuff. That'll work swell against some crazy asshole with a butcher knife."

"Nobody knows me around here."

"Sure, sure. You're in disguise—just like Sherlock Holmes."

Ness had to wince at that; he'd been an avid Holmes reader since he was a kid. He didn't like to think he was acting out some childhood fantasy here. He preferred to consider this good, solid undercover police work.

"You got stubble on your face," Wild said evenly, "and you washed the Vitalis out of your hair. You put some gunk on your teeth, and you slouch, and you swear. But somebody who knows you will *make* you, my friend."

"Who would know me down here?"

"The Butcher."

Ness moved toward the door. "Merlo's waiting, Sam . . ."

Wild was patting the air with one hand, gently. "Eliot, let's not forget that you and the Butcher have something in common."

Ness laughed shortly. "Such as?"

"You're both publicity hounds. Now don't give me that look! I'm all *for* you getting headlines—I've helped out enough, in that line. And I know, I know, it's part of your job to make the papers. It's something you do well. But so does the Butcher."

The truth of that jabbed sharply at Ness, but he said nothing.

"He leaves these bodies out in the open, where they are bound to be found eventually," Wild went on, "when he could be disposing of them in such a way that they *wouldn't* be found—like the heads and hands aren't found, when he doesn't want them to be."

"Make your point," Ness said.

"My point is, this guy probably has a goddamn scrapbook of what he's been up to—he may even bump another victim off, or at least pull a body out of his fridge and dump it, when he's stopped getting as much play in the papers as he'd like. See, he *likes* being the Mad Butcher of Kingsbury Run—not just for the butchering, either. For the celebrity."

"Well, you may have something there."

"Of course I do. And if he's collecting his press

clippings, and believe me he is, he knows all about you declaring private war on him. He hasn't just *seen* your mug in the papers—he's likely memorized it. He ain't no fool, but you, my friend, are bordering on that condition."

"If he recognizes me," Ness said, "maybe he'll come to me."

"Oh, yeah, and cut your head off and go steady with you, till the next idiot comes along."

"Sam . . ."

Wild sighed in frustration, then gave Ness a look so earnest and concerned it surprised them both. "You may also spook your boy. Have you considered that? You might make him take a powder."

Ness shrugged matter-of-factly. "If he's one of the suspects I've narrowed in on, then he'll give himself away if he runs."

Wild shook his head, rolled his eyes. "It's like trying to reason with a fucking brick wall."

Ness took Wild by the arm and led him to the door. "Then why don't you go on your well-meaning way before that brick wall falls on you."

Now Wild put a sarcastic grin on his face. "It's your funeral, buddy boy. I'll see you tomorrow morning, round ten at that joint on East Forty-ninth, to do our vaudeville act . . . if you're still breathing."

And he left.

Ness waited five minutes, or what felt like five minutes at least, and soon was approaching the black Buick parked on a residential side street that was shady in several senses of the word, where more rooming houses, some frame, some brick, huddled like conspirators. He slid in on the rider's side.

Merlo, who hadn't seen Ness in his undercover attire, started for a moment, then smiled and shook his head.

"Hell," Merlo said. "For a minute there, I thought *you* were the Butcher."

Ness, shutting the door, killing the dome light, said, "Sam Wild thinks I'm an easy target—thinks the Butcher will see right through this."

"Maybe," Merlo said, "but I doubt it."

Actually, Merlo didn't look much like a cop tonight,

either. He wore a checkered sportshirt and slacks and no hat. But then Merlo didn't ever look much like a cop with his scholarly glasses and thin, dour face, though tonight he seemed less dour. He was smiling, in fact.

"You look like the bearer of glad tidings," Ness said.

"That I am," Merlo said. "Your notion about checking the patient records of that dead colored dentist with appropriate Missing Persons reports, well . . . it paid off in spades, if you'll pardon the expression."

Merlo handed Ness a manila file folder and passed him a pocket flash. Ness opened the file and lit up the face in the photo: a black woman, attractive if slightly heavyset, about forty.

"Mrs. Rose Wallace," Merlo said. "Lived on Scoville Avenue—that's not far from where the skeleton was discovered. Been missing since August twenty-first of last year."

Ness studied the picture: the face seemed somehow both good-natured and hard. "Do you have anything besides matching the Missing Persons report to her name on the dentist's list?"

"We sure do," Merlo said. "You were right on that account, too. We showed the bridgework to her son and he broke out crying. It was pretty distinctive—three gold teeth and all. He recognized it as hers, all right."

"Good, good," Ness said. "Any rap sheet on her?"

"No. But talking to her son and neighbors, it's clear she ran with a rough crowd—and in the same lowlife parts of town as Edward Andrassy and Florence Polillo. She worked in taverns. Maybe hustled. Heavy drinker."

An old car rumbled by; Ness clicked off the pen flash and the men sat in near darkness.

"Nice work, Sergeant." Ness smiled over at the detective, glad that he'd trusted his instincts and kept the dogged Merlo on the job. "You got right on top of this. I appreciate it. Hell, I admire it."

"Mr. Ness," Merlo said, "I eat, sleep, and drink this case. I go to sleep thinking about it—when I finally do go to sleep—and when I wake up, I'm still thinking about it."

"I know the feeling." Ness lifted a finger to one eye. "These aren't bloodshot for effect."

Merlo laughed shortly, then said, "I also have some preliminary info on your three suspects."

Ness had relayed the names to Merlo through Wild.

"Good," Ness said. "Anything interesting?"

"Nothing on the bartender, this guy Steve Fabian, other than some busts back in speakeasy days. He does own the place. What makes you suspect him?"

"Just that that saloon is his little world. A world where at least two victims—Andrassy and Polillo—did a lot of living before they died. He has relationships with all his regulars—they trust him. And he's pretty cold."

"Cold?"

"I've talked to him about the Butcher a couple of times, and he doesn't seem particularly broken up that the victims include friends of his. And his eyes just kind of . . . glaze over, when the subject comes up. He seems detached. And, he's got a sadistic streak. He's his own bouncer—he tossed a kid out the other night and busted him up pretty good in the process."

"That's not much to go on," Merlo said.

"No," Ness admitted. "And the kind of joint he's running, he's running pretty close to form."

"What kind of joint *is* it?"

"Hangout for petty thieves and prostitutes. But it's more than that—it's a regular latter-day court of miracles."

"Miracles?"

Ness grinned lopsidedly. "Yeah—every evening half the beggars in town stumble in there and get miraculously cured. Backs get straight, missing limbs appear out of empty sleeves, blind guys match quarters with each other for drinks . . . must be something in the water, only nobody's drinking water."

"The dregs of humanity," Merlo said archly. "Perfect stalking grounds for the Butcher."

"One of those beggars was this fellow One-Armed Willie, who apparently knew both Andrassy and Polillo. He sounds like a suspect to me."

Merlo shrugged wearily. "Willie was able to prove he was out of town when several of the murders occurred."

"Willie seems to get around. Word at the tavern is he's hopped a freight to pick oranges in Florida—how many hands he's using, I'm not sure. Maybe we could talk to the Florida authorities. Even if Willie's not a valid suspect, he ran in the same 'social circle' as the others. We need to talk to him."

Merlo nodded. "I'll get on it."

"Anything on Seleyman?"

Merlo shrugged again, not so wearily. "He's a Turk—got a laundry list of a rap sheet, petty stuff but a lot of it. He used to be a professional wrestler, barnstormed all over the country when he was younger."

"I want him shadowed," Ness said.

"I took the liberty of doing that already," Merlo said, somewhat sheepishly.

"Undercover guys?"

"Yes. But I told them to stay clear of that tavern of yours."

"Good. What are their early reports?"

"Seleyman does indeed have a petty shakedown racket going, in East Cleveland. Small merchants—shops, cafés, saloons."

"Tied in with the Mayfield Road boys?"

"Hard to say. You know, we have enough to bust him, right now . . ."

Ness shook his head no. "I want to clip him on more than a petty-racketeering rap."

"If he's the Butcher . . ."

"Let's wait till we have better reason to believe that that's so—then the petty-racketeering charge will keep him off the street, and out of his digs, long enough for us to send a team in and build the Butcher case."

Merlo nodded, looking at Ness shrewdly. Ness could sense Merlo's respect and gratitude—even if the scholarly-looking detective's feathers had been ruffled at first by Ness's intrusion into "his" case.

"What about Dolezal?" Ness asked.

"Well," Merlo said, "he's fifty-two years old, an immigrant. Speaks half a dozen languages, of which English is his worst. A plasterer and bricklayer by trade. Been on some WPA projects. Right now he's working over on Harvard Avenue for the U.S. Aluminum Company, where they say he's a good joe. Apparently was once a fairly well-to-do contractor. What arrests he has, you'll be interested to know, fall into an old category of yours."

"Oh?"

"He was supposedly a very successful if small-time bootlegger. Was in the money at the height of Prohibition—known to everybody in the district. I'm surprised you never ran into him."

"I didn't start working Cleveland till after repeal," Ness said. "But we were rounding up former bootleggers to testify in those police corruption cases last year. He must be one of the ones we were never able to track down."

"That's understandable," Merlo said, "because he's been seriously on the skids. We checked with his brother-in-law, who really is a cop, like that bartender said—a patrolman—which is where a lot of this info came from, incidentally. And apparently Mr. Dolezal hit hard times not so much because of the Depression, but because he keeps looking for the bottoms of bottles, and finding them."

"I've witnessed some of that," Ness said. "He put ten bottles of beer away last night. Have you got him shadowed, too?"

"Yes. For the last three nights. Last night he was in that tavern where you were, of course."

"And the nights before?"

"Various parks, approaching various men. Transient types."

"I see."

"If he's our boy, and we keep him shadowed long enough, we may catch him in the act."

"That's fine, but if so, let's try to catch him before he chops somebody's head off, okay?"

"Speaking of which," Merlo said slyly, "there is *one* other interesting fact about Mr. Dolezal's past."

"Saving the best for last, Sergeant?"

"You be the judge, Director Ness." Merlo smiled nastily. "A few years ago, between bricklaying jobs, the suspect worked in a meat-packing plant."

"Doing what exactly?"

"Slaughtering animals."

The two men sat in the dark and listened to the silence.

Finally Ness said, "The coroner and other experts think the Butcher has surgical training."

"Well, Dolezal obviously has at least some knowledge of carving, knows something about bone structure."

Ness nodded. Then he used the pen flash to study the face of Rose Wallace again, asking, "How goes the search for the murder lab?"

"Nothing has turned up as yet, but five teams of fire wardens, accompanied by detective bureau men I hand-picked, are out in the field. They're reporting to me, until you're back in your office. Oh, and Curry reported in from undercover today, as well."

"What did he have to report?"

"Not much so far. He's been hanging out at the shantytown at Canal and Commerce since Monday. Turned nothing up, to speak of. He came in this morning looking like hell—hasn't been sleeping, and who can blame him."

"Did you send him home?"

"Yes. Told him to get some rest. By now he's probably heading out again."

"To the other shantytown, this time, I trust."

"Right. The more spread-out one, not far from Jackass Hill."

"Good." Ness got out of the car quickly, then looked in the window. "Now, I have further instructions."

Merlo leaned forward eagerly. "Yes?"

"Go home," Ness said. "Get some rest yourself."

Then he walked back to the two-story brick tenement where he was inhabiting suite 3.

As he went up the creaking stairs, he noted a figure seated on the landing, using the top step for a chair. A gathered-into-itself figure, leaning against the wall, crying.

Ness slowed. The sound was eerie—like a child's sobbing. Soft, pitiful, plaintive.

And the man crying was Frank Dolezal.

"Frankie?" Ness said, stopping a few steps from where the blond man sat.

It was dark, but both men had their night vision in full swing. And Dolezal, his unshaven face wet with tears, squinted at Ness, then recognized him, uttering in a guttural slur, "Oh. Hello, Harry."

Harry was the name Ness had made himself known by at the nameless saloon.

"You okay, Frankie?"

Dolezal nodded yes, but said, "Not so good, Harry. Not so good. You want drink?" He offered a wine bottle in a paper bag.

"Thanks," Ness said, and sat on the step next to the man, pretending to drink from the bottle before passing it back.

Dolezal used both hands to clutch the bottle as he drank from it. That was good: Ness wanted both of Dolezal's hands in plain sight. Night vision or no, he wished he and his drinking partner were somewhere other than this unlit hall.

"I need move, Harry."

"What do you mean, Frankie?"

"Can't sleep. Room has ghost."

"A ghost?"

Dolezal nodded. He had a square head and haunted eyes.

"I need move," he said. "That woman still in my room."

"What woman, Frankie?"

"Flo."

"Flo?"

"Woman who get chopped up."

Both of Dolezal's hands held the bottle.

"Oh. Who do you suppose did that?"

Dolezal's eyes flared and he gulped at the wine.

"I think maybe it was that wrestler," Ness said.

"Abe?" He snorted; suddenly the nervousness, the fear, was gone. "I am stronger than him."

"I bet you are," Ness said.

Actually, the man seemed small to Ness, albeit stocky.

"I am very strong. More I drink, more strong I am."

Ness said nothing: he was watching the two hands on the bottle.

"All his fault."

"Whose fault, Frankie?"

"Damn Hoover. That goddamn Herbert Hoover."

Somehow Ness felt the former president would have an alibi for the Butcher killings.

Suddenly Dolezal put a hand on Ness's shoulder; the grip was surprisingly strong. "You drink much, Harry?"

"Too much, sometimes, Frankie."

"You ever . . . wake up and not know what you do?"

"Sometimes. That happens to you, Frankie?"

"Sometimes," he said gravely. He gulped at the wine, wiped off his mouth with a grimy hand, which he'd removed from Ness's shoulder. Then both hands settled back on the bottle, caressingly. "Sometimes I no remember."

"Do you remember Flo, Frankie?"

"I remember Flo. Fat gal."

"Flo Polillo."

"Flo. Fat Flo."

"Did you drink with her?"

"Yes. Many nights. Flo could drink. Rose, too."

Rose!

"Rose, Frankie?"

"Rose."

Ness watched the two hands on the bottle.

"Was Rose fat like Flo, Frankie?"

"Rose was big, but not like Flo. Colored gal."

"I don't think I know her, Frankie."

"Not see her in long time."

"Rose, huh? Can't place her . . . what was her last name?"

"Wallace."

Ness watched the two hands.

"I move tomorrow. After I get my check."

"Move, Frankie?"

"Ghost in room. And they search houses. You not hear, Harry?"

"Who's searching houses?"

"Cops or somebody. Looking in everybody house. Looking in everybody business. I move tomorrow, Harry."

Dolezal rose, shakily, bracing himself on the wall. Ness watched the man's hands, felt very aware of the flight of steps at his back.

But Dolezal only shuffled down the corridor, weaving like the drunk he truly was, and entered suite 5.

Ness entered his own "suite" and gathered his things. He, like Frankie Dolezal, had decided to move.

Only he was moving tonight.

Right this minute.

9

Detective Albert Curry, his face stubbly, his denim work shirt and brown cotton pants raggedy, stood in darkness on the East Fifty-fifth Street Bridge and stared into the ravine that was Kingsbury Run.

Curry knew that the Run had once been a beauty spot with gardens and stone quarries and lakes—his working-class parents, Cleveland natives, had told him so; now it was sumac bushes and trash heaps and a stench-emitting pool. But on this almost-cool, overcast Thursday night, just past nine, you could see nothing more than the yardlights of the railroads. The sickle blade of the moon, glowing behind dark clouds, was no help.

Somewhere down there was the shantytown where he would become a resident. Somewhere down there, possibly, was the so-called Mad Butcher of Kingsbury Run.

Curry walked back to his Ford sedan and began to drive, navigating deserted side streets whose occasional streetlamps were feeble against the night, matches lit in a vast dark room. He felt strangely unrefreshed from his all-afternoon sleep: the three days and nights he'd spent at the shantytown at Canal and Commerce had taken their toll. His apartment had seemed unreal to him, like something in a dream; the reality of the packing-crate world he'd been inhabiting lingered like a bad taste.

He felt hungover from the strange cocktail of boredom and fear: the boredom of long hot days mingled with the fear of long hot nights in the crowded cluster of shacks on a rubbish-strewn hillside just blocks from Cleveland's downtown.

He had met many homeless men, any of whom might be the Butcher, none of whom struck him as such. Some of them were down-and-out and others seemed taken by wanderlust. They were as young as eighteen and as old as seventy; there were a few families, women putting the wash out on makeshift lines, a few raggedy kids wandering about, though mostly the community had seemed male.

What was troubling Curry was something vague, something he couldn't put his finger on. Perhaps it was the lack of structure, which meant so much to a career cop like Curry. Meals seemed to happen now and then, time blurred meaninglessly, men came and went, without a hello, without a good-bye.

Or maybe it was that these men seemed to live in a different world, with its own ways, its own values. They were cleaner than he had imagined, many of them; there was less drinking; some of the men read papers, books, magazines—there was political talk, Red-tinged mostly, predictably. Bums were chased out when they appeared—shantytown welcomed hobos and tramps only. The hobos, he had soon discovered, were migratory workers; his cover story, of coming up from Florida having picked oranges, put him safely in that category. Tramps, it seemed, were migrants who occasionally worked—odd jobs and such—but did a lot of back-door begging at homes and restaurants. Bums were skid-row refuse to be disdained.

That was why the hobos and tramps were cleaner, better kept, than he'd imagined they'd be: you had to be clean to get that job; you had to be clean to mooch that meal.

He wheeled the sedan gently off Bessemer Avenue onto a dirt road, which wound behind the Ferro Foundry to a dump. He stopped beside a delapidated, deserted brick building, its windows dark and many of them broken-out. He locked and left the car here and began to walk, bedroll on his back. In front of him were flatcars; to the right, a sheer drop-off into that dark, stagnant pool, gurgling down there like a drowning man.

He found the least-steep place and made his way down to the banks of the foul pool where one victim's parts (some of them) had turned up; the moon and lights from a nearby viaduct were silver on the water's greasy surface. The pool was separated from the railroad tracks by a narrow strip, thick with sumac bushes, though a footpath of sorts was there. He took it.

Branches reached out for him as he felt his way along. A breeze rustled the bushes, which he began to imagine hid the Butcher himself, and why not? This was the Run, after all, the Headhunter's stomping grounds. . . .

Curry reached into his pocket and gripped his jack-knife, the blade of which was open. He'd rather have been holding a flashlight, though—it would've made his journey simpler—but he didn't figure a hobo would carry one of those. Did the Butcher?

He could hear his own heart beating as he pushed branches out of the way, but after a time the scrub trees and brush let up somewhat, and he found himself in a clearing. And in the clearing, draped in shadows and the cool gray-blue of the cloud-filtered moonlight, was the shantytown.

The shantytown at Commerce and Canal had been crowded in upon itself; this one, though, with perhaps a few shanties less than the thirty-some at the other settlement, seemed larger. It sprawled across the level ground of the gully and began crawling up the embankment. Shacks and lean-tos, sagging like the backs of old men, had some breathing room here—though why anyone would want to breathe this sewer-tainted air, Curry couldn't fathom. Corrugated metal, broken boards, packing crates, provided walls for the hovels; tar paper on roofs was kept in place with stones or chunks of cement. The ground was carpeted with straw and chicken feathers and charred tin cans and discarded rubbing-alcohol bottles.

Several fires were going, with men clustered near them, but not huddling close to the flames; while it was cool, it wasn't cold, and the fires were presumably to keep the bugs away. And the Butcher perhaps. In fact, many of the men here were not sleeping in their shacks; they were stretched out under the stars, using their shoes for a pillow, and now and then a raggedy-ass pet dog slept near its raggedy-ass master. It was a lifeless scene, frozen, like something in a mural. Even when the streetcar-like Rapid Transit trains went roaring by on the nearby tracks, spitting sparks, nothing stirred. The gulley floor might have been a battlefield where corpses were strewn.

Curry approached one of the fires where three men sprawled, leaning back on bedrolls, enjoying the quiet night—quiet but for the rattle and roar of the perodic Rapid Transit trains.

"Mind if I join you, gents?" Curry asked. He smiled mildly, not wanting to come on too strong.

Two of the men shrugged casually, while their eyes studied him. The other man, a heavyset, white-bearded hobo in his late fifties or early sixties, said, "Sit yourself down, son."

Curry placed his bedroll on the ground and sat with his back braced against it.

"There's a couple shacks standing empty," the old man said, pointing. "You can claim one if you like."

"What happened to the former tenants?" Curry asked.

"Spooked by the Butcher," said one of the other men, a tall, thin man in his late thirties maybe, who'd shaved within the last several days. He wore a plaid shirt and his hair was light.

"Lot of that going around?" Curry said.

"Some."

The old man said, "I'm not afraid of this goddamn Butcher. Killing's nothing new to this ol' life."

"How do you mean?" Curry asked.

The old man snorted a laugh; he plucked a corncob pipe out of his shirt pocket and stuffed a couple cigarette butts in and lighted it up. "Shootings, stabbings," he said. "I seen 'em all—over nothing, over some wisecrack, or at most a hijack . . ."

Curry had learned that "hijacking" down here meant robbing a fellow 'bo while he was sleeping. He had also learned that life on the road included frequent irrational, violent outbursts over insults, real or imagined.

"Guys who been pickin' somewhere come in with a pocketful of cash, start flashing it around, pretty soon there's trouble. They get to drinking, then to fighting, and before long somebody's got a knife. A lot of people die in this ol' life, and nobody even keeps track of it. You're on your own here, son."

It seemed death was commonplace in these parts.

"So the Butcher doesn't frighten you," Curry said, "any more than anything else around here does."

"Not many are all that spooked by this spook. Long as a person ain't a fool and goes walking alone in the Run—like you was doing."

"I just hopped off a freight," Curry said.

"I think he kills faggots and whores," said the third man, another gaunt individual, but a younger, not so well-shaven one. His eyes were bright, catching the reflection of the fire. "I think a real man's got nothing to fear."

"That one guy was a sailor, they say," said the clean-shaven hobo.

The bright-eyed one laughed derisively and said, "I never knew a sailor who didn't take it up the poop deck."

"Gets lonely out at sea," the old man said philosophically. Then he looked at Curry carefully, saying, "Where you in from?"

"Down Florida way," Curry said. "Picking fruit."

"Long as there's fruit, there'll be 'bos to harvest it." The old man smiled; he didn't have all his teeth, and what he did have he wouldn't have forever. "You ain't been on the road long, have you, son?"

"No," Curry said, smiling a little. "Does it show?"

"A mite."

Curry knew it showed more than a "mite," though he didn't know what to do about it. These men had earned the road-weary look they carried: eyes bloodshot from the dirt and cinders of riding the rails; leather-dry, sun-brown faces; callused hands.

"You don't look like you been in Florida," said the younger one. "You're pale, like a baby's butt." There was no suspicion in his voice. It seemed merely an observation. He took a small waxed-paper bundle out of his breast pocket; it contained a sack of Bull Durham, rolling papers, and a book of matches.

"The railroad dicks pulled me off a train in Georgia," Curry said smoothly. He'd used this story at the other shantytown and was starting to believe it himself. "Turned me over to the locals and they vagged me. I didn't see the sun in two weeks."

"Cops get your grubstake?" the younger one asked, eyes narrowing.

"No," Curry said, feeling a little wave of panic. Nobody had asked him that before.

"The cops didn't take your dough?" the old man said, astounded. "What kind of cops was these?"

"Well," Curry said, gesturing, improvising, "I had a hundred bucks, and I didn't want to travel with it. So I mailed it to a girlfriend of mine in West Virginia. I seen her the other day and picked it up."

"And she didn't *spend* it?" the young one asked, eyes widening, as he rolled his cigarette.

"She knew I'd beat the bejesus out of her if she did," Curry said with a wicked smile, proud of himself for coming up with this line of malarkey on such short notice.

"Better be careful," the old man said, gesturing with his corncob pipe. "Money's dangerous now, 'cause it's so short. You go flashing a roll around, round here, the jackrollers'll get ya, sure as I gotta take a shit."

And with that, the old man got up and wandered off into the darkness to the designated spot, and Curry turned to the other two and said, "Now, it seems to me a guy wandering off to take a piss or a dump or what have you, in the middle of the night like this, is asking for trouble."

"From that Butcher, you mean?" the clean-shaven one asked. He laughed shortly and waved the notion off. "Not tonight, anyway."

"Why do you say that?"

"Got my reasons."

"Such as?"

"Maybe I know who he is."

"You know who the Butcher is?"

"Maybe."

Curry tried not to let his anxiety show. "There's a big cash reward, you know."

"Not for the likes of me," he said. He reached behind him and withdrew an unmarked bottle of clear fluid; rubbing alcohol, most likely. He swigged at it. Then he offered some to Curry and the young bright-eyed 'bo. Curry declined, but the other did not.

"That burns," the bright-eyed one said, grinning, wiping off his mouth with the back of one hand.

"I live for it," the clean-shaven one said. "Army did it to me. You drink or you go bughouse."

"Were you in the war?" Curry asked.

"Yes," he said, taking his bottle back from the kid. "They made a tramp outa me. Learned to live off what I could carry on my back. Learned I could live anywheres."

Curry couldn't tell whether the man was spiteful or grateful, and he wasn't sure the man knew, either.

Soon the old guy came back and sat back down against his bedroll. A Rapid Transit train went screeching by, sparking up the night.

"Look at 'em," the old man said, "going to their fancy houses. Goin' nowhere!"

"I'd like to be going there," said the bright-eyed one. "I had a good job once." He didn't say what it was.

"They got no independence," said the old man, as if he felt sorry for the commuters heading out to ritzy Shaker Heights. "They own too much. It comes to own them. When the stock market crashed, my life didn't change. Long as I keep moving, something will turn up—another flop, another ride, another handout, another cigarette butt, another odd job."

The bright-eyed kid studied the old man, his expression sober—perhaps he was contemplating the life ahead of him.

The thought of one of his companions knowing the Butcher's identity was gnawing at Curry.

So he said to the old man, "This fella here says he knows who the Butcher is," and he gestured to the clean-shaven war vet.

The old man shrugged, digging out more butts for his pipe. Not terribly interested.

"If you know who he is," Curry said to the vet, "why don't you call the cops or something?"

"The cops," the vet said, "work for the rich. Fuck 'em all, I say."

"I seen the newspapers," the old man said, getting his

pipe going again, "and the two corpses they put names to, neither of 'em is our people."

"A faggot and a whore," said the vet.

"But the other victims might be hobos," Curry said. "The fact that they weren't identified—"

"Look," said the clean-shaven one forcefully. "I *know* who the Butcher is, and he's moved on. I don't think we'll see him again."

That seemed to satisfy the others—except for Curry, who was stewing in his own frustration, not being able to follow up harder on the matter without blowing his cover.

"Think I'll sack out," the bright-eyed kid said suddenly, and he headed for a nearby shack, then disappeared inside. The clean-shaven war vet got up after a while, too, lugging his bottle of rubbing alcohol.

That left only the old man. He smiled with patience and wisdom and bad teeth. He said, "Be careful tonight, son."

Curry smiled back at him. "I thought you weren't worried about the Butcher."

"I'm not. But watch yourself—there's thieves among us. Guys who are nice to your face, waiting till your back is to 'em."

Curry nodded. "Thanks."

"I'd sleep out in the open."

"Well, actually, I'd rather have a roof over my head."

"Up to you," the old man said, and began undoing his bedroll near the dwindling fire.

Curry found a small, vacant shack; you could stand in it, but then you can also stand in a closet, which this was barely larger than. The "floor" was well-worn earth, and Curry unrolled his bedding—two blankets, which held an extra set of clothes, a tin cup, fork/knife/spoon, several pots, a frying pan, and a small, hard block of salt. He wrapped these items in one of the blankets and spread the other out like a tablecloth and placed himself on it like a meal he was serving up; he stuffed his shoes under the blanket as a pillow. The hard ground was uncomfortable, but he didn't mind. This shelter was more than he'd had at the other shantytown. He felt more secure here than he had there. He might even be able to drift asleep.

The man was on top of him, the knife blade pressing against his throat.

Curry's eyes snapped open; he didn't know if it was seconds later or hours. He only knew he was looking up into the clean-shaven face of the war vet who'd been so friendly at the fire. He only knew the point of a very sharp jackknife was poking him in the throat, right under the Adam's apple.

"Give me your grubstake or I'll kill you," the man said.

"I don't have any money," Curry said.

"You been harvesting," he said, lip curling into a sneer, rubbing alcohol on his breath. "You got money. Hundred bucks, you said!"

"Okay, okay. Take the knife away and I'll get it for you; it's in my shoes." He jerked a thumb at the lump behind his head.

The vet pulled back, the blade eased off, and Curry's hand found the frying pan handle and he swung the thing and the guy saw it coming and pulled to one side, catching the impact on his arm. He howled and pitched to one side, no longer atop Curry, but the knife was still in his hand. Curry's hand dropped the frying pan and he fumbled at his pant leg, pulling it back to get at the little revolver in the ankle holster; but the guy was diving at him with the knife again so Curry ducked to one side and kicked, like Ness had showed him, jujitsu-style, and the guy went crashing through the side of the shanty. The little building caved in on Curry, who found himself flailing against the pieces of wood and cardboard and tar paper, a joker caught by a collapsing house of cards.

By the time Curry had shaken himself free from the disassembling shanty, the war vet was running into the darkness of the Run, toward the train yard.

The noise had roused a good deal of the shantytown populace, and the first one to approach Curry was the old man, who was again smiling. "I told you to be careful."

"Damnit!" Curry said. "He got away!"

"Good thing for him he did," the old man said, matter-of-factly. "Hijacks get whipped or kilt in a jungle, if they get ketched."

"He came at me with a knife!"

"Well, sure."

"You don't understand . . . he could be the Butcher."

"No, I don't hardly think so," the old man said, taking Curry by the arm.

"And why not?"

"Remember how he said he knew who the Butcher was?"

"Right—and he was talking about himself!"

"No, no, no. I know who he was talkin' about. Lot of us do."

"You do?"

"Sure. Who do you think told him? I can even show you where he lived."

Now, Curry thought, *I'm getting somewhere.*

"Where did he live?" Curry asked.

"He lived in a cave he carved out, just up the hill. Kind of a hermit type of tramp."

Maybe, Curry thought, *these days undercover have all been worth it . . . maybe I can hand Ness the Butcher on a platter.*

"But we don't have anything to worry about," the old man said. "He never bothered none of us. And besides, he seems to have lit out. Ain't seen him in days."

"Do you know his name?"

The Butcher's name!

"Ben," the old man said. "He just went by 'Ben.'"

10

Ness wore a gun, a Colt revolver, in a shoulder holster under the left arm of his tailored gray suit; he also wore a gray-and-white-speckled tie and a white handkerchief in his breast pocket. A snap-brim fedora shielded him from the

Friday-afternoon sun, except possibly from its reflection in the fifty-cent shine of his shoes. He seemed out of place, standing before the run-down, two-story brick building on Central Avenue, like someone who'd taken a wrong turn from downtown, or better times. If he felt uneasy, however, his wardrobe had nothing to do with it: the gun did. He rarely carried one. Diplomacy was, after all, his preferred ammunition.

Today his ammunition was thirty-eight caliber.

Detective Albert Curry, also wearing a suit and gun, his face clean-shaven, came around the corner and up to Ness, saying, "Merlo has the back stairs covered."

"Good." Ness motioned across the street, where their car, a black Ford, was parked in front of a vacant lot and near a three-story, paint-peeling frame rooming house. "Sit on the rider's side. Pretend to read the newspaper."

"All right," Curry said. "What time do you expect him?"

Ness checked his wristwatch. "It's not quite four. It'll probably be after six. He works till then. You have some waiting to do."

"All right," Curry said again.

"Go on, then."

"Mr. Ness, I still think—"

"I know. You came up with two suspects on your undercover, and they're good suspects. You did good work. But we have no name on one of them, and nothing more than a first name on the other . . . 'Ben.' Both have apparently taken off for parts unknown."

"If I go back in," Curry said, face tight with eagerness, "I might find out more."

"You or someone else will indeed go back into shanty-town," Ness said with a gentle smile and a hand on Curry's shoulder, "no matter how today works out. We have a long list of killings, and the M.O. shifts enough that we may have more than one killer."

Curry nodded, smiled ruefully, said, "So you really figure this fellow Dolezal for our Butcher?"

"It begins to look that way. I had enough to get a search warrant for his premises, and I've got enough to arrest him when he comes home after work."

"You're going up there alone?"

"Yes, but you're to follow him up, when he gets back, remember."

"And I'm to honk the horn twice before I do."

"Right. Once long, once short."

Curry sighed. "Okay. Myself, I think you ought to take a couple uniformed men up there with you."

Ness shook his head no. "If we fill this neighborhood with blue, somebody'll get spooked. Somebody could warn our boy, by phone, or he could warn himself by coming home to a sidewalk full of onlookers."

"Oh-kay." Curry shrugged, smiled faintly, and crossed the street. There was no traffic to speak of.

Ness went in and up the creaky stairs; he had no intention of presenting the search warrant to the landlady. He would go on into Dolezal's "suite" and begin tossing the place and present the document only if somebody asked to see it.

As he neared the top step, he unbuttoned his suit coat. There was always a chance Dolezal, heavily hung over from the night before, might have stayed home from work. Ness had been in law enforcement long enough to know that you never took anything for granted. A surprise could be around any corner.

A surprise was around this corner, but it wasn't Frank Dolezal.

It was a big, pouchy-faced sheriff's deputy in khaki, overwhelming the folding chair he was seated on, reading a racing form, a big .45 revolver on his hip. He was sitting next to a door with a brass number 5 nailed haphazardly to it; less haphazard was a strip of paper, three inches wide, stretched across the portal saying: SEALED FOR INVESTIGATION—SHERIFF'S DEPARTMENT.

Number five was Dolezal's room.

"What's the idea?" Ness asked the deputy.

The deputy swallowed, folded the racing form up, and stuffed it under the chair. Then he stood and smiled; it was a nasty smile, but it seemed a little nervous, too.

"Possible crime scene, Mr. Ness. Sheriff's office is investigating."

Looking at the man through narrowed eyes, Ness said, "Do I know you?"

"Uh . . . I'm Deputy Robert McFarlin, sir."

"I've seen you before."

"I was on the police department till I retired, sir."

A recent retirement, no doubt, Ness thought; one of the corrupt rats who scurried into a pension. This one had scurried further, into a position on the sheriff's staff.

"No, that isn't it," Ness said. "I'll think of it."

The deputy's smile disappeared; his white face seemed to go even whiter.

"What about the man who lives in this apartment?"

"His name is Frank Dolezal, Mr. Ness."

"I know that. Have your people approached him?"

"I'd guess he's been arrested by now."

"What!"

The deputy shrugged again. "The sheriff himself was going to arrest him this afternoon. At his job. Dolezal's gonna be taken over to the county jail for questioning."

Ness fought the anger. "What case are you investigating, Deputy?"

"I'm not at liberty to say."

"What case are you investigating?"

"Mr. Ness—all due respect . . . but you ain't my boss. Your office don't have jurisdiction over the sheriff's office."

Ness moved closer to the man and looked him in the face; the man was taller then Ness, but he seemed to shrink under the smaller man's gaze.

"What," Ness asked, biting off the words, "case are you investigating?"

The deputy swallowed and smiled and said, "Well, if you must know . . . the Mad Butcher of Kingsbury Run. We cracked it. This fella Dolezal is him."

Ness backed away. Fought the anger. Lost.

"What in hell," he said, "are you people doing investigating that case? That case is most definitely under the jurisdiction of *my* office. What in the bloody hell . . ."

The deputy patted the air, and his smile was condescending now. Not at all nervous.

He said, "Not all the bodies was found in the city limits, Mr. Ness. It's not just a city matter. It's a county matter, too."

Ness stood and stared at the sheriff's department seal across the closed apartment door. He clenched and unclenched his fists.

He said, evenly, "That's true, Deputy. Technically, it's true. But your office has not been investigating those murders."

"But we have. We just kept it to ourselves."

"Where have I seen you?"

The deputy swallowed. "I worked in the Fifteenth precinct."

That figured.

"That isn't it," Ness said. "I will think of it, Deputy. I will place you. And now I'm going inside that apartment and have a look around."

McFarlin held up a hand in a stop motion. "I'm afraid I can't let you do that, Mr. Ness."

"I have a search warrant, Deputy."

"I think, all due respect, that search warrant is overrode by us being here first."

"Are you a lawyer, Deputy McFarlin?"

"No, sir."

"Are you a judge?"

"No, sir."

"Are you the safety director of the city of Cleveland?"

"No, sir."

"Well, I am," Ness said, and brushed him aside and removed the sheriff's seal and opened the door and went in.

"Goddamnit . . ."

Ness turned and looked at McFarlin, who stood outside the room, looking in, as if afraid to enter, afraid to violate his own rule. "Did you want something, Deputy?"

McFarlin, his face red, looked as confused as he was angry. And he couldn't find anything to say, though he clearly wanted to.

"Why don't you go find a phone," Ness suggested, "and call your boss. Tell him I'm here, tell him what I've done. Go on. Shoo."

McFarlin was shaking his head, no. "I can't leave the place unguarded . . ."

"I'll look after it for you. I'll keep all unwanted persons out."

"I don't think . . ."

"That doesn't surprise me. Go call the man who does your thinking for you. He's going to want to be informed."

McFarlin, the red leaving his face, said, "Don't touch anything."

"Thanks for the advice," Ness said pleasantly, and shut the door in his face.

The room Ness stood in was in some respects like the one he'd inhabited himself, down the hall, for four nights. The faded, failing floral wallpaper was even the same pattern, and much of the furniture was of the same gray-metal, institutional variety; but there were also pieces of furniture Dolezal had obviously added himself—a comfy sofa here, an oak dresser there.

And Dolezal, who had a job after all, had managed in this tenement to inhabit something almost worthy of the term "suite." The large room was three rooms in one: a bedroom area off to the right, as you entered; a central sitting room area where the sofa was; and at left a kitchen area—a small icebox, sink, kitchen counter with cupboards, wood-burning stove, and table.

Most impressive of all, Dolezal had his own bathroom—toilet and tub. No sink.

Ness nosed around the large outer room carefully, poking with a pencil sometimes, touching things but not anywhere any other print was likely to have been left. He found little beyond Dolezal's well-worn clothing. There were no personal effects—no address book or picture album or family Bible. Perhaps the sheriff's investigators had already confiscated such items.

In the kitchen area he opened several drawers and looked in. Knifes looked back. One he found, poking with his pencil among other silverware and utensils, was a long, slightly curved butcher knife. The whorls of wood in its handle bore dark stains. If the sheriff hadn't discovered and confiscated this yet, the room had probably only had one fairly cursory going-over. Good. He was getting an early look.

He peeked in the icebox. Bare. Cupboards were bare, too, of any foodstuffs. Maybe that made sense: Dolezal was planning to move, after all.

The bathroom was small and dirty, but even so the dark stains on the floorboards stood out starkly. He knelt. Bloodstains? He glanced underneath the bathtub; to the two legs closest to the wall clung a considerable gathering of dirt and something brownish red that might be rust. Or might not.

He stood. Hands on hips, eyes wide, he took it all in. Could this unkempt little chamber be *it*? The "murder lab" his people had been so diligently searching for? This was no soundproof room; the icebox in the other room would hardly provide the refrigeration he had assumed the Butcher would need; and while you could clean this bathroom easily enough, it hadn't been scrubbed down, not lately. It was filthy. Could his theories have been this far off the mark?

He shook his head and took off his suit coat and folded it neatly over the edge of the tub. Then he took a small penknife from one pocket and two tiny manila evidence envelopes from another. With the penknife, kneeling again, he took a small but sufficient scraping of the black-stained wood of the floor and baseboard. He reached an arm way in under the bathtub and took a small but sufficient scraping of the apparent rust and filth collected around one clawed foot of the tub.

He tucked the knife and the two evidence packets in his pocket and rose and put his suit coat back on.

He was exiting the bathroom into the outer room when the door opened and the deputy came in.

"The sheriff says I shouldn't oughta let you out of my sight," McFarlin said.

"Then you're going to have to ride over to my office with me," Ness said, brushing by the man, "because that's where I'm headed."

The deputy followed Ness out in the hall. Called after him. "The sheriff said to tell you we got this case under control. He's going to have a signed confession by morning."

Ness whirled and stared the deputy down. "How can he know that?"

"Well . . . he's just confident we got the right man."

"A little third degree'll do the trick, is that it?"

"He's bein' questioned," McFarlin shrugged. He pointed back into the apartment. "We got bloodstains in there. Human blood."

"Has a chemist checked it already? Identified it as human?"

McFarlin smiled and nodded smugly.

"Too fast," Ness said, almost to himself. "You're moving too goddamn fast."

"Look," McFarlin said impatiently, "he's the guy. You oughta to know."

"I oughta to know? And why is that?"

The deputy looked away. "Just go about your business, why don't you?"

Ness snapped his fingers. "You were in the tavern the other day. You stood right next to me."

The deputy flushed. "What are you talkin' about . . ."

Ness pointed his finger at him. "You spotted me. You've been following me ever since."

"Don't be silly."

Ness grabbed the bigger man by the front of his khaki shirt. "You stole my case from me, you son of a bitch."

"Hey, take it easy!"

Ness let go of him, pushed him hard with the flat of a hand into the wall.

The deputy was trembling with rage or fear or maybe both. With one hand he smoothed the front of his shirt; with the other he pointed toward the stairs. "You just better get out of here. You better get out."

Ness thrust a finger in his face. "Don't louse my case up. Tell your boss. You stole it from me, well, fine. Just don't louse it up."

He turned and went quickly down the steps, making a lot of noise on the rickety boards, and was out on the street. He gestured to Curry, seated in the black Ford across the way, and Curry put his newspaper down and joined his chief.

"What's up?"

"Interlopers," Ness said disgustedly. "Go around back and get Merlo. I don't want to have to tell this story twice."

When Curry came back, Ness was seated in the car, on

the rider's side. Merlo got in back and Curry got behind the
wheel. The three men sat there and Ness told the story.

"It's my own damn fault," he said. "The son of a bitch
made me. He was in that tavern and recognized me."

"What was he doing there in the middle of the
afternoon?" Curry asked.

"Probably collecting graft," Ness said. "He's one of the
sheriff's bagmen, no doubt. This is one area of the city we
haven't cleaned up, you know."

Merlo, in the back, was in shock. Curry seemed
confused.

Ness set in silence, trying to fight off the gloom.

Finally Merlo said, "I don't believe it. I don't believe
it."

They were still sitting there at a quarter to six when
Sam Wild showed up. He noticed them clustered in the car
and leaned in the window on Ness's side.

"I know I'm early," Wild said, wryly apologetic, straw
fedora pushed back on his head, "but I'll keep out of the
way. I got a photographer in the car to take the pic when
you haul him out in cuffs. This is gonna be a big moment,
gentlemen."

"I don't think so," Merlo said.

Wild looked hard at Ness and knew at once it was
scratched. "What the fuck happened?"

Ness, without looking at the reporter, said, "Off the
record?"

"Yeah, yeah. Off the record."

"The sheriff made saps out of us," Ness told him. "Me
especially." And, despite his best efforts, he found himself
telling the story a second time.

"Oh, for Christ's sake," Wild said. "They're going to
muck it up."

"I know," Ness said. "They don't have the evidence
yet. And they don't have the wherewithal to gather it,
either."

"Well," Wild said with a humorless smirk, "they had
the wherewithal to gather your suspect."

Ness said nothing.

"You gotta give me *something*," Wild said, some
desperation in his voice. "I promised my boss a big story."

"Get out your notepad," Ness told him.

Wild did.

"The sheriff is to be commended for his investigation," Ness said. "The leads he has uncovered will, of course, be followed up to see what possible connection the suspect may have with other homicides."

Wild got that, then said, "Which means you're still on the case."

"Yes, it does. Now ask Sergeant Merlo for a quote."

Wild looked toward the backseat.

Merlo looked toward Ness, who glanced back at him and said, "Say what you feel."

Merlo smiled and nodded and said to Wild, "I consider the sheriff's actions an intrusion into a case that was well under way and well under control. The suspect, Dolezal, is known to me and has been under my surveillance for some time. We were waiting for the right moment to slam down on him. Now the sheriff's office has spoiled it."

Writing furiously, Wild got that, too. Then he grinned at Ness. "Between the two of you," he said, "you covered everything—including your own ass."

Ness managed to grin back. "That was the point of the exercise." Then the grin faded and he said, "Now if you'll excuse us, Sam, we have to be getting back to work. I have some evidence to process."

And they left the reporter there, smiling and scratching his head.

11

Frank Dolezal sat in a wooden chair in a large concrete room in the basement of the Cuyahoga county jail. The chair was the only furniture in the room. A single window, high up at right, was barred; beyond the bars was wire and night. A single lamp descended from vague darkness, hanging rather low over the chair, providing a cone of blinding bright light.

Dolezal slumped in the chair, his ruddy face wet with tears and rough with stubble, eyes burning from the light, feet dancing without rhythm, fingertips on knees drumming to no cadence. His blue cotton workshirt was perspiration soaked, and soiled. He was a mess. But even more than a shave and a change of clothes, Frank Dolezal needed a drink.

He didn't know how long he had been in this room. He figured it was hours, but how many, he couldn't guess; he could barely remember not being in this place, this cold, vast, gloomy bunker. Relays of deputies and county detectives, occasionally the sheriff himself, had been trading off questioning him, in pairs. They hadn't hit him yet, but he sensed that was coming. He wished he could tell them what they wanted to know. But the truth was, he couldn't remember.

And he was beginning to think the truth was not what these men wanted to hear.

He grabbed at his stomach; if only it would stop clutching. Every thirty seconds or so a spasm would hit him. He knew what would stop it: a beer. One tiny little beer. Or better, a shot. Or a double; *that* would do it. Then he'd be calm. He'd be able to relax. His head would stop aching. His mouth wouldn't feel dry. As it was, he felt helpless. He felt tired. He felt weak.

Despite this, he got up and began pacing the room, though he had been told not to leave the chair. He just couldn't quit moving. He avoided the bright pool of light where the chair waited and wandered the dark outskirts of the large room.

The heavy steel door—marked: AUTHORIZED PERSONNEL ONLY—swung open and the sheriff strode in. He was a big fat man with a head as square as Dolezal's; his khaki shirt was soaked with sweat. He was bareheaded and had a rubber hose in one hand. Another big man, a deputy named McFarlin, who'd been in here before, trailed after him.

Dolezal's eyes squeezed shut as he willed this sight to go away, knowing it would not. Knowing that the time for beatings had come.

"Frank," the sheriff said with an awful yellow smile, beating the rubber hose casually in a big fat open palm, "you weren't supposed to get outa that chair, now, were you?"

Dolezal swallowed. "No, sir."

The sheriff moved quickly—amazingly so for a man his size—and smashed the top of the chair with the rubber hose; some wood chips flew.

"Sit, Frank," the sheriff said, as if to a dog.

And much like an obedient dog, Dolezal sat.

"You want a smoke, Frank?" Now the sheriff's voice seemed friendly.

Dolezal nodded eagerly.

The sheriff nodded to his deputy, who dug out a pack of Camels and gave one to Dolezal, lit a match for him. Dolezal, shaky as he was, managed to lean in and get the light, then sucked the smoke in like a drowning man gasping for breath; he could taste the smoke so sharply, so cleanly. But a cigarette without a drink was like wearing one shoe when the world was a hot asphalt road.

If he could only have a drink, life would be good again.

"You should talk to us, Frank," the sheriff said.

"I talk plenty," Dolezal said. His voice sounded like a

whine in his ears and he hated it; he wished he could sound strong. He wished he could stand up to these men.

"You should get it off your chest," Deputy McFarlin said. He was standing back, away from the light, a voice out of darkness. "You'll feel better about it."

"We'll give you a meal," the sheriff said, "and let you get a good night's sleep."

"Give me a drink," Dolezal said, and sucked in more smoke. "Drink make me relax. Make me remember."

"First, remember," the sheriff said, lifting a finger gently, the rubber hose limp in his other hand, "then you get your drink."

Dolezal shook his head helplessly. "I no can remember."

The sheriff swung the hose and it made a swooshing sound before it landed with a whump against Dolezal's left rib cage.

Dolezal howled and fell out of the chair, landing hard. The cigarette went flying, sparking into the gloom. He hugged himself, like a fetus, and rolled out of the bright light. McFarlin hauled him off the floor and out of the darkness and back into brightness and the chair.

The sheriff raised the hose again.

"I tell you," Dolezal said, weeping, "I tell you."

The sheriff smiled. "Good. Get it off your chest, Frank."

Dolezal looked at the floor. "I . . . I make sex with boys."

The sheriff whacked Dolezal's chest with the rubber hose. "Christ, you old faggot! We *know* that!"

"You . . . you do?"

"You think we didn't check up on you before we arrested you? Everybody in the Third precinct knows you're one of the Brown family!"

Being "one of the Brown family," as Dolezal in his shame knew all too well, was how the sin of his sex drive was described on the street. He had not wanted to admit his bent to the sheriff, knowing he would be sentenced for pederasty; he had a career to consider, after all.

"Frank," Deputy McFarlin said reasonably, brushing off the shoulders of Dolezal's workshirt, "you've already admitted you knew Ed Andrassy. You've already admitted you knew Flo Polillo. Why not give us the rest?"

Dolezal swallowed and rubbed away some moisture from his stubbly face; he was tapping the floor with one foot. "What rest?"

The sheriff smacked him in the left rib cage with the hose. Dolezal howled again, but did not fall out of the chair.

"Tell us how you killed Flo Polillo, Frank."

Dolezal felt himself begin to shake. Is *that* why they brought him here?

The sheriff grabbed him by the back of the hair and made him stare up into the blinding white light.

"Tell us, Frank!"

He shut his eyes. "I kill Flo?"

The sheriff let go of Dolezal's hair, and the man's head flopped forward.

"Are you askin', Frank, or tellin'?"

"I . . . I know somebody chop Flo up."

"How do you know that?"

"People talk. Cops around, asking questions."

"Was it you, Frank?"

"Me?"

"Did you kill Flo?"

"No! No. I no remember . . ."

"If you don't remember, how can you say no?"

"I drink," he said pathetically, "and no remember."

"Tell us what you *do* remember about Flo, Frank."

He tried to think. "I not see her since January."

The sheriff and the deputy glanced at each other.

"That's when she was killed, Frank," the sheriff said.

"I hear that," Dolezal said.

"When exactly did you see her last?" the sheriff asked.

He'd seen her ghost the night before; but he knew the sheriff didn't mean that.

"We was in my room drinking," he told them. "A Friday night. We drink sometimes. She stay my place sometimes."

"I thought you liked boys, Frank."

"She was friend. We drink together. She got mad sometimes when she drink."

"Really, Frank?"

"She was dressed up to go out. She want some money."

"Go on."

He shrugged. "She grab for ten dollars I had in my pocket. I didn't want to give her. She tried to take my money before."

"What happened then, Frank?"

"We . . . had fight."

"You had a fight?"

He shrugged again. "I have this butcher knife."

"Go on, Frank."

"In drawer at my place, this butcher knife. She went and got it. She came at me with it."

"Tried to stab you? Tried to kill you?"

"I don't know. She had it. She wanted ten dollars. But she was too drunk, I take knife away. I hit her."

"With the knife, Frank?"

"My fist. I hit with my fist."

"Is that when you killed her?"

"I didn't kill her. I didn't kill nobody."

"Tell us the rest."

"I can't remember."

"Did she hit you back?"

"No. I knock her down."

"Did she get up?"

"Can't remember. I drink some more."

The sheriff and the deputy looked at each other and shrugged with their faces.

"I tell you enough now? You give me drink?"

"Frank," the sheriff said, "you're going to have to tell us about it."

"About what?"

"About killing Flo Polillo. About cutting her up, Frank, with that butcher knife."

"No!" Had he done that? Had he killed her?

"You heard about it. You said so. Heard about her body turning up, all cut up, in pieces. Some of her we haven't found yet. Like her head. Maybe you can tell us where her head is, Frank."

"No! No!" Had he? Had he done it? Could he do such a thing? People told him, sometimes, of awful things he did when he was drunk—getting violent, fighting with strangers, beating up on people. He awaited such reports with dread. But had he done *this*? Was he a monster? Was he this Butcher they wanted?

And those other killings—were they something he had done while blacked out with drink?

"You worked in a slaughterhouse, Frank," the sheriff said. He was leaning a hand on the chair just behind Dolezal's shoulder; the rubber hose was hidden behind his back.

"Yes. But that not make me butcher of men."

"Deputy McFarlin's been asking about you, at your rooming house. Deputy, tell Frank what you've learned, from his neighbors."

The deputy said, "They say Flo Polillo wasn't the only visitor you had at your room. You knew a colored woman name of Rose Wallace, too."

He nodded. "Yes. Not see her in long time."

"She's dead, Frank," the sheriff said pleasantly. "She was just identified as one of the Butcher's victims."

"No . . . no . . ."

"And," the deputy went on, "your landlady reports seeing a sailor go up with you to your room. A heavily tattooed sailor."

Dolezal tried to think; he'd known more than one sailor in his time.

"One of the Butcher's victims," the sheriff said matter-of-factly, "was a heavily tattooed sailor, as yet unidentified. Maybe you'd like to see his death mask."

"No . . . I . . . no . . ."

"Frank. You should tell us. You should really tell us . . ." And the sheriff took the rubber hose out from behind his back and began smacking it gently in his palm again. ". . . really tell us what happened."

A bad spasm ripped at Dolezal's stomach, doubling him over; the sheriff stood back, startled, as if an invisible rubber hose had struck the prisoner this time, beating the lawman to the punch.

"Give me goddamn drink!" Dolezal cried out.

The sheriff swung his left, the hand without the rubber hose, and hit Dolezal in the left eye. The fist was so large it eclipsed Dolezal's face.

Dolezal fell out of the chair and landed like a sack of flour on the floor and wept there. "Need it to relax . . . to remember."

The sheriff and deputy traded looks, sighs. Then the sheriff seemed to nod.

Soon Dolezal was back in his chair and under the light, gulping greedily at a shot of whiskey; it went down smooth, burning in his stomach but turning into a glow. He sighed. He was trembling, but that was different than shaking. His left eye was swelling shut, but he didn't care.

"There's more where that came from, Frank," the sheriff said, taking the empty shot glass away from his prisoner.

"Okay," Dolezal said, "I killed her. Bring me 'nother drink."

"Tell us more, Frank."

"Uh . . . I kill her. She fall when I hit her. Uh, maybe she hit her head."

The deputy leaned into the bright light. "There was blood on the bathroom floor, Frank. A chemist checked it out for us—human blood."

"Maybe her head hit bathtub."

"When she fell, you mean?"

"Yes. When she fell, yes."

"Why were you in the bathroom, Frank? Were you drinking in the bathroom?"

"No . . . uh . . ."

The deputy, eyes flickering with thought, said, "She chased you in there with the knife!"

"Yes! She chase me. In bathroom, I hit her. She go down. Hit head on tub." He nodded. Smiled. "I think that is what killed her."

"Why did you cut her up, Frank?"

"Uh . . . I need 'nother drink."

"No, Frank."

"No remember without drink." He folded his arms.

The second whiskey went down just as smooth; the world was coming into focus for Dolezal. His stomach stopped clutching. He felt good.

"Why," the sheriff asked, taking away the empty shot glass, "did you cut her up?"

"I, uh . . . cut her up because I don't know what else to do with body."

"Go on."

"Go on?"

"Tell us what you did."

"I cut up the body."

"Yes, but how?"

"With butcher knife."

"Go on."

"Go on?"

"Go on, Frank."

"Well, I . . . first I cut off head. Then legs. And then arms." He smiled at them. "Can I have drink now?"

"What did you do with the body?"

"I cut it up."

"No, Frank. How did you get rid of it? How did you get all those body parts out of your room?"

"Oh. Well. I . . . I made plenty trips."

"Plenty trips?"

"Two or three trips, carrying stuff out."

"What did you carry it in?"

"Uh . . . in basket?"

"A basket," the deputy said, smiling. He was taking notes, Dolezal noticed.

The sheriff said, "What did you do with the torso?"

"Torso?"

"The trunk."

"I no use trunk. I use basket."

"No, you imbecile. What did you do with the trunk?" And the sheriff gestured to his body from neck to upper legs.

"You left it behind Hart Manufacturing, didn't you?" the deputy said, pencil poised.

"That near where I live," Dolezal said.

"Yes," the sheriff said smugly. "Two hundred and thirty-five yards from your rooming-house doorstep."

Dolezal nodded. "Okay, I leave trunk in alley behind where you said."

"What about the rest?"

"What rest?"

"Arms, legs, head . . ."

"Arms, legs, head. Okay, I dump them in lake."

"Whereabouts?"

"Oh. Uh . . . foot of East Forty-ninth Street. I threw them in lake. Breeze carry them away. Can I have drink now?"

The deputy was smiling; he closed his little notepad and drummed on it with his pencil. The sheriff was smiling, too. They were smiling at each other, like Dolezal wasn't there.

So he reminded them that he was: "Can I have drink please?"

"No, Frank," the sheriff said. "No drinks for a while. You just sit here. We'll have another go-round a little later."

"I tell you everything you want!"

"You didn't tell us about Rose Wallace or Eddie Andrassy."

"I drink with her, I fuck with him! Okay? Drink now?"

"Later," the sheriff said, smiling, tapping his palm with the rubber hose.

The two men left.

Dolezal sat in the bright cone of light.

He sat there and sweated and the two drinks began to wear off. His stomach began to clutch again. His hands and feet could not stop moving; he was on stage alone, dancing in the spotlight of the overhead lamp, performing to an empty house.

He had told them what they wanted, but was it the truth? Had he killed Flo? Had he cut her up?

He could have. He'd seen her ghost in his room, after all. He knew—he shuddered at the thought—he knew he had done bad things during blackout drunks. People had told him. Oh, how they had told him.

Was he the Butcher?

He stood and kicked the chair. He kicked the chair out of the light and into the corner and began kicking it savagely, mercilessly, like he was the brutal sheriff and the chair a suspect he was grilling. But the chair was tougher than he was. It remained intact, except for where the sheriff's rubber hose had chipped it.

Dolezal stood, shaking, waiting for someone to come in from outside and beat him or something. But the noise of his attack on the chair had attracted no one. The cement room, with its heavy door shut, was apparently soundproof.

He sat in the darkness, on the floor, against the cold cement wall, and thought.

I'm the Butcher, he told himself.

Again and again.

I kill all those people. Grotesque images of animal carnage from his slaughterhouse days flashed through his mind. His stomach clutched.

He stood. Shaking. He took off his shirt and tore it into wide strips and tied the strips together with heavy knots, like a sailor might make. Then he went and got the chair and stood on it and tried to reach the barred window. Couldn't.

He was, however, able to reach up above the fairly low-hanging conical lamp, squinting up into the brightness as he tied the rope he'd made from his shirt to the thin shaft of steel from which the lamp hung, and then he tied the shirt-rope around his neck and stepped off the chair.

12

Ness ignored the khaki-clad fellow at the desk in the outer office and went right into the sheriff's sanctuary. Sheriff O'Connell was a whale beached on a leather sofa pushed against a wall decorated with various civic awards from the suburbs he serviced. The sheriff was snoring and a copy of the *Police Gazette* was draped open across his stomach.

Ness slammed the door, rattling its glass, keeping the secretary or deputy or whatever-the-hell he was back out in the outer office, and waking up the sheriff of Cuyahoga County.

O'Connell's tiny dark eyes were wide as he gazed up at

the safety director, surprised and disoriented for a moment; then he sat up on the sofa, his eyes turning hard and his face red with anger.

"Even God needs an appointment to see me," he said, getting up on his feet, looking down at the six-foot Ness.

Ness looked back at him, making no attempt to hide his disgust. "Well, I'm sure the devil can walk right in," he told the sheriff. "So I took the same liberty. Now why don't you sit down. We have to talk."

O'Connell glared at Ness, though the red was fading from his face as he said, "All right. But I think I'd like one of my deputies as a witness. To make some notes."

"I don't think you will." Ness gestured to the sheriff's tidy desk. "Sit down, Sheriff."

Sighing out his nose, the sheriff moved behind the desk with an agility that belied his size and folded his hands on a green desk blotter. His fingers were thick, the hands massive. His eyes were lidded with contempt.

It was the Wednesday after Frank Dolezal's arrest. Dolezal, who had made two suicide attempts, was alive and somewhere in this building, in this jail. In all that time Ness had not been able to arrange a meeting with the suspect—or sheriff, for that matter.

"You have a prisoner I'd like to see," Ness told him.

"We have a suspect in the Kingsbury Run investigation," O'Connel said blandly, "if that's what you mean."

"That's what I mean."

"Nobody sees this suspect but my people."

"Including a lawyer?" Ness asked with mock innocence.

They both knew that if the suspect had seen a lawyer, Dolezal would have been released by now, on a writ of habeas corpus.

"He hasn't been indicted yet," the sheriff said.

"And the court isn't allowed to appoint an attorney until after he's been indicted. Of course. But a suspect is supposed to be indicted within seventy-two hours. You've had Mr. Dolezal in custody for six days now."

"It's an unusual case. Now I'm a busy man, Mr. Ness. If you don't mind . . ."

"I do mind, and I've only begun. Your nap and the *Police Gazette* are just going to have wait."

The sheriff's mouth curled into a sneer, but he said nothing.

"Yesterday you hauled Mr. Dolezal over to the East Cleveland police department," Ness said, "for a lie detector test. Why did you bother driving over there when just across the way we have a modern facility which Chief Matowitz and I would have been glad to make available to you?"

"I prefer to keep my investigation of this case separate from yours."

Ness smiled. "Ah, but Sheriff, there are no rivalries between good men in the pursuit of justice. I haven't been unkind to you in the press, have I?"

"The hell you haven't. Your detectives have been smearing me from—"

"My detectives are men with their own minds and their own way of seeing things and expressing themselves. They have a right to say what they wish, to the press or anyone else. There's a document called the Constitution of the United States, with which you apparently aren't familiar, that guarantees them that right."

The sheriff's mouth twitched. "I have work to do. If you're here to get information about the Dolezal case, I'm afraid I can't give you any. It's confidential."

"Oh, but I'm here to *share* some information with you."

The sheriff arched an eyebrow. "Such as?"

"Certain scientific findings. As Deputy McFarlin may have told you, I was up in Dolezal's 'murder den,' as you've been referring to it in the papers, the very day you arrested the suspect. I took some scrapings from the bathroom floor."

"So what? We had a chemist check that for us. He found human blood. On a butcher knife, too. Everybody knows that."

"Yes, and I understand the chemist is Deputy McFarlin's brother-in-law. He works for a couple of M.D.'s, I understand."

"That's right."

"Well, I had my scrapings checked as well. Dr. Eckert,

a pathologist at Western Reserve University, a completely objective third party, tested them for me. I just got his findings this afternoon."

The sheriff snorted derisively. "What took him so long?"

"He said the high iron content of the deposits around the bathtub feet complicated the tests, made it take days to get accurate results. I have his analysis right here, if you'd like to see it." Ness made a show of reaching for something in his pocket, then abandoned the effort with a wave of one hand, saying, "Actually, it's not complex. I think I can remember exactly the composition of the material, in Dr. Eckert's own scientific phraseology . . . 'just plain dirt.'"

The sheriff's tiny eyes bugged and he half-rose from his seat. "What?"

"Dirt, Sheriff. No blood, human or animal, present."

O'Connell clearly did not know what to say. Slowly he sat back down.

Ness gestured with an open hand. "Of course, experts on such matters do disagree."

The sheriff put on a tight smile and said, "Mr. Ness. All due respect. With or without bloodstains, we got the Butcher, right here in this jail. You may not like it. It may not help your reputation any . . . it may not help you get my job for yourself, for instance . . . but justice, like you said, is gonna be served."

"Do tell."

"Yeah, I do. Those lie detector tests were positive."

"They're not admissible."

"They point to Dolezal's guilt, nevertheless." The sheriff began counting off items on his fingers. "Andrassy, Wallace, and Polillo frequented his room; he admits it, and his neighbors confirm. They all frequented that bar at Twentieth and Central. He's an admitted sexual pervert. He's given to fits of violence and rage during drinkin' bouts. He lived in proximity of where some of the body parts was found. He was fixing to move out of a place where his rent was paid up a month in advance, because the neighborhood was being searched by fire wardens. Most important, he's confessed."

Ness smiled and raised a forefinger. "Ah. His confession. Like when he confessed throwing the Polillo head, arms, and legs in the lake."

The sheriff shifted in his chair.

"Unfortunately," Ness continued, "after you released the confession to the press, some bad sport pointed out to a certain reporter that Dolezal doing that in January was . . . unlikely. Unless he sawed a hole in the ice."

The sheriff sighed heavily. "We checked the records and found the lake was ice-covered at that time, yes."

"From the shore out to beyond the breakwall," Ness said. "Somebody must've got their facts mixed up—perhaps whoever was questioning the suspect—because the arms and legs of Flo Polillo were among the body parts that turned up behind that manufacturing plant."

The sheriff shrugged. "We confronted the suspect with those facts."

Ness smiled pleasantly. "And lo and behold—he changed his story. He remembered leaving the arms and legs in that alley. He remembered it was only the head he'd disposed of eleswhere, and not in the lake."

Another shrug. "Well, he mighta got confused about which victim was which. Body parts of two of the woman victims did turn up in Lake Erie, you know."

"But after you 'confronted' him, he sorted it out. Said he burned Polillo's head and buried the skull."

"Never mind all that," O'Connell said, mouth pursed with irritation, eyes moving.

On Monday the sheriff had taken Dolezal, manacled and surrounded by deputies, to Kingsbury Run, so that he might lead them to where he buried Flo Polillo's skull. A few reporters, among them Sam Wild, had been allowed to trail along, at a distance. The suspect had led them up and down, through the sumac bushes and sunflowers, past the infamous stagnant pool where body parts had once floated, but he just couldn't remember where he'd buried Flo's skull. Then under the East Thirty-fourth Street bridge, a deputy spotted a pile of bones.

Dolezal had become hysterical upon sight of them and began babbling that he was sorry for what he'd done. O'Connell gloatingly displayed the discovery to the accompanying press, who took pictures of the sheriff with his prize pile of bones, which weren't the Polillo skull but sufficed—at least until the embarrassed sheriff had to reveal to the press the next day that the bones were those of a dog.

"What really interests me about your excursion into the Run," Ness said, "was that Dolezal was heard, by the reporters, to complain his ribs were hurting him. And he had an ugly shiner as well, I understand."

And another shrug. "He hurt himself. He tried to kill himself twice—you know that."

"How does a man hurt his eye in a suicide attempt, exactly?"

"The second time he tried to do it was in his cell. He used his shoelaces; they broke and he fell to the cement floor."

"There is an automatic reflex action, Sheriff, which makes anyone falling forward throw his arms out in front of him, to protect his face."

"Maybe he was part unconscious at the time. I don't know. I wasn't there."

"Neither, apparently, was your jailer."

"We increased our watchfulness with the suspect. There haven't been no suicide attempts since."

"That's admirable, Sheriff." Ness picked at a hangnail absently. "What luck have you had with the address book?" he asked, referring to the one found in Dolezal's apartment.

"There were twenty-five names in it, and we're checking them out."

"You announced, with some fanfare to the press last Saturday, that in that book was the California address of a sailor. You implied this sailor might be the tattooed male victim who remains unidentified. What have you found?"

"Our investigation is confidential."

"Is the sailor in the address book still alive?"

The sheriff said nothing.

"Well, is he?"

Reluctantly, O'Connell nodded.

"Sheriff," Ness said, leaning forward, his face expressionless, "your investigation is coming unraveled. Cooperate with my people and maybe you won't wind up looking like a complete horse's ass. If Dolezal is the Butcher—and I frankly don't think he is—you're going to lose him on procedural matters."

O'Connell's eyes slitted. "What the hell do you mean by that?"

"It's known you kept Dolezal without food or sleep for the first twenty-four hours he was in your custody. You have held him for six days without charging him, refusing to permit relatives to see him, making no effort to get him an attorney. It's obvious that you've used outrageous third-degree tactics, which will undoubtedly come out when Dolezal *does* finally get a lawyer, whose first move will be to have his client repudiate those confessions as having been made under duress and without counsel."

"The lie detector—"

"Is inadmissible, as I said. Further, Dolezal is an alcoholic, and you've either kept drink from him or provided him with some, or some combination of the two, to get him to admit to anything you wanted him to. I spoke to him before you arrested him, and my feeling is he's a blackout drunk, and these confessions you've wrung out of him may have convinced him that he *is* the Butcher, when he isn't. Hence, suicide attempts and positive lie-detector results."

The sheriff swallowed thickly; he seemed a little stunned.

"Today," Ness continued evenly, "I spoke to a representative of the civil liberties committee of the Cleveland Bar Association. They're preparing a report on your conduct of this case. I'm helping them."

"You self-righteous bastard . . ."

Ness pounded the desk with a fist and the sheriff jerked back with surprise. "You stole my case. Your man followed me around and stole my goddamn case. Now you've loused it up, and you're going to pay. I don't want your job—I don't want to be sheriff. But I can guarantee you one thing: They won't elect you dog catcher after this—even though you did manage to track down one dead dog."

The sheriff was trembling with rage, but he said nothing.

Ness stood. "If you cooperate with my office," he said, "perhaps you can salvage your career—and perhaps I can salvage Dolezal as a suspect, or at least as a witness. If he *isn't* the Butcher, he undoubtedly *knows* the Butcher—and that's too important for me to allow you to louse up."

Ness walked to the door, and paused. "And one last thing: Get your man off my tail."

Mild surprise crossed the sheriff's face. "What do you mean?"

"I don't know what purpose you think is being served by keeping me shadowed at this point. But stop it. Or I'll 'confront' the next stooge you send and send him home with the sort of swollen eye and sore ribs you can only get in a suicide attempt. If you catch my meaning."

"Look, Ness, I honestly don't know what the hell you're talking about."

"Take your nap and think it over."

Ness slammed the door and rattled the glass again.

After a session with Chief Matowitz and Merlo at Central headquarters, filling them in on his meeting with the sheriff, Ness walked up the cement ramp into the elevated parking lot where his black Ford waited. It was late evening now, and balmily breezy; it had rained this afternoon. He felt good about having unloaded on the sheriff, but wasn't sure how the man would react. It was, to him, one of the great mysteries of life how a man that corrupt could still be proud.

He stopped at a diner on his way home and had a meat loaf dinner. He ate slowly, using a piece of bread to collect all of the gravy, leaving a plate so spotless there was no evidence a meal had been there. A pretty waitress flirted with him a little, talked him into a piece of pecan pie; the girl reminded him of Viv. It gave him a pang that all the meat loaf and pie in the world couldn't cure. Nonetheless, he ate the pie, drank a second cup of coffee, and read the final edition of the *Press*, in which the sheriff's handling of the Dolezal case rated a skeptical sidebar.

On the way home he thought he was being followed again. It was after dark, as usual, when the car showed up in his rearview mirror; when he slowed to try to identify the driver or vehicle, the car turned off. Goddamn that O'Connell, anyway.

Just approaching nine o'clock, he reached suburban Lakewood. The booth at the mouth of the private drive was empty; the guard had been fired for drinking last week and hadn't been replaced. Ness had been asked, by the Homeowners Association of the small group of boathouses and cottages clustered along Clifton Lagoon, to find a replacement. He hadn't got around to it. Finding an honest retired cop in the Cleveland area was a job for a detective better than himself, Ness feared.

The boathouse was small but massive, a weathered, gray-stone, two-story castle with turrets and a squat central tower and a short stone fence that walled off the modest yard; the castle had a stark, masculine beauty in the moonlight, and was quite unlike its more conventional frame-building neighbors. One of Mayor Burton's financial angels had provided Ness with this hideaway, as a fringe benefit. He parked the Ford in front, right behind where Viv had parked her car (why, even now, did he leave space for her?), and gazed out on the endless gray-blue of the lagoon and the lake beyond. It was a peaceful moment that he enjoyed just about every night—a moment of feeling smaller than the world around him, a feeling that, for some reason, comforted him.

Inside, he slipped out of his suit coat and tossed it over a chair; he was usually neater than that, but was suddenly quite tired. The investigation of recent weeks had been draining, though this was the first he'd really noticed it. He made himself a Scotch off the liquor cart and collapsed on the couch before the fireplace. He sipped the drink till it was gone, and then stretched out on the sofa and soon he was gone, too.

A noise woke him.

For a moment, just a moment, he thought he was back in the Central Avenue rooming house. He sat up on the couch and listened. What had the noise been? The wind? A car going by? He went to the nearest window and looked out and saw nothing but the narrow band of pavement that was the private drive of the division, and the lagoon beyond. And a moon and a very clear night.

A night that he and Viv might well have enjoyed.

It wasn't as if he hadn't missed her. She hadn't been constantly on his mind by any means, but at night, at least, when he had to go upstairs to that double bed without her, he missed his sweet, sassy society girl.

And it wasn't only in bed that he missed her. She was wonderful, crazy company, and smart, so smart. He went up the stairs and sat on the bed and checked his watch. Not quite ten-thirty. She'd be up. He could call her. But did he want to? Did he want her back in his life?

He got up and went to the window. He looked out at the moon. At the lake. Someone was down there.

Standing. On the small space of ground, between the private drive and the lake.

A man. He was tall and looked massive, but Ness couldn't make out a single feature or even what his apparel might be. He was just a dark male shape against the lake.

Ness's mouth tightened; so did his hands, into fists.

That goddamn sheriff had not called off his shadow. Who was it down there? McFarlin?

He rushed down the stairs and was out the front door, ready to challenge the son of a bitch.

But no one was there.

He backed against the door. Listened carefully. He could hear a car; at left, on the winding pavement going up the hill, was the twin glow of taillights. The sheriff's man?

He walked across the paved drive to where the man had been standing. The earth was damp enough from the rain earlier to leave an impression of rather large feet. Ness could see where his shadow had walked to this one spot and stayed put. On the other side of the road were more footprints and a tire track that indicated a car had been parked there.

Back inside, he got himself another Scotch and sat studying the unlit fireplace, wondering why the back of his neck was so prickly. Something—nothing rational, he'd be the first to admit—said to him that the man out there had not been a sheriff's deputy.

He was stretched back out again, on the sofa, just barely asleep, when the phone rang. It was on a stand not far from him, but he had to rise to reach it and was fully awake by the time he said, "Ness," into the mouthpiece.

"This is Merlo."

The voice sounded depressed. Earlier, the usually somber, professorly Merlo had seemed damn near cheerful, when Ness had told him about reading off the sheriff.

"What's up?"

"Dolezal's time," Merlo said glumly. "He got the job done tonight."

"What do you mean?"

"Prisoner requested some cleaning rags, to tidy up his cell."

"So?"

"The sheriff gave them to him and then left him alone there. Third time was the charm."

"Hung himself?"

"How did you guess?"

Ness sighed. Closed his eyes. "I'm a detective."

But it didn't take a detective to figure that the Butcher had, in an oblique way, taken another victim.

With the help, that is, of the sheriff of Cuyahoga County and, Ness bitterly knew, the safety director of the city of Cleveland.

13

Stalking Ness was fun.

It had been something of a challenge for Lloyd. Something different. He was tickled by the idea of following—or "shadowing," as the detective magazines called it—this supposed great sleuth who had made such a show in the papers about "tracking down the Butcher." Oh, really? Well, maybe Lloyd would just have to track *him* down.

For days now Lloyd had followed Ness around, on foot—from City Hall to various public buildings and restaurants—and by car, "tailing" him (another good detective magazine term!) back to Lakewood. Tonight Lloyd had even followed Ness down into the private development of cottages and boathouses where the King Detective lived in his little stone castle. Lloyd had parked the car on Ness's side and crossed the road and stood with the lake at his back, looking up at the turreted roof of the tiny fortress.

He stood, his hands in the pockets of his raincoat, one hand grasping the handle of the jackknife, its long blade out. He had practiced last night, practiced withdrawing the knife in one swift motion, without tearing the coat. There was a breeze and the faintest mist in the air; Lloyd wasn't sure if it was from the lake or a bit of rain. When he glanced behind him, at the lake, it was a beautiful thing: an expanse of ripply gray-blue with ivory overtones from the full moon. He liked to kill in the moonlight, though sometimes he had to settle for indoors.

Then he glanced up and saw a shape in the window—Ness!—and for some reason (which now, upon reflection, eluded him) he ran to the car and raced away. As if frightened! Frightened . . . him! Lloyd. The Mad Doctor of Kingsbury Run.

That was how he thought of himself: he rejected, resented, the appellation "Butcher." Butcher! With *his* skill? "Mad" he could accept—loosely, that might just mean "daring" or even "creative," and after all, he *was* seeing a psychiatrist, so the other meaning of "mad" did have *some* bearing, being objective about it. But "Butcher," hardly!

That was the newspapers for you. Those hack news-hounds had no pride in their own work; how could you expect them to understand the pride another person had in his?

He kept their clippings nonetheless. He liked getting press, getting credit where due. He could easily have disposed of the bodies without a trace. Instead he left them where they'd be found, eventually, to thumb his nose at the world in general and the police in particular.

It made him smile to think of the public praise his father had heaped upon him. The smile quivered on his face and his eyes brimmed with tears. It was an approval he had sought for so long.

Right now Lloyd was sitting in the same downtown diner to which he'd earlier followed Eliot Ness. He'd sat just two stools down from the great, meat-loaf-eating safety director, in fact. Had restrained laughter at the thought of how stupid the safety director was, sitting two stools down from the prey he sought so avidly but whose presence his bloodhound nose could not begin to detect.

Now, several hours later, Lloyd was back in the diner again, sitting at one of the small tables along the row of windows, with only a narrow aisle separating him from the counter, where the pretty young brunette waitress who had made eyes at Ness earlier was still at work.

What did she see in him? Lloyd knew, from society gossip, that Ness was something of a ladies' man. He used to date Viv Chalmers, for Christ's sake! What did they *see* in him? Ness was just a nondescript, almost Milquetoast of a paper pusher.

That's how Lloyd saw it. Lloyd saw himself as handsome, and some people would have agreed, while others would have found the six-three, blue-eyed blond to have oddly babyish features for a man of twenty-six. As a matter of fact, Lloyd was eating a bowl of cereal right now—Wheaties—though it was nearly midnight.

Lloyd associated breakfast with his mother. It was a meal they would share together—his father always had a quick cup of coffee and skipped the morning meal and was gone. Mother would pour the milk gently from a white pitcher, and her smile would be as white as the pitcher and her beautiful complexion as pale as the milk itself. Her hair had been blond—as blond as Lloyd's—and she wore it in a bun. She was very beautiful. She was very kind.

Father had been less kind. Lloyd's dark, severely handsome father believed in education above all else, and he believed that punishment was a form of education. The strop had taught Lloyd many lessons as a child.

One of the lessons had been that where punishment is concerned, it is better to give than receive.

He had two sisters, both older than him. He was the baby, to his mother; the son, to his father. He had been very ill with rheumatic fever as a young boy, and his mother would not allow him to play at sports. He'd taken some ribbing over this, at school, because he was a big, strapping kid and should have been a natural for baseball and football.

But he preferred to read, anyway. He was a very good

student (he took ribbing about that too) and had hoped this would please his father, who didn't seem to notice. The only time Lloyd's father seemed to notice his son's grades was the time he got a B in geography; the strop was an incentive to improve.

Bookworm though he was, Lloyd did have his athletic side. He loved to swim and as the family had a summer home at Ashtabula, he got plenty of practice. And he loved the out of doors, loved to hike, loved nature—he was an Eagle Scout with merit badges to spare. Father said nothing about that accomplishment, one way or the other.

The only hint Father ever gave that he took some pride in Lloyd was the casual comment he would make, to family and friends, that his boy would "one day be a finer surgeon than I." This comment, which his father began to state as a fact as early as Lloyd's junior-high years, meant the world to the boy.

Appropriately, science was his favorite subject. He had begun to experiment on animals, on his own, while in grade school. He had found a cat in the street that had apparently been struck by a car; the cat was half-dead, so surgical experimentation couldn't do any harm. He had set up a little lab, a little workshop, in the garage, which was a freestanding building away from the large main house. Here he dissected living animals for the pure science of it. For the educational value.

He'd been fascinated by Kingsbury Run since he was a kid; he would see the lovely desolation of it out the window of the Rapid Transit train, which he and Mother occasionally took from Shaker Heights into the city, for a day of shopping together. An an older boy, in the Scouts, he would sometimes take the train and get off at Seventy-ninth or Fifty-fifth Street and explore the Run by himself, catch animals and experiment on them, right out there in nature.

The younger of the two sisters once caught him carving up a small dog and told their mother, and he explained that he was experimenting scientifically and she understood, though she asked him not to operate on living things again. Henceforth, out of deference to his mother, he would kill the animals first—though it limited the range of his experimentation, and the sense of power he so enjoyed.

Unlike Father, his mother had never struck him a physical blow, though she had hurt him once, in another way. She had walked in on him, when he was masturbating in his room, and had reacted with shock, with horror, and then tears. She later told him she had never been so disappointed in anyone in her life.

She had been pregnant at the time, and even now Lloyd could see her, standing in the doorway, a fat silhouette, choking with horror.

She died trying to have that fourth child. While his father had not been the attending physican, Lloyd was filled with anger toward Father. Not because his father had caused the pregnancy, no; but because medicine, surgery, had failed her. This exhalted profession to which his father gave so much time and energy, to which his father expected him to give his own life, had not been able to save the one person on the face of the earth worth saving.

He'd been thirteen when she died, and his father— whom he never saw cry over his mother's death, what a cold, cold bastard he was!—had responded to the change in the household by sending Lloyd off to military school. His oldest sister was married, and the other sister was off at college, so Lloyd—out at last from under the spell of his "sensitive" mother (that was how Father would often describe his late wife, giving the word a distasteful ring)— would finally be made a man.

And the academy was where Lloyd had been made a man, all right. He had learned that the feelings of tenderness he'd had for other males, feelings he'd tried to repress until now, were welcomed by other horny young men whose sexual awakenings were taking place in an all-male world. And while he was haunted by vague memories of his father having contempt for "queers," Lloyd enjoyed, in his first year, being the favorite of an older cadet, a loving son to a loving father, so to speak. And upon that older cadet's graduation, Lloyd became loving father to several young sons.

Did Father sense something in his manner? Home for the summer, Lloyd felt his father's eyes on him, suspicious eyes that seemed to strip him naked. His military bearing, his crisp politeness, somehow did not fool Father. Father seemed to know—though of course nothing was said—that the rifles and bayonets Lloyd had been drilling with were not always made of steel.

So on his sixteenth birthday, Father gave him one of two very special gifts that Lloyd would receive in an upbringing characterized by little fatherly attention. In the dead of one memorable night, his father took him to a brothel in the Flats, where a heavily made-up whore of perhaps twenty-two literal years and a hundred figurative wound up bringing him off with her mouth, because he couldn't do it otherwise. When Lloyd returned to his father—who was waiting in a chauffeured Lincoln out front—the old man had said, "Well?"

Lloyd, stiffly military, had said, "Thank you, Father. It was a perfect birthday."

And, as the boy climbed in, his father had bestowed a rare smile on his son and an even rarer pat on the shoulder.

For reasons Lloyd never knew, his father had pulled him out of the academy and put him back into public school for the senior year of high school. And the summer before his senior year, on his birthday, his father gave him the other memorable gift.

In the chauffeured Lincoln once more, they had driven in the dead of night, not to the Flats this time, but to Western Reserve University, where his father taught anatomy. In a vast, white, but dimly-lit classroom littered with lab benches, his father walked him to a wall of refrigerated drawers and pulled one out. Father flipped back the sheet and revealed the gray corpse of a man of perhaps forty.

"For you," he told his son.

"For . . . me?" Lloyd began to smile; his eyes began to tear. "My own . . . my very own ca . . . daver?"

"Your own." And again Father bestowed a smile and a hand on the shoulder. "This will be our secret."

Father had even given him a set of shining stainless-steel surgical tools in a leather pouch.

And throughout the school year ahead, at least one night a week, his father would take him to Western, and while Father prepared lesson plans and corrected papers, Lloyd practiced on his cadaver. To have power over the living, Father told him, one must first learn the secrets of the dead.

It was the most time that father and son ever spent together.

Lloyd never forgot those two gifts, those two thoughtful, personal gifts his father had given him: the live female body and the dead male one.

Even now, that rare tenderness on his father's part brought tears to Lloyd's eyes. It made him feel all the more ashamed that he had let Father down.

He hadn't at first. He'd gotten in at Harvard, no problem; between his grades and Father's connections, it had been a snap. But he hadn't exactly been an honor student—the drinking, the carousing with his fraternity brothers had taken a toll; he also had several affairs, with boys and girls, and was confused about who he was, exactly.

Sex with girls was something he could manage—like a duty; it required affection and care and time. Sex with a guy was animal, basic, in a hurry. He didn't think it was sissified conduct—he felt more a man with a man. Like the Greeks. He was a fraternity brother, wasn't he?

Anyway, his grades were good enough to get him into med school, and that was when disaster struck. He found himself drinking more and more, and his hands began to shake—it was from the drinking obviously, but how could he tell his instructors that? How could he explain to them that the lack of dexterity was temporary?

And how could he explain to his father that this temporary lack of dexterity, and this alone, had caused him to flunk out?

For several months his father said nothing to him. Literally nothing. Any communication between the two men in the large dark house was done through hand gestures or the servants. Finally Lloyd threw himself on his knees before Father, in his study, and begged forgiveness.

Father hadn't granted forgiveness, exactly, but he did say he would find "something constructive" for his son to do.

And what Father had done was, gradually, turn his investments and business dealings over to Lloyd, who found he had a complete and immediate knack for it. At first just a bookkeeper, he soon began doing some of the actual investing and, even in these hard times, made money for his father. Of course Father said nothing by way of approval, but he eventually turned virtually everything of a business nature over to Lloyd for his managing. Father and son began to speak. Civilly. Hardly warm. But if the war would never be over, at least there was a truce of sorts.

Among the matters Lloyd managed were various rental properties. These included a number of rooming houses in some rather unsavory parts of the city, as well as the bungalow where his father had begun his career, years ago, over on Central Avenue. Father—supported by his own father, whose money was in oil—had set up a practice in that neighborhood, an office/surgery, and abandoned it as he became more established and the neighborhood declined.

In dealing with these properties, Lloyd—who had been suppressing certain of his desires—began to mingle with the lowlife scum who dwelled there. He found that for a few dollars, sometimes less than one dollar, sometimes for a beer or some smokes, he could get those desires satisfied.

But he did not want to go down that road anymore. He wanted to please his father, who after all hated queers. Lloyd began to date females of his own social class. He had been engaged to Jennifer Wainright for a year now. She was a lovely girl and innocent; very religious; steel money. She agreed with him that they should wait until after they were married to "consummate their love."

The engagement seemed to make his father very happy. He had smiled several times, touched Lloyd's shoulder once.

Lloyd's life had really come together in the last few years. His father was accepting him, in a limited way admittedly, as the family business manager. He was engaged to be married. He had been seeing a psychiatrist—something his father had insisted upon about the time he turned over the business affairs to his son (had somebody at college said something to Father?)—and his doctor told him he could, with therapy, overcome his "homosexual tendencies."

And, of course, the truly satisfying thing, the most wonderful thing, was his return to surgery.

It had begun as a disaster. It had begun with one of the lowlife sex partners attempting to blackmail him—a woman he'd had various kinds of unnatural acts with. Lloyd had made the mistake of using his real name, and this lowlife bitch had tried to turn a buck because of it. Lloyd had pretended not to be upset by the demand, and drove the woman to the bungalow on Central Avenue, which was going unrented at the moment. On the pretense of getting the money for her, he led the cheap whore down into the cellar, where his father's surgery had been, and stabbed her in the chest repeatedly with one of the scalpels from the surgical gift set.

There was a lot of blood, but, oddly, he'd had an orgasm—the most intense he'd ever had with a woman.

Maybe he wasn't queer after all.

He had laid her on the dusty, dented white-enamel examining table his father had left behind and decided the best way to get rid of the evidence was in pieces. And, for the first time in a long time, he performed surgery.

He found it very satisfying.

Late that night he drove the pieces—some of them wrapped in newspaper, some packed away in an old suitcase—up to Euclid beach and tossed them out into the water. When they washed up on shore, they would (he assumed, correctly) be thought to have washed in from the lake.

And, so, simply, elegantly, it had begun: his return to surgery, and a second sexual awakening. Sometimes the sex would be with men, but he was moving away from that; he would turn them into women sometimes, and that would make it better. He felt there was nothing at all wrong with dispatching these human derelicts—they were just so much flotsam and jetsam, after all. Faggots and whores who could serve mankind best as lab specimens.

He would keep the bodies, at least parts of the bodies, and practice both surgery and sex on them—surgery to make his father proud, and sex to improve his performance with Jennifer, when they eventually married.

He was not a "butcher." He was a surgeon. Hadn't his

father said so, at the Torso Clinic? "No layman could have attempted such meticulous incisions." His father *was* proud of him! "We are dealing with an intelligent human being—most likely *not* a denizen of the lower strata." Yes! Father recognized breeding when he saw it!

In addition to its medical import, he saw his adventuring in the Flats, in the Third precinct, as another kind of research—sociological and psychological. In fact, that was how he maintained a "cover" (he did so enjoy the true-detective magazines); he told the landladies of the various rooming houses he oversaw that he would be keeping one room for himself and using a pseudonym. He was doing scientific research and it was crucial they not reveal to any of the other tenants that he was anything but another worker (or out-of-worker) in the neighborhood.

He had become "Andy," and it was a tribute to his intelligence and social skills that he could blend in with this rabble so effortlessly. They trusted him. They became his friends. For as worldly as they were, they were naive fools.

Like Frank Dolezal. Had Frankie mentioned his friend "Andy" to the cops, he wondered? Lloyd doubted it. Knowing Frankie, the poor bastard had spent most of his time begging for a drink, and thinking he'd committed the murders himself. That was a laugh! Frankie Dolezal, bricklayer, blackout drunk, and onetime slaughterhouse stooge, pulling off "meticulous incisions." Not in this lifetime, Frankie!

But the sheriff (and Ness) now made Frankie for the "Butcher." Which presented Lloyd with a dilemma.

Should he at this point wish to give up surgical and sexual experimentation, he could; the blame, the "Butcher" title, would forever be Frank Dolezal's. Part of him hated the idea of that—that such an untalented lowlife should get credit for *his* brilliance—but there was much to be said for quitting while you were ahead.

That was where shadowing Ness came in. But Lloyd had a problem with killing Ness. First, doing so would tip to the world that Dolezal was not their "Butcher"; and second, Lloyd was not a murderer. He was a surgeon, a sociologist, a psychologist, a bold and creative experimenter in the laboratory of life; but not a murderer. He did not kill to protect himself, but for science, and for love.

Killing Ness would be neither scientific, nor sexual, and Lloyd wasn't sure he was up to that. Even if Ness *had* been spouting off in the papers.

Oh, if it were a matter of self-defense, if Ness came at him with a gun or something, Lloyd would not hesitate to kill. This had begun when he had killed that blackmailing whore, after all, which was self-defense of a sort. But cold-blooded murder? And of someone more or less from Lloyd's own social class? That was not Lloyd's style; he was no fiend, after all. He had standards.

Perhaps it was time to end all experiments. He would be married soon.

He wondered if, by now, he could perform adequately with a woman—a live woman, a whole woman. He thought so. Practice, as they said, made perfect.

Now, as he finished his third bowl of Wheaties, he approached the counter, where the slim, pretty brunette waitress was leaning against one elbow, fooling absently with the gold filigree ring on her right pinkie.

"You look tired, beautiful," he said, and smiled.

She smiled back at him. "Been a long day."

"When's your shift end?"

"About ten minutes, thank God."

"Doing anything after?"

"Just collapsing somewhere."

"How about collapsing at my place?"

She studied him. He knew he looked good: he was not in scummy attire tonight, but wore a light-blue Arrow shirt and black slacks. He imagined he looked rather like an Arrow shirt ad come to life.

"I don't think so," she said unconvincingly, playing nervously with the gold filigree ring.

"Aw, come on. What's the harm? I got a nice bottle at home."

"Maybe . . . maybe we could go to a bar or something."

"Well, sure."

"I'm not that kind of girl, you know."

"Oh, I know."

"I'm not some easy pickup."

"I'm sure you aren't!"

They went to two bars and ended up back at his place, the reconverted surgery on Central. She was a pretty girl, and he hoped he could do the deed with her. They drank some more, especially her, and finally she passed out, probably due to the morphine he slipped in her Scotch. Having her pass out made it easier. He took her clothes off and did it to her while she was passed out. She didn't move at all while he was on her. That helped him do it. She was snoring a little when he climbed off and put his clothes on.

He was whistling when he went downstairs, flipping the light switch, illuminating the very white room below. The examining room cum surgery was spotless, probably cleaner than when his father had been practicing here. Lloyd had gone over the floor with a scrub brush to make it surgically disinfected as well as to destroy any evidence. He went to the large steel refrigerator and got out the lower torso of a woman and set it down upon the white-enamel examining table. He took from the lab bench his leather pouch of surgical tools that Father had given him and began to cut.

He didn't hear her on the steps.

The first thing he heard was her saying, in a slurred voice, "What are you up . . ."

Then he turned, scapel in hand, and she was standing there, on the stairs, slim and nude, with her eyes and mouth open very wide.

". . . to," she finished. Breathlessly. Frozen there.

He sighed, and moved quickly toward her.

INTERLUDE
April 8, 1938

14

Nine months had passed since the discovery of victim number nine—or victim number ten, if you counted (and Ness did) the 1934 torso that had washed up, half of it in a suitcase, on Euclid beach. Nine months since that startled tender in his tower on the Third Street Bridge had seen a dressmaker's dummy float by, only it hadn't been a dressmaker's dummy.

With the death of Frank Dolezal, and the apparent halt in killings, Eliot Ness had handed the Butcher case over to Merlo and Curry and returned to his duties as safety director. It had not been his idea: the Mayor had suggested that he "distance himself" from the investigation, what with the waters muddied by the sheriff's involvement.

Still, the Butcher remained a major concern of his, and he kept close tabs on his two detectives, who were (among other things) trying to track several suspects, including the hobo named Ben, the beggar called One-Armed Willie, and the nameless tramp who'd attacked Curry with a jackknife in the shantytown on the Run.

But none of this was on the mind of the young safety director on this pleasantly cool Saturday in April. Wearing a tux, looking and feeling spiffy, he was in the company of Evelyn MacMillan, a slender, lovely brunette of twenty-five years.

Ev's father was a well-fixed stockbroker in Chicago where several years back Ness—then head of the Justice Department's Prohibition Bureau in Illinois—had first encountered the MacMillan family socially. He'd been attracted to the girl then, but she'd been just a kid, a student at the Art Institute.

Last October he and Bob Chamberlin had taken the train to Ann Arbor for the Michigan/Chicago football game. He'd run into Ev and some friends at the stadium, and they'd all gone out to dinner afterward at his hotel. That was where and when Ness got the word that his mother had died in Chicago that afternoon.

He'd been close to his mother, very close, and it hit him hard, though he didn't think it showed. It showed to Ev, who insisted on taking the train back to Chicago with him. She stayed at his side throughout the next several days. She'd been a good friend to him; settling his family's affairs required several more trips home to Chicago, during which time a warm friendship with Ev blossomed into something even warmer.

Earlier this week, after much urging from him, she had moved to Cleveland. She was a gifted artist and had already illustrated several children's books for major New York publishers; so he didn't have to pull many strings to get her the job as fashion artist for the Higbee Company, one of city's major department stores.

This was their first night out on the town together, after her move. Ev wore a sleek black gown with pink and green satin ruffles at the bust, her creamy shoulders bare. She was quiet and rather modest personally, but she always dressed dramatically for an evening out. The fashion illustrator side of her, he supposed.

"This is a lovely place," Ev said, sipping her after-dinner champagne cocktail.

They were seated in yellow leather chairs at a corner table near a blue-mirrored wall in the Vogue Room off the lobby of the Hollenden Hotel. The Vogue Room was a streamlined, stainless-steel-trimmed nightclub with subdued, reflected illumination. The only light fixture visible was a steel chandelier over the central dance floor.

Ness, his back to the mirrored wall, sipped his Scotch and smiled and said, "Not what you'd expect of Cleveland, I guess."

"The town's not living up to its dull reputation. Very cosmopolitan, if you ask me." She touched his folded hands. "Eliot . . . I don't know what to say. I don't know how to thank you."

"You'll find a way, doll," he said, and smiled again.

She smiled big, showing pink gums above tiny white teeth; it was not a very cosmopolitan smile, but it appealed a great deal to Eliot Ness. "It sounds so corny when you call me that. 'Doll.'" She shook her head.

"Do you mind?"

"I don't mind it at all. It's just . . . it sounds like something some . . . *movie* tough guy would call his 'moll.' Jimmy Cagney or somebody. I'm glad they didn't serve grapefruit tonight."

He laughed. "Well, I'm supposed to be a gangbuster. Haven't you heard?"

"Of course I've heard," she said, gently swirling her champagne in its glass, looking down into the liquid as if it were a crystal ball she was trying to see the future in. "It's just that I've never heard it from *you*."

"I don't like to bring my work home."

"I can understand that. You work long hours. But my work is something I can and really *have* to take home with me."

"I told you, doll. You can have the tower for your studio. You can cloister yourself there all you want."

He was referring to the upper floor of the boathouse.

She squeezed his hand. "Oh, Eliot . . . I wish I could move in tomorrow."

"I wish you could, too. We need to wait awhile."

She nodded. "Till after the municipal election."

"I think it would be wise." His divorce hadn't been publicized, but it would be if he remarried, particularly if he remarried soon. He wouldn't care to give Mayor Burton's political enemies any ammunition; Burton had won by a landslide last year, but crucial council seats were at stake.

"November seems so far away," she sighed.

"Well, it'll give us a chance to get you acquainted with the city, and the city acquainted with you."

"I suppose. But darling . . . how much distance do we have to keep?"

"Well," he said, leaning toward her, whispering in her ear, "I expect you to stay on your side of the bed tonight."

She kissed her fingertip and placed it on his lips. "I think I can manage that."

Soon they were out on the dance floor, gliding to the strains of "The One I Love Belongs to Somebody Else" as performed, and nicely, by Ina Ray Hutton's all-girl band. The world was bathed in coral lighting. They held each other close; she was a rather tall girl and they made a nice fit.

As the number was concluding, Ina Ray announcing the band's break, he felt a tap on his shoulder, as if someone were cutting in.

He turned and looked into the jade-green eyes of Vivian Chalmers.

"Am I going to have to ask to be introduced?" Viv's voice was cordial and her smile pleasant and white and dazzling; but Ness recognized something hard and hurt lurking in her eyes.

"Of course not," he said, and gestured. "Vivian Chalmers, this is Evelyn—"

"MacMillan," Viv finished, smiling tightly but sincerely, shaking Ev's hand. Ev seemed a little embarrassed. "You're the talk of the town."

"Am I?" Ev asked ingenuously.

"Why, of course, dear," Viv said. "That's a plum job you pulled down at Higbee's. You must have friends in high places."

Neither Ness nor Ev knew what to say to that. They just gave her polite smiles, and finally Viv slipped an arm around Ev's shoulder and said, "Come on. Let's not be enemies."

"Enemies?"

The two women physically were quite similar; only their hair color and apparel differed. Where Ev wore an evening gown, Viv's slender shape was tucked away in a crisp white flannel mannish suit, pin-striped black, over a black blouse.

Viv looked sharply at Ness. "Hasn't this insensitive heel even mentioned me to you?"

"I can't say that he has."

Ness wished he were anywhere else. Picking torso pieces out of the Cuyahoga, for instance.

"We were an item," Viv said, walking Ev toward a side table. Ness followed like a pet. "I don't say this to be bitchy. But some bitch will tell you about it—I'm surprised you haven't heard already—so let's get it out in the open."

"F-fine," Ev said.

"It's over between this big sap and me. Okay?"

"Okay," Ev said tentatively.

"Now why don't you join us," she said, "for a drink."

Ev glanced desperately at Ness. He shrugged. This was one rescue he couldn't manage.

And they approached the table where a dark, vaguely dissipated young man in a tux sat gloomily nursing a double Scotch; next to him was a couple, sitting close to each other, holding hands, apparently very much in love. The woman was older than twenty, but not by much, a pretty redhead who worked hard though not successfully at covering her freckles with makeup; she wore a rather low-cut, shiny green gown and, hidden freckles or not, was a fine-looking woman. Her beau was a husky, towheaded guy in white dinner jacket with black tie.

"I'm sure you folks know our celebrated safety director," Viv said with a casual, almost dismissive nod in Ness's direction, "but I know you haven't yet had the pleasure of meeting his lovely young dinner companion, Evelyn . . . what was it, dear?"

"MacMillan," Ev said, a little confused, since Viv had known her last name a few minutes ago.

"She's a fashion illustrator with Higbee's," Viv said. "And this dashing drunken young fellow is Kenneth Morrison—his father is the real estate Morrison, a business which Kenneth seems also to be in, as coincidence would have it."

The young man smirked at her and lifted his glass.

"And this charming couple is Jennifer Wainright and Lloyd Watterson. They're engaged, they're in love, they're disgusting."

Watterson, whose blond, sunburned handsomeness was of a baby-face variety, stood and reached a hand out to Ness.

"This is a real pleasure," he said with a big white smile. "I've long been an admirer of yours, Mr. Ness."

Ness shook the somewhat sweaty but very strong hand and smiled back and said, "Call me Eliot. Isn't your father professor of anatomy at Western Reserve?"

"Why yes he is," Watterson said, his smile turning crooked. He sat back down.

Ness held a chair for Ev, and then took a chair himself, with his back to the wall, while saying to Watterson, "Your father was of some help to me, not so long ago."

"Really?" Watterson said. He was sipping at a glass of red wine. "He's very civic-minded, father is. What exactly did he do?"

"Well," Ness said, sorry he'd brought it up, "that really isn't suitable table conversation."

Watterson snapped his fingers. "It was that Torso Clinic! He helped you on that 'Mad Doctor of Kingsbury Run' affair."

Viv laughed. "I never heard him referred to as a 'doctor,' before, Lloyd. Isn't it 'butcher'?"

"Not according to Lloyd's father," Ness said. "He studied the . . . evidence and said he felt the Butcher had surgical training. But I'm really not so sure this is proper cocktail-party conversation."

Ev touched his hand. "Eliot doesn't take his business along on social occasions."

Viv studied the couple over the rim of her glass. "But he always sits with his back to the wall, doesn't he?"

Ev gave Ness an odd look, realizing that what Viv said was true.

Ness grinned and shrugged and said, "Old Chicago habits die hard."

"Does this mean," Kenneth Morrison said, with a sneering little smile, "that our safety director's packing heat?"

"Oh, no," Viv said, putting her Bacardi glass on the table next to two other empty ones. "He never carries a gun. It's against his philosophy."

"Is that right?" Watterson said with an interested smile. "Now why is that?"

Ness smiled shyly back and shrugged.

Viv said, "Something about people being disinclined to shoot an unarmed man. Besides, he knows judo. Don't you, Eliot?"

Ness leaned over to her and said, very softly, so that no one else at the table could hear, "Stop it, Viv."

Viv's lips trembled and her eyelids fluttered nervously. "I'm just a little drunk," she said.

He smiled charitably. "Happens to the best of us."

They leaned back away from each other.

"Do you think the Mad Doctor is dead, Mr. Ness?"

He turned his attention to Lloyd Watterson, who had posed the question.

"Lloyd," Ness said firmly, "I don't think this is a topic of conversation that's really suited for—"

"No! No!" Kenneth Morrison was gesturing rather drunkenly. "It's a fascinating topic! Share the inside dope with us poor outside dopes."

Ness felt ill at ease, but as he glanced around the table, he saw all eyes on him, none of them belonging to anybody who seemed to feel uncomfortable about the subject.

And now Viv got into the act.

"The newspapers," she said, "and the public, too, assume that the Butcher is dead. I mean, he *is* dead . . . what was his name?"

"Dolezal," Ness said softly.

"He hanged himself in the jailhouse," Morrison said cheerfully. "Spared the state the expense and the trouble."

"I don't know about that."

All eyes turned toward the pretty redhead at Watterson's side, whose small, high-pitched voice had finally entered the conversation.

"Everyone seems to think," Jennifer Wainwright said, "that the reign of terror is over. But it seems to me a lot of questions died unanswered with that poor man."

"Poor man?" Morrison said. "He was a maniac!"

"He never had a trial," she said reasonably. "How do we know he really was the Butcher?"

Watterson, his face blank but for intensely interested eyes, said, "Do *you* think this fellow Dolezal was guilty, Mr. Ness?"

"Eliot," Ness corrected with a smile. "I have my doubts. The evidence is less than overwhelming."

"Well, hell, man," Morrison said. "Didn't he confess?"

"Those confessions were beaten out of him."

"I thought," Watterson said, "that the coroner's inquest cleared the sheriff in Dolezal's death."

Ness smiled gently. "Not exactly. In fact, Coroner Gerber's autopsy established that four of the suspect's ribs were broken while he was in custody. It's just that those injuries could also be attributed to Dolezal's two failed suicide attempts."

"Come on now, Ness," Morrison said, his smile nasty, "aren't you just a little tiny bit bitter?"

"Bitter?"

"Hell, man—the sheriff stole your thunder! I remember all that press you got, coming out saying you were personally going to take on the Butcher. Well, the sheriff caught him, and that left you with a whole handfull of nothing."

Viv said sharply, "Kenneth, I hardly think the demise of the prime suspect in the Butcher case made Sheriff O'Connell a hero. The press, the Cleveland Bar Association, the American Civil Liberties Union . . . they were *all*, all over him, like a bad smell!"

Ness was struck by the bittersweet expression Ev wore as she studied Viv. It seemed to both please and sadden her to see Viv stick up for him.

"Come on, Eliot," Viv was saying. "Defend yourself! Admit it—you think the sheriff got away with murder. *Literal* murder."

"Maybe," Ness said, his voice barely audible. "But my office can't do a damned thing about it."

"Well," Viv said, "your pal Sam Wild has. He and half the reporters and editorial writers in town gave O'Connell hell. And they still are, months later."

"I would say," Morrison said, lifting his glass to Ness, "that the sheriff's reelection possibilities are just about nil."

Ness raised an eyebrow and his glass to Morrison. "I'll say this much—whether the sheriff killed Mr. Dolezal or not, he's killed his own political future."

Watterson slid his arm around Jennifer and said pleasantly, "So is the Butcher case open or closed, Mr. Ness—Eliot?"

"Lloyd, the mayor feels that unless or until bodies begin turning up again, the case should be considered closed—unofficially."

"Don't you have *anyone* working the case anymore?"

"Officially the slayings are unsolved—and I've kept two good men on it."

"Ah," Watterson said, smiling, as if reassured.

Ev, who'd been largely silent throughout the conversation, said, "Eliot, you haven't said what you really think. Do you think the Butcher is alive or dead?"

"Oh, I think he's still out there."

Viv smirked and said, "So do I. But he'll stay in hiding. He won't be back."

Ev turned to Viv and asked her why.

"It's obvious, dear," she said. "He can hide behind a dead man—this fellow Dolezal. Right, Eliot?"

"I think you're right to this extent, Viv: that's why we haven't heard from him in a number of months. But he'll be back. We have not, I'm afraid, heard the last of him."

Watterson seemed interested and almost amused by that. "Why's that, Eliot?"

"Because of the killing. That'll bring him back out in the open."

"The killing?" Watterson asked, confused. "What about it?"

"He likes it. Now, if you'll excuse us . . . I think the band is coming back from its break."

They bid the group their good-byes; Ness could feel Viv's eyes on his back as he headed out to the dance floor with Ev. Ina Ray Hutton and her girls were playing "Star Dust" and the lighting had shifted from coral to blue. He held Ev close, but she pulled gently away and looked at him with dark, searching eyes.

"Are you still in love with her?" Ev asked.

"Don't be silly, doll."

"She's still in love with you."

"I don't think she ever was in love with me."

"Oh, Eliot—don't you be silly."

"Look, we just had a fling. I'd rather not talk about that. That's the past. I'm interested in the present."

"And the future?"

"And the future."

He held her close and she let him.

They were headed back to their table when a waiter stopped them.

"Mr. Ness," he said. "Telephone for you in the lounge."

He left Ev at their table and walked to the bar in the dimly lit, walnut-paneled lounge. He hadn't left word where he'd be, but he wasn't terribly surprised to have been tracked down. It didn't take much of a detective to figure Ness would be in the Vogue Room on a Saturday night. The only other two possibilities were the Bronze Room at the Cleveland Hotel or his country club.

The bartender directed him to the one of the overstuffed davenports where a table with a phone waited. He sat and spoke his name into the receiver.

It was Curry.

"Chief, he's back at it again."

"You don't mean the Butcher?"

"That's exactly who I mean."

"Christ. Tell me."

"We got an arm without a hand; a lower leg, from ankle to foot. Clean dismemberments with a sharp knife, I'd say."

"God. Where?"

"Washed up on the riverbank near the foot of Superior Avenue, below the Run. Not far from where some pieces of the last two turned up."

"An arm and a leg at the foot, huh," he said wryly. "Where are you now?"

"Merlo's still at the scene. I'm calling from a saloon that I don't imagine is quite as nice as the one you're in."

"Can you tell anything from what you've seen? Man or woman?"

"Woman. Not much decomposition. It's either fresh or refrigerated. One new twist."

"Oh?"

"He might've tortured this one, some."

"How?"

"The arm's scarred up, blistered. They look like sores or acid burns or something. Suppose that means something?"

"I'm sure it does," Ness said. "I just wish it did to me."

He told Curry he'd meet him at the crime scene and hurried in to make his apologies to Ev. She would understand. They always did at first.

TWO

August 17–22, 1938

15

Sam Wild was standing in a rock- and refuse-strewn wasteland near the intersection of East Ninth Street and Shore Drive. It was five-thirty in the afternoon, within spitting distance of the business district, though you'd never know it, judging from these several desolate sloping acres of rubble and rubbish. He was perhaps twenty-five feet from Shore Drive, where homebound traffic was clogged, many motorists stopping there and on East Ninth, perhaps two hundred feet away; a cordon of uniformed cops was keeping hordes of onlookers back.

Word of the latest torso find had spread fast.

Scouting the vast dump was a handful of plainclothes detectives, including the youngish Curry and older, haunted-looking Merlo. The slabs and chunks and hunks of cement beneath their feet, and the occasional concrete pillar that lay about as if discarded by some nonchalant Samson, were debris from the expo. All that was left of a once-proud city of the future.

In charge, of course—and in this summer heat the only man in a vested suit rather than shirtsleeves—was the safety director himself, who was at the moment bending over the headless body of a woman, waving away flies.

The upper and lower arms and upper and lower legs and hands and feet had all been neatly severed from the torso by an unknown party; but the pieces had been put back where they belonged, assembled like a puzzle, by Ness and Coroner Gerber. The small pale coroner, with his salt-and-pepper hair and mustache, and wire-frame glasses, all in medical white, seemed strangely out of place in this desert of garbage and stones. He was kneeling over the reassembled corpse, raising a hand over it like a priest making a benediction.

The remains had been discovered, less than an hour ago, by an out-of-work young man named James Beason, who'd been searching the dump for scrap metal; at the moment he was being questioned just within Wild's earshot by Curry.

Wild, who'd been in Ness's office when the call came in, had been allowed along on the condition that he didn't take any notes; otherwise, other reporters—not invited along—would take offense. That was okay with Wild. He had a hell of a memory.

Beason, a man of average build in dungarees and workshirt, seemed calm, considering.

"I was getting ready to gather up the scrap iron I found and put it in my wheelbarrow," he was saying. "You know . . . so I could sell it to a junkyard? Then I seen what looked like a real colorful coat sticking out from under these rocks that was piled up neat."

"Go on," Curry said, writing it down.

Beason shrugged. "I took a couple of rocks off the pile and then I noticed these human limbs. So I went to call a policeman at a filling station on East Ninth Street. And that's all I know, I swear."

"Well, you're going to have to repeat this at headquarters. We'll have some more questions."

"What about my scrap metal?"

"We'll make sure nobody takes it."

Curry walked Beason to a uniformed cop and gave some instructions that Wild didn't hear; then the cop took Beason away.

Wild moved closer to Ness and Gerber.

Gerber was standing now, saying, "The technique is unmistakable, Eliot. Hesitation marks are all too familiar. This is no copycat. It's the genuine article. Our man is back at it. Butcher victim number twelve."

"An even dozen."

"I should think a butcher's dozen would number thirteen," Gerber said with a grim smile. "Let's hope he doesn't reach that tally."

The most recent corpse (till now), as yet unidentified, had turned up—actually washed up—in April; an arm and a leg first, then both thighs, one foot and the torso in two halves, wrapped in potato sack burlap, floating in the Cuyahoga.

Truth be told, Wild was glad this case was active again; it made for hot copy.

Ness was saying, "What can you tell me about her, Doctor?"

Good. Mentally, Wild began taking it all down.

Gerber scratched his chin, glancing down at her. "Well, she was white."

That was a hell of an observation, Wild thought.

"Between twenty and thirty-five, I'd say," the coroner continued. "Five feet five—allowing for the absent head."

Ness nodded, then said, "I'd put her weight at around one twenty."

"Yes," Gerber said. "Again, allowing for the head. Small hands." He bent down and picked up a severed foot, studied it. "Size nine shoe."

"Large foot," Ness said.

"Maybe they just seem that way," Wild offered, "when you pick 'em up and look at 'em close."

The coroner gave the reporter a quietly withering look. Wild smiled at him pleasantly, lit up a Lucky.

"We have a piece of jewelry," the coroner said. "The first time for a clue of that nature, I believe—a gold filigree ring that apparently was on so snug it would have to've been cut off for removal. Though why that would have stopped our man is beyond me."

Ness said, "Can you tell me when this woman was killed?"

"I will if you don't hold me to it," Gerber said. "My estimate at the moment is a year."

"A *year*?" Wild blurted.

The coroner glanced at Wild darkly.

Ness gave Wild a warning look but said, "Sam, if you'd like, take a closer look at the body."

Wild pitched the newly lit Lucky away and moved closer.

Ness pointed and said, "You can see that while the decomposition is limited, portions are dry and hard—as if preserved. And the stench is modest."

"Yeah, right," Wild said, nose twitching.

Gerber said, "She's been kept in a refrigerator, I'd say."

"Then," Wild said, "she was dumped here recently."

"Yes," Ness said. He pointed over to some cardboard boxes nearby. One of them bore the bright colors of the Quick-Frozen Seafood Company and the other the labels of the Boston Biscuit Company; two others had markings that indicated they were from the Central Market area.

"The arms and legs were wrapped in butcher paper and twine," Ness said, still pointing to the boxes, "and left in those. Only the torso, wrapped in that quilt, was under the pile of rocks."

The colorful gingham patchwork quilt he referred to was also nearby.

Ness was saying, "If those boxes had been sitting out here for a year—"

"They wouldn't look so brand-new," Wild finished, nodding. The boxes indeed were not at all weathered. "So—where the hell's her head?"

"Who knows?" Ness said, and sighed, glancing wearily about the littered landscape.

Gerber said, "Six out of twelve, this makes, where he hasn't left us the head."

"Maybe," Wild offered cheerfully, "this guy's got a collection in his attic."

"Maybe," Ness said.

Wild took off his straw fedora and wiped his brow. "If so, in this weather, it's gonna smell choice."

Gerber, with no apparent irony, said, "That's what refrigerators are for, Mr. Wild."

"Hey!" somebody called.

About one hundred and fifty feet to the east, somber Merlo was waving his straw hat frantically.

"Got something!" he called.

They walked briskly over, where Merlo was pointing to another cardboard box, a big one. As if a present had been unwrapped, butcher paper was peeled back to reveal what the box held: an assembly of bones. Dozens of them.

Gerber poked inside the box. "Human, all right . . . neck vertebrae . . . dorsal vertebrae . . . ribs . . . pelvic bones." He rummaged around in there like a kid searching for the toy in Crackerjacks. "No skull."

"Man or woman?"

"I don't know. Small person—that is, not tall. Big rib cage, though. Barrel chest. Probably a man. Five six, maybe. Dead a year, perhaps."

Wild said, "But not refrigerated."

Gerber ignored that. "Somebody get something . . . a container . . . a bucket or something. I want to sort a few of these out."

Ness gestured. "There's a can over there. Get it, Sam, would you?"

Wild went over and picked up the can; it was an old gallon container of some kind, with the lid on. He tried to pry it open with his fingertips, then asked around for a pocketknife. Curry had one and handed it to him.

Ness was saying to Merlo, "There may be more bones scattered about this dump. Gather as many reliable volunteers as you can and go over this rock pile. Pick up every tin can, board, rock—look under and in everything. Examine every possible place of concealment."

Wild pried off the lid and looked inside the can and said, "Oh, Christ."

It was a skull.

Wisps of blondish-white hair clung to it.

Wincing, he handed it, still in the can, to Gerber, who beamed; this was the first time Wild remembered ever seeing the man look happy.

"That's what I mean," Ness said, as if Wild had performed this feat to prove his point, "about places of concealment."

"I think this is a man," Gerber said, looking in at the skull. He drew it out and looked at it; its hollow eyes stared back at him. "He's not young—blond hair turning white."

"No kiddin' he's not young." Wild shuddered.

Ness left Gerber and Merlo to deal with the box of bones and the can with the skull and returned to the pieces of the woman, Wild following along. Ness again knelt near the body, again waving flies away.

He gestured to the severed right hand, which seemed to reach for an empty soap box not far away, fingers stretched toward the Gold Dust twins.

"We got a few breaks this time," he said. "The Butcher hasn't always left us the hands. So this gives us fingerprint possibilities—even if the Bertillion boys do have one hundred thousand thumbprints to sort through in a given category."

"And there's that nice specific piece of jewelry to try to trace," Wild said, gesturing toward the hand with the filigree ring.

"Not to mention those cardboard boxes, which clearly come from the Central Market area."

"Where all the finer transients go shopping," Wild said archly.

Ness stood. Smiled grimly to himself. "Think I'm going to have to throw a little party tonight."

Wild frowned in mild confusion. "What, that little shindig at the country club tonight, you mean?"

"No. This party's *after* the one at the country club. Later tonight—at Kingsbury Run."

A few minutes later Curry hollered out.

He'd found the girl's head, wrapped in butcher paper and twine. She was brunette and had been pretty. Ness said the girl looked vaguely familiar to him, but he just couldn't place her.

That didn't surprise Wild.

Ness knew his share of women.

Out on the country club terrace the ten-piece band was playing Cole Porter and a balmy breeze from Lake Erie was playing with the women's hair. Wild considered the surroundings a considerable step up from the lakeshore garbage dump of this afternoon. There were plenty of good-looking women present—low-cut dresses, bare shoulders—and lots of men in evening clothes for them to dance with. But some of the golfers were still here from late-afternoon rounds, so there were sports clothes and a few business suits—like Wild's white seersucker number—mixed in.

Even some of the women were dressed casually—for instance, the tall, slender blonde in pink shirt and pale green pleated skirt who sat down next to Wild at the little white-mesh metal table. The air smelled like a flower garden: some of it was flowers, and some of it was her.

"Buy you a Bacardi, Viv," Wild said.

"No," Vivian Chalmers said, touching his arm. Her
de-color eyes were looking for trouble. "You're just a poor
orking stiff. Seeing as how I'm of a moneyed class, I'll
uy."

"Seeing as how you're of a moneyed class, I'll let you."

Eliot was dancing with his girl, Ev, an attractive
runette in her mid-twenties; Wild liked her, but she was a
ttle quiet for his tastes. But then so was Eliot, for that
atter. After all, the guy was a bit on the dull side.

Not in terms of brains, of course. Wild considered
'ess about the savviest detective he knew, or anyway the
avviest honest one he knew. And he was well aware that
less had led—and continued to lead—a life filled with the
ort of adventure and danger that little boys dreamed
ould one day be theirs.

Maybe that was the problem. Maybe Eliot continued
) be a little kid living out a Sherlock Holmes/Rover Boys
antasy. The man seemed, in certain respects, oddly naive
) Wild. An innocent dedicated to tracking down the guilty.

Vivian brought two Bacardis over, set one of them in
ont of Wild, and smiled.

"You are alone tonight, aren't you?"

"Oh, yeah," Wild said. "I rarely come out to these
nings, with or without female company. I don't know how I
t Eliot talk me into joining this silly-ass sewing circle in
ne first place."

"I heard he got you a complimentary membership,"
'iv said, smiling wickedly. "Like his."

"Here's to friends in high places," Wild said, smiling
rookedly, toasting glasses with her, "and the fringe benefits
ney bring."

"Well, now that you're hobnobbing in society circles,"
he said, "if you want to hold out for a dame in an evening
own, I'd understand. You'll have to take me come-as-I-are.
just had to get an extra nine holes in."

"Yeah, well if you were looking for a guy in a tux," Wild
aid, "I'm not it, either. And I've never been on a golf
ourse in my life. What else do we have in common?"

She had a nicely wry smile, which continued as she
ipped the Bacardi. "Eliot, I suppose."

"We're both undercover agents of his, in a way," Wild
aid.

"Each in our own way, of course," she said.

"There's a double entendre in there somewhere tha I'd better not go looking for."

Her smile turned melancholy. "Maybe I wish yo would, Sam."

The band began playing a tango.

Pretty soon, Ness came over to see how Wild an Vivian were getting along, while Vivian and Ev were bot in the powder room.

"What's this Kingsbury Run party I'm not invited to' Wild asked.

"It's private."

"More private than the country club?"

"Yes. You can only attend if you're a bum or a cop.

"There's a difference?"

"Sometimes not," Ness admitted. "Here comes Vi Keep her entertained for me."

"Gee, I'll do my best."

Wild and Vivian sat at a table on the terrace and talke about her "undercover agent" days.

"Things have slowed to a boring halt," she sa nostalgically. "Eliot doesn't want to use me anymore."

That had an ambiguous ring.

"An undercover agent can only be effective so long Wild said. "Pretty soon the other side gets suspicious."

"I gave him something big this afternoon," she sa almost bitterly, "and he just shrugged it off." Then sh shrugged it off herself, with resigned frustration, and l Wild, who was wondering about the "something big" sh mentioned, buy the next round.

They took a walk in the dark, around the golf cours and ended up sitting on a green. Wild liked the bree almost as much as he liked Viv. The flag on the hole—13— flapped.

"Thirteen," he said.

"Huh?"

"Victim thirteen."

"Oh. Yes. Today. It's a goddamned shame."

"A goddamned shame," he agreed.

"Shame they haven't found the son of a bitch and kille his ass. If that stubborn prick Eliot High-and-Mighty Ne would just listen to me . . ."

She was a little drunk, and so was Wild, but it still surprised and amused him to hear a woman, particularly a "society" woman, speak that way.

"Viv, you wouldn't happen to still be in love with that lucky bastard, would you?"

She seemed taken aback for a minute, then her face wrinkled into a got-caught-with-her-pants-down grin. "Maybe a little. But he's got a girl."

"I don't."

"You might."

She leaned forward.

They kissed for a while, and she felt good in his arms; she was firm, almost muscular. But she smelled like flowers. And the sky was midnight blue and scattered with stars above them, as they lay back on the golf green to look up. Even to a man as cynical as Sam Wild, it seemed like a nice world, at the moment.

Long as you didn't recall it had a Butcher in it.

16

Only the green and red switch lights along the railroad tracks disturbed the perfect blackness of the night. Only the gurgling pulse of the underground sewers broke the between-trains silence. Three hours before dawn, Kingsbury Run was a blot in the city's midst. In the two shantytowns of the Run—the crowded one off Commerce and Canal, the slightly smaller but more sprawling one near the Thirty-fifth Street Bridge—hobos and down-and-outers slept in their shacks. No fires remained lit in either camp in these early hours of the predawn morning to keep away bugs or butchers. The darkness seemed to shield the shantytowns' very existence from civilization proper.

On the street above the hillside where the larger

shantytown nestled, a fire engine glided almost silently into place. Already parked on nearby streets of the Flats were eleven unmarked police cars. Five police vans, called paddy wagons by some, Black Marias by others, sat silently, each tended by a driver and a jailer. Twenty-five cops—a dozen plainclothes, a dozen uniformed, and the man in charge—were massed on the street above the hill like a small army. Their commander in chief was the city's safety director, who wore a dark suit and no hat. He had a revolver in one hand and an oversize, switched-off flashlight in the other.

"Bob," Ness said quietly to the man at his side, "get your men into position."

Robert Chamberlin nodded and broke off with nine other plainclothes men; in the midst of a huddle, tall, mustached, lantern-jawed Chamberlin—a man with considerable military bearing—was pointing in various directions into the darkness as if he could see into it, and men were nodding, looking back where he was pointing, as if they could, too.

Earlier, just after one A.M., all of these men had met at the fire department headquarters at the east end of the Central Viaduct, where Ness had briefed them, mapping out the raid in detail.

Chamberlin's men divided up and a few took positions along the top of this hillside, and the rest, with Chamberlin, disappeared down the ridged slope, veering this way and that, into the darkness. Like Ness, each man had a gun in one hand and a flashlight in the other—though their flashlights were not oversize, clublike objects like that of the safety director's. Each was taking up a post at various approaches to the raiding zone; this would, Ness hoped, prevent any alarm from being given and keep anyone from entering or departing the shantytown.

He didn't like all this brandishing of guns; but he'd figured the conspicious presence of firearms, in the hands of men who'd been warned to be anything but trigger-happy, would help keep order among the army of hobos whose camp they were about to invade. Only the plainclothesmen would carry guns: the uniformed cops would be threatening enough in badges and blue and nightsticks-on-belts.

Ness broke the remaining men up into groups of five,

putting Merlo in charge of one squad and Curry in charge
of the other, and sent them off to the right and left, keeping
four men with him.

Several minutes crept by, of which Ness could feel
every slow second. The blackness below seemed to have
swallowed the men without so much as a belch. Ness
waited. He brought the hand with the gun in it up near his
face and chewed a hangnail on his thumb.

Then a flicker—on and off, on and off—signaled one
man was in place.

More flashlight flickers followed, down in the darkness, like so many oversize fireflies, signaling that the rest
of Chamberlin's men were in place as well.

Ness thumbed on his massive flashlight and swept a
beam across the area below in one broad swing, signaling
those guarding key positions down there, and those waiting
up top, that he was about to move in.

And move in he did, the other raiders moving with
him, rushing through the darkness and the brush and the
wild trees, sliding, stumbling, tumbling at times. As they
reached the outskirts of the sleeping shantytown, barking
dogs announcing the raiders' impending arrival, Ness
swung his flashlight arcing through the night behind him in
another signal.

A blaze of white light banished the darkness and left
the shabby village naked in its glare. A giant searchlight
mounted on the fire truck above swung its beam slowly
across the landscape, as if giving the hillside hovels a
collective third degree.

Cats scurried away, screeching, but dogs held their
ground and howled.

So did their masters.

"Goddamnit!"

"What the fuck—"

"What in the name of God are you—"

"Sons of bitches!"

Those outraged occupants who rushed out of shacks in
protest and surprise were grabbed and cuffed by uniformed
cops. The charge was vagrancy, and basic personal information, mostly just names, was quickly taken down; as per
Ness's instructions, each bum was tagged with a number,

and the shack that bum belonged to was tagged with the same number. Then the alleged vagrant was dragged up the hill and tossed in a waiting Black Maria. Once a uniformed cop had deposited a 'bo in the back of one of the vans, said cop would head back down the hillside and repeat the process.

Other doors required kicking in, much of which was done by Ness himself; if he seemed to have knack for it, he certainly took no pleasure in it on this raid.

Gun in hand, Ness would kick in a makeshift cardboard-tin-and-wood door and throw the flashlight beam into the eyes of a just-awakened man, blotting out the man's face with light, jerking him from his sleep on his bed made of boards atop battered steel drums, and a cop would rush in and grab the guy, yanking him out of the security of his packing-crate home.

Those whose slumber was a drunken one sometimes required carrying out; one heavyset, bad-smelling 'bo took two cops to hoist him, like a sandbag, up the hill.

There were a few women and children. Not many. They were treated gently, though one woman screamed and kicked worse than any two of the men. She outswore them, too. The kids were quiet, scrawny things. One of the plainclothesmen present, Gold, was with the juvenile bureau, and he took charge of the ragamuffins.

It sickened and saddened Ness to see how these poor bastards lived. These men weren't criminals, not in the sense that he considered a man a criminal.

What was criminal here was not the shantytown's inhabitants, but that such a town needed to exist; what was evil was men somehow becoming faceless noncitizens who could be preyed upon by a Butcher made anonymous by the very anonymity of his victims.

The fire-truck searchlight continued its all-pervasive swing, casting dark shadows, making this ragged world seem unreal, here sharply white, there sharply black. A cacophony of screams, curses, barks, yowls, commands, provided a tuneless sort of background music. For better than an hour Ness moved across a landscape littered with refuse, some of it human, cops like garbage collectors of humanity hauling screaming men away. He felt like a man moving through a nightmare.

"Eliot, *jeez*, look . . ."

Ness turned quickly; saw the shovel blade coming and ducked.

". . . . out!"

It was Curry who yelled, and a massive, wild-eyed, bearded hobo who had swung the shovel; and he was still swinging it. It cut the air, slashing, swooshing.

Ness, still dropped in a crouch, kicked a foot out and up and caught the man in the stomach; doubling him over.

The 'bo was groaning on the ground when Curry cuffed him, kicking the shovel away.

"I'll get him out of here," Curry said.

"Don't forget to tag him, and his home," Ness said, standing, brushing himself off.

Curry nodded.

Ness returned to kicking down doors; nearly another hour passed. Now and then a siren would rend the night, as a filled Black Maria would head back to Central headquarters.

Merlo came over; he looked like a ghost. A tired one.

"We've rounded 'em all up," he said. "Thirty-nine of 'em."

"Good," Ness said, tucking his revolver in its shoulder holster and glad to do so. "Link up with Bob Chamberlin and have him turn over his men to you. It's going to be a long morning."

"And it's not even dawn yet," Merlo said with a sorrowful roll of his eyes.

Ness intended to have the detectives begin grilling the vagrants immediately and at length, at Central headquarters. Each one of them would be questioned regarding the torso slayings—sorting out the suspects from the witnesses, gathering whatever information about the Butcher these men might have.

As Merlo was leaving, Ness called out, "I want them all fingerprinted! Make sure."

Merlo turned and a confused look crossed his face. "But we don't have any fingerprints to compare them with," Merlo said. "The Butcher's never left us anything to . . ."

A few last vagrants were still in the process of getting tagged and having basic information taken down.

Ness walked to Merlo and spoke softly. "That's not what I'm thinking of. I'm thinking of the future."

"The furture?"

"Future victim identification."

Merlo's smile was mirthless; he said with grim admiration, "You *are* a detective, Mr. Ness," and went off up the hill.

Ness called Chamberlin over and said, "Round up your men. It's time to make the trek down to the other settlement."

"Are you coming?"

"No. I'll keep Curry and half a dozen others here. We're going to sort through the shacks for evidence. Now, keep the procedure identical, Bob—I want every vagrant and his shack tagged. Once you've emptied the settlement of its squatters and had them hauled away, then search the shacks, bagging up any possible evidence or personal belongings."

"And tagging that with the same number," Chamberlin said, nodding. "Right. Do you really expect to find the Butcher among these fellows?"

Ness lifted his eyebrows in a facial shrug. "It's possible. If we can find a ringer . . . somebody who doesn't belong here among them . . . some rich guy slumming . . . we may have our Butcher."

"An undercover maniac," Chamberlin said. He glanced at the clustered huts around them. "But there's no place here that our friend could be keeping the bodies of his victims for months on end."

"Yes, precious few refrigerators in *these* modern homes," Ness noted wryly. "Even if he's been living here, he has to have some other place to store the bodies . . . and do whatever else he does to them."

Chamberlin's tiny black mustache twitched in a moment of disgust. Then, matter-of-factly, he said, "Well, we know for sure those cardboard boxes in the dump, with the human bones in them, came from the Central Market area. There's no doubt of that." He made a clicking sound. "I think this raid was needed."

"It was time," Ness nodded.

Chamberlin, with his customary precision and speed, gathered his men and left.

Soon, with the exception of the fire truck, its search light still shining, most of the vehicles had moved out. The Black Marias were already gone; they would deposit their human cargo and meet up with Chamberlin at the Thirty-fifty Street Bridge.

Ness, Curry, and several other men went through the shacks; it was a pathetically easy job. There were few possessions, and nothing resembling evidence at all, with the exception of a few cardboard boxes from the Market area, which were tagged and kept.

When the job was done, Ness went up to his car and radioed for several more fully manned fire trucks.

As he waited for them to arrive, he noticed that Curry was down amongst the shacks, wandering, hands in pockets, looking glum, like a lone performer caught in the spotlight of the huge searchlight, which was stationary now, no longer probing.

Ness worked his way back down the hill.

"What's wrong?" he asked Curry, walking alongside the restless young detective.

"Wrong?"

"You seem . . . out of sorts."

Curry shrugged. Then he shook his head. "*It's* wrong."

"What is?"

"What we did here. These people live here."

"I know that."

"I know it doesn't look like much . . . it isn't much . . . but it was home to these people."

Ness put a hand on the detective's shoulder. "Albert, I know you lived with these people for a while. So it's understandable, how you feel. But don't forget we're helping get them out of harm's way."

"I know," he sighed, shaking his head. "What you said earlier made sense."

What Ness said earlier, in the briefing, was: "The removal of the vagrants is for their own protection since, should they remain here, they might well become victims of the Butcher." But Ness knew the reality was many of

them would stay in the Flats, in the Third precinct—
somehow, somewhere—and would remain the Butcher's
meat.

Curry was saying, "This effort *should* help us nail the
Butcher. Maybe we nailed him here tonight. Maybe he's
being questioned at Central headquarters this very minute."

"It's possible," Ness said.

Curry's youthful features contorted. "But what do they
do now? Or anyway, after we spring 'em loose? Where do
the poor devils go?"

"They're going to have a choice," Ness said. "We're
offering one-way train tickets out of town—Mayor Burton
got me the money for that this afternoon. Or they can have
their cases turned over to the Relief Department, and with
a little luck wind up with a CCC or WPA job."

Curry nodded. Sighed heavily. "Yeah. Maybe this'll
help some of 'em get back on their feet, at that. Still . . ."

"I know, Albert. Look, why don't you go on home. Get
some sleep."

"What about all the questioning we're supposed to
do?"

"I've got the vagrants covered. I don't need you. I
need you on that other suspect."

"The one you got the tip on? You think he's a good
prospect?"

"Reliable source," Ness said. "We're doing a thorough
investigation of the guy, soon as we've got this raid behind
us, but in the meantime, you keep him under surveillance."

"Starting when?"

"Starting when you wake up about noon after going
home and getting some sleep. Get going. Right now."

Curry nodded, smiled wearily. "Okay, Chief. Soon as
we're done here."

"We're done. Take the car. The fire department will
give me a ride."

Curry nodded again and trudged up the hill. He
looked back a couple of times at the deserted city of huts,
frozen in the searchlight's now-motionless glare.

And now Ness wandered the ghost shantytown, feeling as melancholy as Curry.

It was still dark when, atop the hill, fire engines pulled up, five of them, manned to the hilt. Ness went up and gave instructions all around.

Two companies under Battalion Chief Reece dragged the tin-wood-and-cardboard shacks to the very bottom of the hill, some of the structures disassembling on the way, trailing pieces of themselves. The firemen gathered all of the pieces and tossed them on the pile, poured on coal oil, and torched the whole shebang.

Fingers of flame clawed the air; burning wood crackled and snapped. Soon the sound built to a roar, and the flames to a conflagration—albeit a controlled one. The night turned orange.

Ness stood staring down into what he'd wrought.

The fire was so bright, Ness barely noticed dawn. A cloud of gray smoke hovered over Kingsbury Run. Onlookers began to gather at the top of the hill.

"Just like Anacostia," a middle-aged, stubble-cheeked man in a workshirt said to himself. Hands in his pockets, eyes glazed. He was standing next to Ness.

"Anacostia?" Ness asked.

The man glanced at Ness's suit and tie and smiled knowingly, said, "You don't look like you was in the Bonus Army."

"I wasn't," Ness said.

"The big boys burned *that* Hooverville, too," the man said expressionlessly, then turned and disappeared into the crowd.

17

On Thursday, just after noon, Sam Wild sat at a small white-metal triangular table under a colorful umbrella and waited for Vivian Chalmers. The little outdoor café in the shadow of Terminal Tower was doing a brisk business; and the predominant topic of conversation here, and elsewhere in Cleveland for that matter, was the burning of shantytown.

Most folks appeared pleased that the city's worst eyesore had been removed, but others were annoyed at the rashness of the safety director's action. The sky was clear now, but all morning a gray smoke-cloud had hung over Kingsbury Run and drifted over downtown Cleveland as well. In the areas bordering the Run in the early morning hours, people awakened by the noise and/or glare ran to windows and thought the city was on fire. Telephones at police headquarters and at the local papers had rung off the hook.

As for Sam Wild, he was pissed off.

Specifically, he was pissed off at Eliot Ness, whose ass he wanted to chew out, the way his own ass had been chewed out all morning by his city editor. It really steamed him, thinking about all those coy remarks of Eliot's about private parties and bums and cops, at the country club last night. . . .

As yet today, though, Wild hadn't been able to see the safety director, who was still burrowed in at Central headquarters questioning the dozens of vagrants pulled in on the two shantytown raids.

Vivian breezed in around twelve-fifteen. She was smiling and looked girlishly fresh; but something off-kilter lurked in the jade eyes, and her usually smooth brow was creased. She wore a pale orange dress; she sat, crossing her pretty brown legs.

"Thanks for meeting me," Vivian said.

"My pleasure."

"Speaking of which . . . about the other night . . ."

Wild waved it off, saying, "We were both a little drunk. Forget it." Then he grinned at her. "Just don't ask *me* to."

They were served lemonade and little ham-and-cheese and lettuce-and-tomatoe sandwiches with the crusts trimmed off the toasted bread. He wondered if there was a story in the missing crusts; he could use a scoop right now.

She smiled as she nibbled her sandwich.

"Looks like Eliot was a busy boy last night," she said.

"Yeah, right," Wild said disgustedly.

"Don't you approve of his actions?"

"Hell, I could care less about makin' the homeless homeless," Wild said, biting off half a sandwich.

"You sound cruel, Mr. Wild."

"Guys like that are used to life dealing 'em a lousy hand. Anyway, don't kid yourself—most bums were bums *before* there was a depression."

"Then why are you so put out with our mutual friend?"

"'Our mutual friend' screwed me, if you'll pardon my French. He didn't invite me along on that little hayride and that put my ass in a sling with my city editor. Me, who's supposed to be his right-hand man."

"Well, you work for the *Plain Dealer*, not the safety director's office."

"True. But Eliot knows that he's my only assignment. When he goes out on something *this* big, I *got* to get a piece of it."

She smiled to herself. Sighed. "He does have a selfish streak, our Mr. Ness."

"Our Mr. Ness sees things one way: his."

She rolled her eyes like Eddie Cantor. "You're telling me."

"Why do I have the feeling Eliot gave you the short end of the stick, too? And why do I have the feeling that's what you wanted to talk about today?"

She smiled impishly. "Because he did, and I do. Want to talk about it, that is."

He smiled at her shrewdly; tapped the air with a forefinger. "It's that 'something big' you mentioned last night, isn't it? The information you gave Eliot yesterday that he just 'shrugged off,' I think you said."

"My. You're very perceptive, Mr. Wild."

"I'm a reporter, and flattery will only get you the key to my apartment."

"Really?"

"Lady, the only thing I'd like more out of life than being city editor myself someday is marrying a beautiful heiress."

That seemed to amuse and please her. "Is that right? And I qualify?"

"Well, as soon as you fall head-over-heels over me you will. Didn't you see *It Happened One Night*? You're perfect for the Claudette Colbert role."

"Gee," she said mock wistfully, "I'm usually told I'm the Carole Lombard type. As for you, you look about as much like Clark Gable as our waiter."

"Actually," Wild said, "I thought our waiter looked a little like Carole Lombard."

She laughed, sipped her lemonade. "If we're going to go on with this giddy repartee, we'd better move to a bar so we have alcohol as an excuse."

"Vivian—"

"Viv."

"Viv, I like you. You're a good kid, for a rich girl. But sometimes I get the feeling . . . hell. I don't know how to say this without spoiling a beautiful friendship."

"Sam, say what you think. As if you didn't always."

"Last night was . . . well, it was last night. Only here it is today, and you still seem interested in me. Now, maybe you got a yen for impoverished newshounds, I dunno; I realize, of course, I have this striking resemblance to Clark Gable that attracts you wildly. But we don't exactly come from the same worlds. In fact, we only got one thing in common."

She nodded. Looked down at her lemonade.

"Eliot," she admitted.

"Eliot Ness," Wild confirmed. "So I have to wonder if

your wanting to be around me doesn't have something to do with that."

"Sam . . ."

"I guess in my tactless way, I'm asking if last night might've had something to do with wanting to . . . 'show' Eliot?"

If she weren't so sophisticated—or trying to be—she would've looked hurt; but her expression managed to get something else across: disappointment in him.

"Last night had to do with showing *you*," she said. "And . . . it had a little to do with too many Bacardis."

"Okay," he said. "Why don't you tell me about it?"

"About what?"

"About what you told Eliot yesterday that he's ignoring like the stuffy, stubborn bastard he is."

She smirked to herself, sighed elaborately. "It sounds crazy but . . . I think I know who the Butcher is."

"What?" Wild's eyes narrowed to slits. "I can't picture Eliot ignoring *that* . . . it's not like it's just *anybody* approaching him—you worked for him."

"Not lately. And he thinks I'm just . . ."

"Looking for an excuse to be around him?"

She nibbled at a little sandwich. Nodded.

He reached across and patted her hand. "Well, I'm prepared to listen. Tell me about your Butcher."

She smiled, pleased to be taken seriously, even if a bit condescendingly. She pushed her plate aside and sat forward, green eyes flashing. "You know how the experts, Eliot among them, have been harping on the 'professional' way the bodies have been cut up—they say again and again there's a 'surgical' look to the dismemberments."

Wild nodded, suddenly glad he'd had such a light lunch.

She went on: "They've been saying that a doctor— anyway, somebody who'd at least been in medical school for a time—would be a likely candidate for the Butcher."

"Sure."

"And medical school's expensive, so, it stands to reason, the Butcher just might run in the same social circles as yours truly."

"Well, I don't know about . . ."

"For the sake of argument?"

"For the sake of argument." He shrugged. He fired up a Lucky.

"Do you know Dr. Watterson of the Western Reserve?"

"We're not exactly close. He's a big shot, I know that . . . top surgeon, top anatomy professor, serves on various boards of directors, widely respected . . . hey, you're not suggesting—"

"No! No."

"Good. I mean, Viv—Watterson is one of the experts who's worked the case, for cryin' out loud. He was on Eliot's goddamn Torso Clinic!"

"Not him. Not the father. The son."

"There's a son?"

"A son named Lloyd." She seemed embarrassed suddenly; gestured nervously. "I know him socially. He's cheerful, seems like a nice enough guy, if just a little . . . off."

"Well, now I guess he'd have to be, if he went around cutting people up, wouldn't he?"

She frowned; she looked like a little girl whose dollhouse had been messed with. "If you're not going to take this seriously . . ."

"I am. I am. Go on, go on."

"Well. He's a big man, very strong—the kind of strength it might take to do some of the things the Butcher has done."

"The same could be said of thousands upon thousands of men in this city, Viv."

"Are you going to listen? Lloyd's an only child, and his father always expected him to be a doctor." She smiled wickedly. "But a few years go, guess what Lloyd did? He flunked out of medical school."

Wild sat forward.

"He's engaged to a friend of mine. But the engagement keeps getting postponed. She's confided in me, a couple of times, that she's afraid they're never going to get married. She says . . . she says Lloyd never touches her."

"Touches her how? You mean . . . ?"

"Sexually. They're very affectionate in public, but in private, he gets all high-tone about waiting until after they're married to 'consummate' their love."

Wild blew out some cigarette smoke. "Maybe he's old-fashioned."

"He's also seeing a psychiatrist. Jennifer . . . that's his fiancée . . . told me that, too."

"A lot of people see psychiatrists, Viv."

"Sam, I was on a double date a few months ago . . . this guy I was seeing for a while, a typical society loser, never mind about him . . . we were out with Jennifer and Lloyd at the Vogue Room, and we ran into Eliot and Ev. They stopped by the table. Well, the conversation got around to the 'Mad Butcher,' though Eliot was reluctant to talk business, as usual; but, anyway, Lloyd seemed overly interested in it, it seemed to me."

"Surely Eliot would've picked up on that, if that were the case."

"I don't think so. Eliot was . . . well, distracted by having both Ev and me around. Also, he wasn't aware of Lloyd's background. And, hell, I didn't think about it much till later, because shortly after that . . . actually that same night . . . the first body in some time turned up. So then I found myself going over the conversation again and again in my mind."

"Maybe you've blown it up out of proportion."

"Maybe. But one of the things that stuck with me was the way Lloyd referred to the Butcher that night . . . he consistently called him the 'Mad Doctor.' Not the Butcher. *Doctor*."

Wild nodded slowly. "There've been a lot of nicknames for this killer in the papers . . . the Headhunter, the Torso Killer . . ."

"But not 'Mad Doctor.' Sam, Lloyd is a failed doctor. A failed *surgeon*."

Wild scratched his chin. "I don't know, Viv. He's a big healthy guy, he flunked out of medical school, he's seeing a psychiatrist, he wants to wait till after he's married to make whoopee with his wife. That doesn't add up to a mass murderer, exactly."

"There's something else. You see, I . . . I did a little investigating of public records. Frankly, I think that's what made Eliot a little . . . well, not angry but put out with me. That I was taking it upon myself to investigate this, when I'm no longer on the city payroll as any kind of investigator."

"Well, it's a hell of a dangerous case to go poking around in, unofficially. He's probably concerned for your safety."

"Yes," she said archly, "he's the *safety* director, after all. Sam, he just listened blankly—didn't write a thing down. Just told me, firmly—almost, God, angry—to stay out of the case. That I was no longer associated with his office. Period. Damn, he was cold."

"Viv, like I said, this is a hell of a dangerous—"

"Let me tell you what I found out. Lloyd Watterson manages his father's business affairs. These include certain properties in the Flats and in the Third precinct. Rooming houses."

The skin on the back of Wild's neck began to tingle.

"He oversees them," she said. "Collects rent and such from the landladies who manage them. And do you know where he lives?"

"At home with daddy?"

"No. He lives on Central Avenue. In the Third precinct. In a building that used to be his father's."

"His father's?"

"Yes. It's where his father first hung out a shingle. It's a goddamn doctor's office, Sam."

Wild swallowed, stabbing out his cigarette. "Christ. It could be this 'murder lab' they've been looking for. . . ."

"Eliot Ness doesn't seem to think so," she said tightly. "And you know something else?"

He was almost afraid to ask, but he did: "What?"

"Lloyd told Jennifer what he's being treated for. By the psychiatrist. It's what made her start crying and break down in my arms and confide so much in me."

"So what is Lloyd being treated for, anyway?"

Her smile was small and smug. "Homosexual tendencies," she said.

And she sipped her lemonade.

Lloyd Watterson lived just off Kingsbury Run on Central Avenue in a rooming-house district. From the small but weed-overrun lawn and the boarded-up basement windows, the modest bungalow, its white paint curling off, might have been abandoned. There were signs of inhabitation, though, namely the draped front windows and some mail sticking out of a box by the front door.

It was midafternoon, and Wild was having second thoughts.

"What if he comes home?"

"He isn't home," Viv said. "He and Jennifer are at the club today; I checked it out thoroughly, Sam, and anyway, if he comes home unexpectedly, I'll start honking the horn."

"Swell. Then what? I'm unarmed."

"I have a gun," she said, simply, and showed him a small pearl-handled automatic in her purse.

"Do you know how to use it?"

"I'm the best female skeet shooter in town."

"Well, hell—anybody who can shoot female skeet with a twenty-five automatic is jake with me." He sighed. "Here goes."

She stayed behind in her little shiny blue Bugatti sports car, which couldn't have been more out of place in this neighborhood. Hers was one of the few cars parked on the street, and the sidewalks were relatively empty as well.

The game plan was for Wild to get inside that bungalow and snoop around enough to see if there was any possibility that the residence, reconverted from a general practitioner's office years ago, might still be a surgery of sorts. To see if it might indeed be a possible "murder lab."

If Wild felt that was the case, he would tell the director of public safety.

Wild's say-so, both he and Vivian felt, would be enough to get Eliot off the dime. And if Lloyd turned out to be the Butcher, there would be the scoop of a lifetime in it for Wild. He—not Eliot Ness—would be the man who "got" the Butcher.

Which was all well and good, but what if there was more substantial evidence of butchery? What if he found a stock of torso parts in cold storage, a virtual human meat locker? What if a half-carved victim lay on a surgical table?

It was a warm day, but Wild shivered.

He had a cynical nature, and he had seen about all

there was to see in his time. But the small, unprepossessing frame house before him chilled him like nothing he'd ever faced.

Reluctantly, pitching a spent Lucky behind him into the street, he climbed the half dozen steps, his hand on the rusting rail.

He didn't care what Viv said, he wanted to make sure Watterson wasn't home; so he knocked. Should Lloyd come to the door, Wild might ask directions to the nearest gas station, or maybe do a man-in-the-street (or on-the-porch) interview about the Butcher. *How does it feel living in this neighborhood when it's under the cloud of these killings.*

Of course, right now the cloud the neighborhood was under was from the shantytown fire. The acrid smell of smoke was everywhere.

He knocked again.

Nothing.

Like any good reporter, Wild carried several skeleton keys, and the first he tried worked. Wasn't this his lucky day.

Just inside, in the foyer, he noted several built-in coat hooks on the wall. What had been the waiting room was off to the right, converted to a small, well-furnished living room. The furnishings looked comfortable but not cheap, and the oriental artwork and tapestries on the walls were more expensive than you would expect to find on Central Avenue. Nothing suspicious, exactly, but this place clearly was a bachelor hideaway of some sort.

A door off the reconverted waiting room stood open on a room that was larger, but strangely empty. It had been, perhaps still was, an office; a rolltop desk, like Eliot's, and several half-filled bookcases. Several wooden chairs. On the desk, Wild noted, was a stack of ledgers; also an adding machine. In the bookcase, medical texts, books on anatomy. That, and the emptiness of the room, after the homey coziness of the adjacent living room, unnerved him.

But he stayed with it. He peeked into what he thought would be closets, but turned out to be cubicles with examining tables. The tiny rooms were clean but smelled musty; they didn't seem to have seen recent use.

He went back through the small living room and into

the hall and walked down to the kitchen. It was white and clean, smelling of disinfectant. There was a kitchen table with a newspaper—Wild's paper, the *Plain Dealer*—folded open to the funnies. Otherwise, there was no sign of anyone's living here. No dishes in the sink or food out on the counter.

Years ago this place had been set up to be a residence in back and a doctor's office in front; so the bedroom and a small dining room were off the hall and the kitchen respectively. Those rooms remained to be inspected, but, for a moment, Wild thought he should just get the hell out. It wasn't that he was scared: the only thing thus far that really disconcerted him was that big, mostly empty office. And why shouldn't it be mostly empty? Lloyd wasn't a doctor; the only item of any use to him in that room was the desk, and his business ledgers had been on the desktop, just as they should be. Nothing suspicious.

No, Wild was thinking he'd made a mistake coming here. Lloyd was not a suspect. He was just somebody Viv knew who fit parts of the Butcher's projected profile. And both Wild and Viv had axes to grind against Eliot, at the moment, impairing both their judgments.

He was trespassing for no good reason. He ought to just get the fuck out.

As he stood in the kitchen contemplating all this, he found himself facing the large Frigidaire refrigerator.

And now he felt a little nervous. Now his tongue felt thick and his hand trembled as he reached out for the door handle. This would be the test, he told himself. If Lloyd's refrigerator shelves bore nothing more than common everyday groceries, Wild would hightail it out of here and write this one off to bad judgment and getting laid.

He cracked the Frigidaire door, then yanked it open all the way, and the cold air hit him in the face. He bent to look in.

And saw nothing more than common everyday groceries: some vegetables, milk, eggs, bottles of beer. No meat at all, human or otherwise. Wild felt relief, and chagrin, and a hand on his shoulder.

He wheeled and the hand fell away, and he looked up at Lloyd Watterson's smiling face. Wild was tall, but Lloyd was taller, a blond man about six three with a baby face and ice-blue eyes and shoulders nearly as wide as the Frigidaire. He wore a kid's grin, on one side of his face. He also wore a white polo shirt and short white pants; he seemed about to say, "Tennis, anyone?"

But he said nothing, as a matter of fact; he just appraised Wild with ice-blue, somewhat vacant eyes. Wild now knew how it felt for a woman to be ogled—and it was not a good feeling.

Wild said, "Look, I can explain," knowing he couldn't, brain scrambling for some excuse, coming up with nothing, and Lloyd's hand reached out and grabbed the front of Wild's shirt and pitched the reporter like a horseshoe across the room.

Wild smacked into a white-tiled kitchen wall and slid down it like food flung there by a brat. His head, the back of his head, hit the tiled wall hard, and he blacked out.

When he woke up, he had no sense of how long he'd been out, and found himself tied in a chair in a blindingly white room.

He knew at once he was in the murder lab of the Mad Butcher of Kingsbury Run.

It was in the basement—the ceiling above showed the open beams and wiring of a basement, though painted out white, and a white-painted wooden stairway that rose to somewhere; the only window was painted out black. There was a white-enamel examining table and white metal medical storage cabinets and a counter with neatly arranged glass vials and tubes and beakers of substances of various colors. A large glass jug on the counter bore a label saying only: FORMALDEHYDE.

He felt his breath coming fast.

He turned his head and saw a large, stainless-steel refrigerator; it was humming. He saw his reflection in its door. Clutched by the horror of the moment, bound tightly to the chair, he looked at his own wide-eyed reflection, wondering what—who—was in cold storage, wondering if he would be there soon himself.

Then he shook his head, pulled himself together, telling himself, *You're not dead yet*, *you asshole*, and began straining at the ropes.

They were snug; not so snug as to cut off his circulation, but snug enough.

Feet came tromping down the wooden, white-painted stairs. He saw bare legs first, in tennis shorts; unlike the room, the legs weren't white. They were as suntanned as Viv's; and where the hell *was* Viv?

Wild hoped to Christ she wasn't in that goddamn refrigerator.

Lloyd Watterson was grinning. The white tennis outfit, with its short pants, was like some absurd doctor outfit made for a child. He walked over to the counter and opened a drawer and his hand rustled around amidst metal objects. Then he withdrew something. Held it up in his right hand, catching the electric light.

A cleaver.

He turned. Smiled pleasantly.

"I'm no butcher," he said. His voice was soft, almost gentle. "Don't believe what you've heard. . . ."

"Do you want to die?" Wild asked.

Lloyd started. "Of course not."

"Well, then cut me loose. There's cops all over the place, and if you kill me, they'll shoot you down. Do you know who I am?"

"Certainly. You're a reporter. It said so in your wallet, and I recognize your name from the paper."

"Then you know I work with Eliot Ness."

He thought that over, nodded.

"If you touch me," Wild said, "Ness and his men will shoot you down like a fucking animal."

Standing just to one side of Wild, holding up the cold polished steel of the cleaver, in which Wild's frantic reflection looked back at its source, Lloyd said, "I'm no butcher. This is a surgical tool. This is used for amputation, not butchery."

"I . . . I can see that."

"Why did you insist on calling me a butcher, then? In your stories?"

"Do you want to be caught, Lloyd?"

"Of course not. I'm no different than you. I serve the public in my own way."

"How . . . how do you figure that, Lloyd?" Wild's feet weren't tied to the chair; he could move his legs from the knees down . . . if Lloyd would just step around in front of him . . .

."I only dispose of the flotsam. Not to mention jetsam."

"Not to mention that."

"Tramps. Whores. Weeding out the stock. Survival of the fittest. Punishing the wicked. Experimentation. Does anyone mourn a guinea pig?"

"The guinea pig's mother?"

That stopped Lloyd short for a moment.

Wild filled the silence: "You make a lot of sense there, Lloyd. I think I did misjudge you. But I'm not flotsam *or* jetsam. I'm a reporter. I'm like you—I serve the people, in my way."

Lloyd thought about that.

"I could help you tell your story," Wild said. "So people would understand. So they'd know you aren't a—"

"I don't think so," he said, shaking his head no. "I don't think I have any choice in this."

He moved around the chair, stood just to one side of Wild, his expression troubled, the cleaver gripped tight in his right hand, held about breastbone level. Then his mouth tightened and his eyes narrowed as he made his decision.

Lloyd leaned forward and put his hand on Wild's head, grabbed him by the hair.

"You shouldn't have called me a butcher." he said.

"I'm sorry, Lloyd," Wild said, and kicked him in the balls.

Wild was surprised how much power he could muster, tied in a chair like that; but people manage some amazing feats when circumstances are extreme. And circumstances rarely got more extreme than being tied to a chair with a guy with a cleaver coming at you.

Only Lloyd wasn't coming at Wild now: now he was doubled over, and Wild stood, the chair strapped to his back, and butted Lloyd in the face.

Lloyd tumbled back, gripping his groin, cleaver tumbling from his hand, clattering harmlessly to the floor, his head leaning back, tears streaming down his cheeks, cords in his neck taut, his nose bleeding like a fountain, spilling onto the formerly spotless floor.

That's when the window shattered, and Vivian squeezed down in through, pretty legs first.

And she gave Wild the little gun to hold on Lloyd while she untied him, got the chair off his back.

Lloyd was still soiling the spotless floor with his blood, moaning like a sick child, when Wild and Viv went up the stairs and through the small neat house out into the sunny day, into a world that wasn't white and antiseptic and full of death.

She was helping Wild across the lawn, toward the Bugatti, when detective Curry came running up, gun in hand.

"What's going on?" he demanded. "What the hell's going on?"

Wild pointed back to the house. "Lloyd Watterson's the Butcher. He's in there—and I wouldn't . . ."

Curry went rushing up the front stairs, where they'd left the door open hurrying out, and into the house.

"I didn't see him come home," Viv told Wild breathlessly. "I'm sorry, so sorry—I was getting worried about you, and checking around back, I saw Lloyd's car was in his garage. He must've gone in one of the back ways. . . . God, I'm sorry, I'm sorry."

Wild couldn't think of anything to say to her. He just stood there, an arm around her, hugging her to him, for minutes that seemed like hours. Finally he said, "Damnit, give me that little popgun—he's been in there too long."

But as Wild was reluctantly approaching the house, Curry came out.

"There's nobody in there," he said, putting his own gun away. "And no car in the garage."

"You better put a call out on that sick son of a bitch," Wild said.

Curry looked pale, shaken. He glanced back at the bungalow and said, "If that isn't the murder lab, I'm Charlie McCarthy."

"Then *do* something!" Viv said.

"I've already done something," Curry said. "I radioed for the chief when I first spotted your fancy little car. You'll have to answer to him."

"He'll be grateful to us," Viv said, chin up.

"I don't think so," Curry said, looking past them.

The unmarked sedan with the EN-1 license plate screeched up to the curb, and an uncharacteristically rumpled-looking Eliot Ness sprang from behind the wheel and bolted across the weedy lawn toward them. His eyes were hard and ringed with lack of sleep; he was unshaven, pulled from the midst of a long day of interrogation.

"Explain," he demanded of all of them.

Viv flushed with anger, but Wild felt suddenly sheepish, as if he'd just noticed he'd stepped in something and was tracking it all the hell around. Curry filled his chief in.

"Maintain your watch," Ness told Curry. "In a few minutes I'll take this pair downtown and question them along with the rest of the vagrants." He looked sharply at Viv. "This is about the stupidest stunt you've pulled yet."

Her eyes flared; nostrils, too. "Well, you should've taken me seriously, you big sap!"

"I did take you seriously. That's why Lloyd Watterson is under twenty-four-hour surveillance. That's why I'm spending the day quietly showing his photograph to half the bums in creation. That's why my personal assistant is launching a full-scale investigation into the suspect. You two have tipped our hand, and most likely tainted the evidence."

"You're welcome," Wild smirked.

Ness glared at them both and motioned them toward the Bugatti.

When they were seated within, he told them, "Wait," lifting a forefinger like a lecturing parent. Then, typically unarmed, he advanced upon the house.

He was inside perhaps ten minutes; he was ashen when he came out. He walked to the driver's side of the Bugatti and reached in and touched Viv's shoulder.

"If anything had happened to you," he said, to Wild as much as to Viv, "I'd have killed you."

Then the little sports car, trailing after the sedan licensed EN-1, leaving Curry and his Ford behind, drew away from the Run, under the shadow of the black, hovering cloud of shantytown smoke.

18

Two days later, at eleven in the morning, in a warmly appointed suite on the fourteenth floor of the Hollenden Hotel, Eliot Ness sat at a massive library-style desk near a bay window overlooking Superior Avenue. Of simple boxlike design, with a broad, shiny surface, the dark wooden desk had a central, rectangular panel—where a blotter might normally be—that obviously concealed some device within. Electric wires and rubberized cable were connected to one lower side. To the right of where Ness sat was a comfortable-looking brown leather armchair. It was positioned forward somewhat, so that anyone sitting in it, while facing the same direction as Ness, would not be able to see him without a turn of the head.

Detective Albert Curry, his shirtsleeves rolled up, stood nearby and said, "Well, is that where you want it?"

Standing behind and to one side of Curry were two uniformed officers, who'd helped him haul the desk and chair over here from the Standard Building, where they'd borrowed it from federal friends of the safety director.

Ness, who sat and then sat again in the chair behind the desk, as if making a test, smiled tightly and said, "This is fine." And to the two uniformed men he said: "Thank you, boys. You can go."

They nodded and left.

Curry stood with folded arms and narrowed eyes and said, "What the hell is this all about?"

"I'm going to administer a lie detector test." He checked his watch. "In about half an hour."

There was a knock at the door.

"Should I get that?" Curry asked, and Ness nodded.

Bob Chamberlin, nattily attired as always, came in and went over to the desk and chair and said, "I see you're all moved in."

Ness nodded and gestured to a couch along the wall. "Sit down, Bob. Albert."

The two men did.

"We have an awkward situation," he said, coming out from behind the desk, "and for the time being it has to be . . . contained."

"Contained?" Curry asked.

Ness pulled up a straight-backed chair and sat across from them. "The mayor has made it clear that we need, at least for the time being, to keep the Watterson investigation under wraps. Now, what does Sergeant Merlo know about the events of the last several days?"

Curry shrugged. "Nothing. He got that lead from one of the shanytown vagrants that One-Armed Willie was doing time in the county jail in Cincinnati. He left by train Thursday afternoon to check it out. He got back this morning, I understand, but he doesn't work today."

"Albert," Ness said, "much as I dislike it, we need—for the present at least—to keep Merlo in the dark where Watterson is concerned. And every other active cop on the case as well. We're keeping this in-house—within the safety director's office."

"Well," Curry said, obviously somewhat confused, "I had to use several homicide detectives to gather some of what we put together yesterday. You did tell me to move quickly."

"Yes," Ness said, "and you've done very well. But only we three know of the significance—the seriousness—of the Watterson investigation."

"Chief, I don't understand . . . why are we . . ."

"Several reasons," Ness said. "First, I made a rather major mistake. When Vivian Chalmers gave me the lead on Lloyd Watterson, I immediately knew it was of possible, even probable, substance. But knowing how rash Viv can be, I didn't tell her so, playing down its importance. And at the same time, in no uncertain terms, I told her to stay out of the Butcher investigation."

"And naturally," Chamberlin said wryly, "that only served to light a fire under her."

Ness nodded wearily. "Yes. I should have known better than to tell that particular child to keep her hands off the cookie jar. And then she drafted Sam Wild to help her out, and he was just irritated enough at me, for not asking him along on the shantytown raid, to go along with her on that boneheaded fishing expedition."

"They *did* find the murder lab," Curry said.

"Did they?" Ness said. "We may never know. From what I saw, it certainly could have been—but the cabinets and refrigeration units I looked in were noticeably free of spare body parts. Of course, if we could get a crime-lab team in there . . . well. The family's lawyers are, for now at least, keeping us out."

"Can't we get a warrant?" Curry asked. "He did come after Wild with a cleaver, after all."

"Did he? That's Wild's word against Watterson's. Do you know what Watterson's stand is, on that little incident? Wild broke into his home—which is the truth, incidentally—and Lloyd only protected himself from an intruder. He overpowered Wild and tied him up until he could call the police. If anything, Sam Wild may face charges on breaking and entering, and assault—Lloyd is pretty bruised up around the face, I understand."

"But he threatened Wild with a goddamn *cleaver!*"

"Wild's word against Lloyd's. And, too, Wild is well-known to be 'unofficially' attached to my office. Evidence resulting from his intrusion into Watterson's home could be viewed as having been illegally obtained."

Chamberlin said, "Eliot, for Christ's sake—Wild isn't a cop, he's a reporter."

Ness smiled and shook his head. "Wild was there with Vivian Chalmers, remember—who for the last several years has been on the payroll of the city, via the safety director's office. No, gentlemen, we are screwed royal on this one. We don't even have enough yet to get a warrant to search that house."

Frustration walked across Curry's features. "But he *is* the Butcher."

"I think he is," Ness said flatly. "But much as I dislike it, we have to take his social standing into consideration."

Curry's face reddened. *"Why* in hell?"

"Because that social standing means the Wattersons can afford the highest-priced lawyers the country has to offer—we will have to mount a cast-iron case before we go to court on this one."

"There's another reason, too," Chamberlin said somberly, looking sideways at Curry.

"What?" Curry asked.

"The mayor," Ness said.

"The mayor?"

Chamberlin said, "Dr. Watterson is a personal friend of the mayor's. He was on the mayoral reelection campaign committee. He was a major contributor to His Honor's campaign coffers."

Curry smiled mirthlessly. "You're not saying the mayor would want us to cover this up, just because—"

"No!" Ness said. "No. We've just been requested to be careful to make sure the Wattersons are not unduly, unnecessarily embarrassed. By the press or otherwise. Until we are ready to charge Lloyd Watterson with murder, we have to keep this tightly—*tightly*—under wraps."

Curry's eyes locked with Ness's. Then the younger detective nodded and looked away.

"That," Ness said, standing, gesturing over to the desk, "is one of the reasons why I'm going to administer a lie detector test today, in this hotel suite, rather than take the suspect to Central headquarters and do so. It's why we borrowed the latest federal equipment."

"Also," Chamberlin said, "it's good procedure."

"How?" Curry said. Sarcasm faintly etched his tone.

"The federal approach to polygraph testing," Ness said, "keys off maintaining the composure of the person being questioned. That's why I wanted one of the federal polygraph 'desks,' where the testing apparatus is largely hidden. Intimidation by scientific gizmos only serves to screw up the testing." He gestured about the hotel suite. "This is ideal—pleasant, quiet surroundings for a friendly interview."

"And," Chamberlin said, "the fourteenth floor is empty at the moment. We're the only guests."

Ness checked his watch. "They'll be here momentarily."

"They?" Curry asked.

Ness nodded. "It's the father and son. I didn't call Lloyd, you see—I called the father. Dr. Clifford Watterson. I told him we had certain evidence agains his son in this matter and I wanted to give his son the opportunity to clear himself via lie detector. No lawyers, no police. Just myself, a polygraph, and two citizens cooperating unofficially."

"Well, hell," Curry said, "lie detector testing isn't infallible."

"I know it isn't," Ness said. "We might be dealing with a subject whose rationalization and self-deceit enables him to pass with flying colors. And I didn't mean to imply to Dr. Watterson that I was offering a deal, that I would drop the matter if his son passed the test."

"But," Chamberlin said with a nasty little smile, "if Dr. Watterson chose to interpret it that way, that's up to him."

Ness walked to a doorway not far from the brown leather chair by the lie-detector desk. "This is to the adjoining room. Keep the connecting door unlocked. If Lloyd Watterson *is* the Butcher—and we have reason to believe that to be the case—anything could happen in here. You are my backup, gents."

Curry nodded.

"Also," Ness continued, "I had this room wired. You're going to be listening in, next door, recording everything."

"It won't be admissible," Curry said. "The son of a bitch could confess, and we couldn't do a thing about it."

"Sure we could," Ness said. "If we have something of that nature, we can pressure the father into doing the right thing. Otherwise we'll make the tape public and watch all hell break loose."

Curry lifted an eyebrow and nodded.

Ness went to him and put a hand on the younger man's shoulder, smiling gently. "Don't despair. We're going to get this bastard. It won't take long to build a solid chain of circumstantial evidence—look what you've dug up in less than forty-eight hours. We'll get him."

Curry smiled faintly, nodded again, and went into the next room.

Chamberlin sighed and smiled. He stood close to Ness and said, "The kid's an idealist, Eliot."

"I know," Ness said. "And I agree with him one hundred percent."

"We work for the mayor," Chamberlin reminded him.

"Yes," Ness said, "but we mostly work for the people. I'll put up with this political bullshit only so long as it doesn't interfere with *that*."

There was a sharp knock at the door.

Chamberlin scurried into the adjoining room, and Ness went to answer the door.

Dr. Watterson's darkly handsome features were a mask: if any emotion had touched him upon hearing his son was suspected of being the worst mass murderer in midwestern memory, it was not apparent. Tall, sturdy, dressed impeccably in a three-piece brown silk suit, Watterson offered his hand and a small polite smile.

Ness shook the hand and gave a polite smile in return. For a moment he thought Watterson hadn't brought Lloyd, but Lloyd was there, standing behind his father, hiding, a little boy's smile dancing on his lips. Ness felt suddenly like a grade-school principal.

They stepped inside. Lloyd was equally well-dressed, though his suit was undertaker black. The area around his nose, beneath his eyes, was bruised from the battle with Wild. He said, "Hello, Eliot," and gave his hand to Ness. Ness shook the powerful, clammy hand and studied the man's twitching smile.

"I appreciate your giving us a chance to clear this matter up," Dr. Watterson said, following Ness into the suite.

"Well, I appreciate you and your son giving us the chance to do so," Ness said, and smiled in a businesslike manner. He gestured to the sofa where minutes before Chamberlin and Curry had sat.

Ness again sat in the straight-backed chair. He looked at the father and son and noted that, apart from their size, there was no family resemblance between dark doctor father and fair failed-doctor son.

"We have a certain amount of circumstantial evidence," Ness began, speaking to the father, "suggesting

hat your son may have some knowledge pertaining to the
ongoing investigation of the so-called Mad Butcher of
Kingsbury Run."

Dr. Watterson's smile was a twitch, too, but not a
nervous one. "I'm well aware of the case, Mr. Ness. You
know very well I've been involved in the pathological
workups on several of the victims."

"Yes. I just feel we should begin at the beginning. I
want both you and your son to understand why we find it
necessary to trouble you with this. I don't have to tell you of
the level of concern in the community over these crimes."

"You certainly do not," Dr. Watterson said.

"Also," Ness said diplomatically, "we have a report of
violence at your son's home yesterday."

"I told you on the phone," the doctor said curtly, "what
my son's position is on that matter. We're discussing with
our attorneys whether or not to bring charges against Mr.
Wild and Miss Chalmers."

Ness nodded slowly. "I can understand that. That
might be appropriate. However, it might simply serve to
open an embarrassing can of worms."

Dr. Watterson's patronizing mask slipped just a bit; and
Ness noticed that the man's eyes did have some spiderweb-
bing of red. Lloyd seemed to be trying to suppress the urge
to giggle.

"There can be no doubt," Ness said, "that your son is
living in a building once used as a doctor's surgery."

"We don't deny that," Dr. Watterson said. "It's where I
first worked."

"Yes. And, having been involved with the Butcher
investigation, you know that we have been searching for a
'murder lab,' for want of a better term, somewhere in the
areas adjoining the Run. Now, and I'm afraid this is a little
embarrassing, Dr. Watterson . . . but I've done some
checking with the fire wardens."

Dr. Watterson frowned. Lloyd smiled.

"You see, I wondered how it could be that my search of
those areas by fire wardens, accompanied by homicide
detectives, might have missed such an obvious 'murder lab'
candidate. I have since learned that you own a number of
properties, in addition to your former residence cum

surgery, rooming houses, all of which are in the less-tha
prosperous areas bordering Kingsbury Run. I have als
learned that Lloyd, as the manager of your business affair
is in charge of those properties; that he calls regularly upo
the landladies tending those properties; that he keep
rooms at those properties where he often stays und
assumed names."

Dr. Watterson's pale face became paler. Lloyd was n
longer smiling.

"When the fire wardens were canvassing Centra
Avenue," Ness said, "one of them received a call from you
Dr. Watterson. Do you recall making it?"

"I do," Dr. Watterson said stiffly. "I assured the fir
warden that my properties were well-maintained and not i
need of inspection."

"You asked that these properties not be disrupted b
the rather thorough searches other buildings in the are
were being subjected to," Ness said.

"Yes."

"And the fire warden with whom you spoke agreed
take care of it."

"Yes he did."

"How much did you pay him?"

"That's an impertinent question."

"Well, perhaps it is. The fire warden in question ha
admitted complying with your wishes—apparently yo
dropped some big names, if not dollars—and I'm incline
not to 'subject' this city employee to further investigatior
since he's cooperating with us. Why did you make that cal
Dr. Watterson? Why did you make that request?"

"Well . . . I . . ."

"Your son asked you to. Didn't he?"

Dr. Watterson said nothing. Then he glanced at hi
son, who smiled nervously.

"Yes, he did," the doctor said. "But it seemed to m
then, and seems to me now, a reasonable request. Th
searches were an invasion of privacy and a disruption c
business."

"Fair enough," Ness said, nodding again. "But yo
should also know that a number of shantytown denizen
have identified Lloyd's picture, confirming that he wen

among them under an assumed name, posing as one of them."

Dr. Watterson gazed unblinkingly at Ness. "My son's avocation is sociological research."

"Fine. But I think you can understand that we have the disturbing beginnings of a possible case against your son. Or at least the suggestion that in his 'sociological research' in these slum areas, he has encountered evidence that, for whatever reason, he's withheld."

The father looked at the son again. The son had a blank, vaguely sad expression, as if Ness's evidence—circumstantial though it was—had worn him down.

"So," Dr. Watterson said. "You're suggesting my son submit to a lie detector test."

"Yes," Ness said.

The doctor narrowed his eyes. "Perhaps it would be a good way to put this ridiculous assertion to rest."

Ness looked at Lloyd and smiled pleasantly. "What do you think, Lloyd? You've been strangely silent about all this."

Lloyd brightened. "Why, Eliot, I think it's a splendid idea. But, uh . . . why don't we get some lunch first? We can chat a little about this situation."

Ness shook his head gently no. "I don't really think dismemberments are proper dinner-table conversation, Lloyd."

"Well, I'd just like you to explain the lie detector to me. I'm interested in science, after all. I don't intend to submit to something that I don't understand."

"I don't expect you to," Ness said.

"I only believe in the scientific," Lloyd said. "The proven. Why should I put my life on the line for something pseudopsychic? This smacks of mind reading and fortune-telling to me."

"All right." Ness said. He looked at his watch. "It *is* noon."

Dr. Watterson said, "We could go downstairs to the dining room. Perhaps it would do us all good to talk like civilized people."

Ness had thought he'd been extremely civilized, considering that in these past minutes he'd lost whatever shred of doubt he might have had about Lloyd's guilt. The big blond young man was the Butcher of Kingsbury Run. Ness would have staked his life on it.

"Why don't I call down to room service," Ness said, wanting to keep the meeting contained to this room, where it was being taped. "We can eat up here."

That seemed agreeable to all, and Ness ordered three steak plates.

"They'll be up soon," he said, and returned to his straight-backed chair. "Why don't you let me explain to you some of the principles of the polygraph, Lloyd."

Lloyd shrugged. "Why not?"

Ness explained that the polygraph was a scientific instrument, stressing the word "scientific," measuring physiological reactions of the body to emotion and stress.

"These measurements," Ness said, "are provided by monitoring blood pressure, heartbeat, and changes in body chemistry, as reflected by an instrument that records the electrodermal changes in the skin."

Lloyd sat forward through this, clearly interested. He said, "I agree that emotions do affect the body—fear, anger, grief, joy, they can all make the heart pump more rapidly. But I wouldn't think *lying* would."

"The mental process of lying," Ness said, "upsets the emotional balance ever so slightly—but not so slightly that the polygraph can't pick up on it."

"It sounds improbable," Lloyd said.

"Here. Let me show you."

Ness stood and gestured Lloyd over to the polygraph desk. Lloyd seemed the kind of subject who needed to understand the machine before submitting to it, and that was fine with Ness. He removed the central, blotterlike cover and revealed a rectangle of light brown metal with many dials and knobs, as if on an elaborate ham radio outfit, next to which was a roll of paper cross-ruled in brown ink in chart fashion, about five inches wide. Three slender arms, tipped with red ink, extended from the brown metal panel to the chart paper.

Ness pointed to the nearest of the three slender arms. "This stylus records heart action." He reached across the desk and threw a switch. A motor hummed; machinery whispered into action. The chart paper began to slowly move, as each stylus point, though motionless, traced continuous red lines.

"The middle stylus," Ness said, "connects with the electrodermal unit."

"What does *skin* have to do with it?" Lloyd asked, smiling smugly, as if proud of knowing what "dermal" referred to.

"Because liars tend to sweat, Lloyd—and that varies the conductivity of saline-impregnated electrodes placed in contact with the skin."

"Oh. And this final stylus?"

"It monitors breathing. The emotions affect breathing, just as they do the heart."

"What would happen," Lloyd asked slyly, "if you encountered someone in complete control of his emotions?"

Ness gave him a broad smile. "Well, Lloyd—I suppose he'd beat the machine, now wouldn't he?"

Lloyd smiled. He turned to his father. "I'm not afraid of this thing."

The father nodded solemnly.

A knock at the door announced room service, and the steak luncheons were brought in and trays were set up, the three men sitting to their meals and eating them in near silence. Neither Ness nor Dr. Watterson ate much at all; but Lloyd, brandishing his shiny stainless-steel steak knife like a scalpel, ate his rare steak quickly, greedily, cheerfully.

Lloyd dabbed his mouth with a napkin and his smile was very white in his suntanned, bruised face. He stood and rubbed his hands together as if about to tackle some challenging project for dessert.

"Let's get it done," he said. "Let's put these silly notions about the 'Mad Doctor of Kingsbury Run' behind us." He turned and looked at his father. "Right, Father?"

Dr. Watterson, still seated behind his tray, his meal practically untouched, nodded gravely.

"Remove your coat, Lloyd," Ness said, and Lloyd did. "Roll your sleeve up, your right sleeve, clear to the shoulder." Lloyd did that, too.

"Now take a seat in that easy chair, and relax. Just relax."

Lloyd settled into the brown leather chair, hands o either arm of it, and his smile once again was that of naughty child. Ness wrapped a cloth and rubber bandag similar to a doctor's blood-pressure apparatus, snug around Lloyd's bare arm above the elbow. Then h positioned a rubber cylinder, capped with shiny metal either end, across Lloyd's chest, fastening it in place. Lloyd's left hand, with small tonglike clamps, he attache saline-dampened sponge-pads on the palm and below th knuckles.

Then Ness took his position behind the desk. He s with one hand poised near the dials and knobs, the othe with pencil near the slowly moving chart paper.

"Now, Lloyd, I'm going to ask you questions that ca be answered yes or no. In fact, I'd like you to limit yourse to those responses."

"All right."

"You mean, 'yes.'"

Lloyd grinned. "Yes."

"All of my questions will be asked only in relation the events under investigation. Do you understand?"

"Yes."

"Now I have to establish a normal level of response, s we're going to perform an experiment—with your interes in science and medicine, I think you'll find this interesting Is that all right?"

"Yes."

"It's going to allow me to show you the capability of th machine. All right?"

"Yes."

"We're going to do a little card trick. Actually, Lloyd you're going to do it."

Ness withdrew a deck of playing cards from his sui coat pocket. He handed the cards to Lloyd, who seeme somewhat surprised, but accepted them.

Dr. Watterson seated himself on the couch an watched as if hypnotized.

"Now, Lloyd," Ness said, "I want you to select a card Don't show it to me."

Lloyd, grinning goofily, did so.

"I'm going to ask you some questions about your card. And no matter what the true answer is, I want you to answer 'no.' Do you understand?"

"Yes."

"You're to answer 'no,' in each instance. Understood?"

"Yes."

"Is it a red card?"

"No."

"Is it a black card?"

"No."

"Is it the number ten?"

"No."

"Is the card below the number ten?"

"No."

"Is the card above the number ten?"

"No."

"Is it a face card?"

"No."

"Is it a spade?"

"No."

"Is it a club?"

"No."

"Is it a jack?"

"No."

"Is it a queen?"

"No."

"Is it a king?"

"No."

"Is it an ace?"

"No."

"All right, Lloyd. The experiment's over. Incidentally, that card you're holding is the jack of spades."

Lloyd's mouth dropped open and his eyes were wide and round. He swallowed dryly. His hand, holding the card, was trembling. He looked helplessly at his father, showing his father the card, which was indeed the jack of spades.

Then Lloyd stood up, tearing away the wires and pads and cloths and tubes attached to him, rising like the waking Gulliver caught in the net of the little people.

Ness stood and said, "Lloyd . . ."

Lloyd made an animal sound, tearing himself free; he lurched away from the brown leather chair and dove for the tray where he'd eaten the rare steak and grabbed the shiny steak knife. He stood there, between his father, who had risen from the couch, and Ness, who had come around the desk—stood there with the juice-stained knife tight in his fist and the expression of a cornered beast distorting his features.

Then he hurtled toward Ness, steak knife raised like a dagger.

Ness stepped back but Lloyd was fast and on top of him. The hand with the steak knife slashed and tore Ness's coat sleeve and shirt, without tearing flesh, and Ness got his hand around Lloyd's wrist and with a jujitsu twist sent the knife tumbling from Lloyd's fingers.

But Lloyd's weight and strength pressed into Ness, pushed him backward, into the desk, across the polygraph, the arms of the stylus digging into Ness's back as Lloyd climbed on him, hands clawing viciously at Ness, at his face, Ness trying to bat the hands away, trying to get his own balance so he could use Lloyd's weight against him.

Then they were toppling behind the desk, onto the floor, and Lloyd sent a massive fist crashing toward Ness's face, but Ness slipped to one side and Lloyd's fist smashed into carpet; with an animal cry Lloyd lifted Ness by the lapels and hurled him against the window and glass crashed and the air of the outside was on him and even without looking Ness knew the street was fourteen stories below him.

Then Lloyd suddenly wasn't on him anymore, and Ness almost toppled out the window from lack of being held, and braced his hands on the sides of the window cutting his right palm on the broken glass.

He dropped back into the room and saw that Dr. Watterson had pulled Lloyd away, was pulling him from behind, by both arms. Lloyd, his face red and distorted, was squirming under his father's grasp, but the father was strong and Ness took advantage of it and swung a hard right hand that seemed to take half of Lloyd's face off.

Lloyd crumpled, the fight gone out of him, and began to weep; he tried to talk, but couldn't.

His father, holding on to him, but more gently now

more holding him up than holding him, said, "I'm afraid you've broken his jaw."

Angry, Ness ran to the adjoining door and flung it open.

The connecting room was empty. No Curry. No Chamberlin. What the hell . . . ?

He went back and picked up the steak knife Lloyd had dropped, put it back on one of the trays. He found a clean napkin and wrapped his bleeding palm with it. Lloyd was sitting on the floor now, weeping, and his father was crouched beside him, examining the son's jaw clinically.

"What do you think now, Dr. Watterson?" Ness said.

"We'll handle this," he said. Very softly. "We'll handle this."

Lloyd was trying to say something, but Ness couldn't understand what it was.

"Eliot! What in the hell happened in here?"

Ness turned and Chamberlin, followed by Curry, both of them stunned by the disheveled area by the window, entered quickly from the connecting room.

"Where the hell were you two?" Ness demanded.

Chamberlin shrugged. "We heard you say you were going out for lunch. We figured we better get down to the dining room before you did."

"We went down there," Curry said, "but you never showed."

"No kidding. Well, I hope you boys had a nice lunch. Mine was medium rare." Ness nodded to them to go back in the adjoining room, which they did, closing the door behind them.

Ness walked over to Dr. Watterson, but it was obviously not a time for further discussion. The father was cradling the son in his lap, stroking his head, trying to comfort him. Lloyd was still trying to speak, without any success; between the broken jaw, and crying like a baby, Lloyd just couldn't manage it.

Then suddenly Ness got it: he figured out what word it was that Lloyd was trying to form.

"Father."

And Dr. Watterson must've understood it at the same time, because he began to cry, but not like a baby.

Like a father.

19

The following Monday, midafternoon, Sam Wild strolled into a dimly lit, hole-in-the-wall bar called Mickey's, on Short Vincent Avenue, not far from City Hall. He had been told by Wanda, the safety director's secretary, that her boss might be there.

And indeed he was, in a back booth, sitting quietly cradling a Scotch in two hands, with a slightly droopy-eyed look that told Wild his friend was half in the bag. Sitting across from Ness was Sergeant Martin Merlo, drinking nothing, speaking rather animatedly (for Merlo, especially), gesturing as if to make the quiet, quietly drinking man opposite pay him some heed.

Wild stood by them and said, "If I'm interrupting something, fellas . . ."

Ness smiled faintly and said, "Not at all," and Wild slid in on the same side of the booth as the safety director. Merlo, whose solemn face seemed even more tortured than usual, clearly did not relish the reporter joining them, but was, after all, outranked.

Then Merlo, with a barely discernible sigh of disgust, leaned forward and continued to plead his case. "This is no time to pull back on the investigation," he said. "We have the best clue we've had in four years."

"Which clue is that?" Ness said.

"The quilt!"

Merlo was referring, Wild knew, to the many-colored, gingham-patched quilt in which had been wrapped the torso of the girl found in the lakefront dump.

"We picked up Elmer Cummings today," Merlo was saying, "a fifty-six-year-old junk man. We located him through a tip from a barber who saw the newspaper photo of the quilt and identified it as one he gave Cummings when the junk man came around his house, looking for rags."

Ness said nothing.

Merlo, obviously exasperated by the lack of response, pressed on. "Cummings says he sold the quilt to the Scoville Rag and Paper Company. We interviewed the owner, a William Blusinsky, and his six employees, today."

"And?"

"Well, they say the quilt may have been stolen from a large quantity of material delivered to the warehouse last week."

"Do Blusinksy and any of his employees have criminal records?"

Merlo's confidence faded. "No. They seem to be respectable workingmen."

Ness sipped his Scotch. "Sounds like another blind alley to me. Any luck tracing the girl's gold filigree ring?"

Merlo stared bleakly at the tabletop before him. "No," he said. He looked up. "But it's early yet."

"And you've established that One-Armed Willie is not a viable suspect."

Merlo nodded. "He was in various jails at various of the key times. He's clean."

"What about those two shantytown suspects? 'Ben,' and the guy with the jackknife who tried to jackroll Curry?"

"We haven't ascertained the identities of either— although Coroner Gerber feels the man whose remains were found in the dump fits Ben's description. Blond, five six, broad-chested, and so on."

"More blind alleys."

Merlo's expression was pained. "I know, Mr. Ness, but that's no reason to pull the plug on the investigation."

"I'm not pulling the plug on the investigation." Ness swirled Scotch in its glass, studied the dark liquid. "I'm just returning it to the homicide department. You're still assigned to the case, I understand."

"Yes, but we had greater resources with your office behind the investigation. Detective Curry and I were developing into a good team. Now, damnit . . ."

"What?"

"He seems almost . . . evasive. Doesn't even want to talk about the case."

Ness finished his Scotch. He waved for a barmaid to come over and ordered another, a double.

Then he said to Merlo, "It's my feeling that the case is closed."

"Not officially . . ."

"No. But after examining the evidence carefully, I feel the Butcher is, in all likelihood, out of commission."

Merlo's frustration was palpable. "You're not serious in saying that you think Dolezal was the Butcher . . ."

"It's the consensus of opinion," Ness said with an easy shrug. "The coroner has confirmed that all of the victims whose remains were discovered after Dolezal's death were very likely murdered before his death."

"That's an iffy assumption," Merlo said, "and anyway, those bodies were dumped *after* his death." Merlo paused to let that sink in. Then he said: "It was evidence to that effect that led us to raiding shantytown."

"And did we find the Butcher? Or any significant evidence of him or his possible whereabouts?"

Merlo sighed. Swallowed. "No," he admitted.

Ness sipped his Scotch.

"Well, if Dolezal really was the Butcher," Merlo said, "then he must have had an accomplice, who dumped the bodies later."

Ness seemed to consider that for a moment, then nodded. "Perhaps you'll turn that accomplice up."

"I mean to," Merlo said tightly, and slid out of the booth and turned to go.

"Sergeant," Ness said.

Merlo glanced back, his features hard.

"You've done excellent work. I admire your dedication."

Merlo's expression softened, slightly. "Thank you, sir."

"Good hunting." Ness raised his glass to Merlo.

Merlo smiled humorlessly, briefly, turned, and went up the narrow aisle out of the gloomy bar into sunshine.

"Only there is no accomplice," Wild said, moving to the other side of the booth, where Merlo had been sitting.

Ness sipped his Scotch.

"You oughta thank me, friend," Wild said pleasantly, lighting up a Lucky.

"What for?"

"For not busting out laughing when you said Frank Dolezal was the Butcher."

Ness smiled faintly again, swirled the Scotch in his glass, then drank some more, not sipping this time.

"Eliot. I've seen you drink plenty of times. But I don't remember seeing you drink before six o'clock. Not like this anyway."

"I gave myself the afternoon off."

"Well, I guess that's one of the fringe benefits of being the boss."

Ness winced. "Yes. I guess it is."

Wild gestured with cigarette in hand, making trails of smoke. "We're all alone back here. You care to tell me what the hell is going on?"

Ness locked eyes with Wild. "What do you know about it?"

Wild shrugged. "I know I was called in this morning by the publisher—not the city editor, not the managing editor, not the editor in chief—the goddamn publisher. And I was told not to write word one about Lloyd Watterson."

Ness smiled the faint smile again and looked away.

"Why hasn't he been arrested, Eliot? Why is Merlo still working the Butcher case without any knowledge of Lloyd Watterson at all?"

"Lloyd Watterson," Ness said evenly, "was committed to an asylum for the insane this morning."

"What? Where?"

"In Dayton. Maximum security. Under twenty-four-hour lock and key."

"Jesus."

"Can you think of a better place for him?"

"Sure! Death fucking row!"

Ness shrugged with his eyebrows. "Good point."

Wild sighed and stabbed out his smoke. "I need a drink myself."

He went up to the bar and got himself a boilermaker and returned to the booth.

Then he said, "So it finally came due, huh?"

"What did?"

"The bill from the mayor's financial angels."

Ness said nothing.

"The slush fund, the country club, the boathouse . . . all those nice perquisites. I told you they wouldn't come free, Eliot."

"Yes, you did."

The two men sat and quietly drank.

Then Ness said, "The mayor asked it as a favor. It was no backroom meeting, Sam. There was really nothing that smacked of . . ."

"Being touchable?"

Ness smiled again, wryly this time. "Nicely put. But then you reporters do have a way with words. What about you, Sam? Are you going to blow the whistle?"

"Are you kidding? When the publisher asks a favor, he isn't asking. And I never did have a conscience."

"The important thing is we got the Butcher."

"Yeah. We did at that."

They toasted glasses.

Wild grinned. "Ha! This is a sweet irony."

"What is?"

"Here I sit with the biggest scoop of my life, and I can't write it up. There you are, old publicity-hound Ness, cracked the biggest case of your career, something to make old Scarface Al look like a footnote in your scrapbook, and you can't make the bust. You can't take the credit."

Ness smiled on one side of his face. "It's called poetic justice, Sam."

"Where I come from it's called getting screwed, but what the hell."

Ness laughed silently.

"Look," Wild said, "you shouldn't feel bad about this. We did get the bastard. He's out of circulation, and that's what counts."

Ness nodded.

"It might be different," Wild said, "if the city believed the Butcher were still at large. But with Dolezal as a scapegoat, that really takes a load off. Lloyd is getting denied *his* 'glory,' too, you know. You don't have to live with the thought of the good people of Cleveland looking over their collective shoulder, wondering if sometime the Butcher's gonna pop back out at 'em again."

Ness nodded.

"Don't let it get to you," Wild said with a dismissive wave. "What's the harm in it?"

"The harm," Ness said tightly, the rage bubbling under his apparent placidity suddenly evident, "is that good cops like Merlo are going to keep working this case, for months, possibly years, wasting their time and the taxpayers' money, when their safety director knows they are on a fool's errand. The harm is that a good cop like Albert Curry has to live with looking the other way on something that bothers him morally."

"It's called being a grown-up," Wild said with a smirk. "Curry will get over it."

"It will change him. Not for the better."

"Is it going to change you, Eliot?"

Ness said nothing. His jaw muscles clenched and unclenched. His eyes seemed cold, yet haunted, eyes that had seen too much. He sipped his Scotch and said pleasantly, "Of course maybe Sergeant Merlo will find out about Lloyd Watterson."

"You think so?"

"He's dedicated and he's obsessive. Someday, a week from now, a month from now, a year from now . . . Merlo may come lay Lloyd Watterson at the city's doorstep. I don't think Merlo gives a good goddamn about social standing and politics and such assorted bullshit."

Wild drank some beer. "You might be right. Does it worry you?"

"No," Ness said. Then he smiled. "It's kind of nice knowing your conscience is out there somewhere, working for you."

"Better your conscience at large than the Mad Butcher of Kingsbury Run."

They drank in silence for a while.

"Sam . . . are you still seeing Viv?"

"Yeah," he said, firing up another Lucky. "I don't know if it's going to amount to anything serious or not . . . we're not exactly from the same side of the tracks, you know."

Ness studied his Scotch. "One of us is going to have to tell her."

"About Lloyd escaping to the madhouse, you mean?"

"Yes. Do you want me to?"

"No," Wild said. "That's a cross I can bear."

"Think she'll keep quiet about it?"

"Oh, yeah. She's from that world. She understands it."

"I'm glad somebody does," Ness said.

And he ordered another double.

Outside, the sun was shining, on rich and poor alike—even over Kingsbury Run, where the ashes of two shantytown settlements were smoldering still; but it was dark by the time Wild and Ness stumbled out of Mickey's. Wild caught a cab. Detective Curry was waiting at the curb in an unmarked car, waiting to drive his chief home to the castlelike boathouse on Clifton Lagoon.

A Tip of
the Fedora

As was the case with my previous Eliot Ness novel, *The Dark City* (1987), I could not have written this book without the support and advice of my friend and research associate George Hagenauer. George and I made a research trip to Cleveland, where we visited many of the sites of the action in this novel and stopped in for a session at the Western Reserve Historical Society, where the Ness papers are kept. George made several additional trips alone and visited (and took reference photos of) virtually all of the death sites in the Mad Butcher of Kingsbury Run case.

We are both grateful to the helpful staffs at the Historical Society, City Hall municipal reference library, and Cleveland Public Library, and we wish to especially thank Karen Martines and Joe Novak.

While much of the research for this book was culled from the files of various Cleveland newspapers of the day, several remarkable in-depth articles provided valuable background material and insight into the Kingsbury Run slayings. These include "The Mad Butcher of Queensbury Run" by A. W. Pezet and Bradford Chambers in their book, *Greatest Crimes of the Century* (1954); "The Head Hunter of Kingsbury Run" by William Ritt in Oliver Weld Bayer's book, *Cleveland Murders* (1947); and "The Mad Butcher of Kingsbury Run" by James Purvis in his book *Great Unsolved Mysteries* (1978). Also helpful was the "Mad Butcher" entry in *Open Files* (1983) by Jay Robert Nash, and an article in *Daring Detective* (December 1949), "Cleveland's Jack the Ripper," by Seymour J. Ettman. Useful, too, was a 1960, ten-part Cleveland *News* series, "Where is the Mad Butcher?" by Howard Beaufait.

The most detailed nonfiction account of the Ness role

in the Mad Butcher case is a twelve-page chapter in *Four Against the Mob* (1961) by Oscar Fraley, coauthor (with Ness) of *The Untouchables* (1957). Unfortunately, Fraley was asked by his publishers to fictionalize names and dates, and, apparently at the behest of Ness's widow, he tended to present Ness only in the most favorable light. All of this has made his book as frustrating as it is valuable as a research tool.

However, I have increasingly found in my research that Fraley's book is a dependable source. There have been those who doubted Fraley's claim that Ness solved the Butcher case (which remains officially unsolved in Cleveland police records); and I was one of the doubters myself, until I examined the Ness papers and scrapbooks and held in my own hands the various crank postcards and letters apparently sent to Ness over a period of years by the institutionalized Butcher, just as reported by Fraley in his book. The apparent Butcher signs himself as "your paranoidal nemesis" and as an M.D., and addresses the cards to Ness variously as "Eliot Direct-Um Ness" and "Eliot (Head Man) Ness." Vague but distinct death threats characterize the postcards; strange clippings are pasted to them: "Handbook for Poisoners," one says; another is an ad with a "pansy" plant whose petals seem to form a skull-like shape. Another shows a man in a cowboy hat sticking out his tongue, and yet another is a scene from the film *Riot in Cell Block 11* in which two prisoners clutch prison bars in crazed anger (one of the actors shown in the clipping, oddly enough, is Neville Brand, who would later play Al Capone in *The Untouchables* TV series).

I did not know what these items were, at first, as examined them in the safe confines of the librarylike Western Reserve Historical Society. But when I realized was holding missives likely written by the Mad Butcher of Kingsbury Run to Eliot Ness (and saved by him!), I dropped them as if they were on fire; and I did not sleep worth a damn that night in my room at the Hollender House hotel.

Incidentally, if Fraley is to be believed, a Hollender meeting between the Butcher and Ness, not unlike the one described here, did take place—right down to the backup men in the adjoining room going down for lunch and leaving Ness unwittingly alone with the dangerous suspect and his steak knife. (It is my assumption—and the indication of other sources—that the meeting involved someone else other than just Ness and the suspect; my speculation, of course, is that that someone was the suspect's prominent father.)

According to Fraley, the Butcher died while institutionalized—apparently in the mid-1950s.

Despite its extensive basis in history, this is a work of fiction, and some liberties have been taken with the facts; the remarkably eventful life of Eliot Ness defies the necessarily tidy shape of a novel, and for that reason I have again compressed time and used composite characters.

Some characters, such as Sam Wild and Albert Curry, are wholly fictional, although they do have real-life counterparts. Wild represents the many reporter friends of Ness, particularly Clayton Fritchey of the *Press* (who, like the fictional Wild, was assigned to cover Ness full-time) and Ralph Kelly of the *Plain Dealer*. Sheriff O'Connell and his deputy Robert McFarlin are fictional, but the rivalry between the sheriff's department and the safety director's police is not—including the sheriff's unwanted intrusion into the Mad Butcher case. The depiction herein of the suspicious circumstances surrounding the possible "third-degree" questioning, and alleged suicide, of Frank Dolezal (his real name) is based on fact.

Sergeant Martin Merlo is a composite character, based largely on two dedicated homicide detectives, Martin Zalewski and Peter Merylo. Merylo never gave up on the case and spent much of his spare time, until his death in 1959, searching for the killer. He believed the Butcher to be responsible for torso killings in other American communities, including perhaps the most famous torso slaying of all, the Black Dahlia.

Among the historical figures included here under their real names are Coroner Samuel Gerber, Chief George Matowitz, Mayor Harold Burton, and Executive Assistant Safety Director Robert Chamberlin. While their portraits herein are drawn from research, those portraits should be viewed as fictionalized. In some cases, a single newspaper "personality profile" provided the basis for my characterization, so I request that these depictions not be viewed a definitive.

Vivian Chalmers and Evelyn MacMillan are fictiona characters with real-life counterparts.

The real names (when known) of the actual Butche victims have been used, as have been the details surround ing their deaths (with some minor, occasional fictiona reshaping).

Both Lloyd Watterson and his father are fictiona characters. They would seem, obviously, to have factua counterparts.

The polygraph sequence was suggested by material i Men Against Crime (1946), John J. Floherty; Crimina Investigation (1974), Paul B. Weston and Kenneth M. Well and Basic Law Enforcement (1972), Harry Caldwell.

A number of books proved helpful in depicting th world of the hobo, including The Hobo (1923), Nel Anderson; The Second Oldest Profession (1931), Dr. Ben L Reitman; Sister of the Road: The Autobiography of Box Car Bertha (1937), Dr. Ben L. Reitman; and Goo Company (1982), Douglas Harper. Always helpful are tw first-rate "oral histories" of the Depression, Hard Time (1970), Studs Terkel, and First Person America (1980), An Banks.

Numerous books on mass murderers, specifically seria killers, were consulted, but two in particular deserv singling out: Mass Murder (1985), Jack Levin and James A Fox; and Buried Dreams: Inside the Mind of a Serial Kille (1986), by Tim Cahill with Russ Ewing, which deals wit John Wayne Gacy, upon whom Lloyd Watterson is pat terned to a degree.

I continue to find extremely helpful the excellen article on Ness by Peter Jeddick, collected in his Cleveland Where the East Coast Meets the Midwest (1980). Anothe basic tool is the Ness chapter in Cleveland: The Best Kep Secret by George E. Condon, who recently published a fin Ness article, "The Last American Hero," in Clevelan Magazine (August 1987). Other Ness material has bee drawn from Cleveland: Confused City on a Seesaw (1976 by Philip W. Porter, who—like Condon—was a Plai

Dealer reporter who knew Ness. Also consulted was the unpublished article written in 1983 for the Cleveland Police Historical Society, "Eliot Ness: A Man of a Different Era," Anthony J. Coyne and Nancy L. Hubbert.

Also, I continue to read and reread the unpublished, twenty-two-page article written by Ness himself on his Capone days, provided to his coauthor/ghost Oscar Fraley as background material for *The Untouchables*. It remains a valuable link to this private public man.

I perhaps should note that this novel has its roots in a short story of mine, "The Strawberry Teardrop," published by Mysterious Press in the first Private Eye Writers of America anthology, *The Eyes Have It* (1984) edited by Robert J. Randisi. In that story my detective hero Nathan Heller (who made an appearance in *The Dark City*) fulfills the role that Sam Wild plays in the final section of this novel. Readers who are following both the Nathan Heller and Eliot Ness stories may find this continuity glitch troublesome; I apologize to them and can say only that the needs of this novel superseded any such concerns.

I would like to thank my editor, Coleen O'Shea, for her tough-mindedness and dedication, as well as her assistant Becky Cabaza, who has been unfailingly helpful; and my agent, Dominick Abel, whose advice and friendship I value.

And, as always, the final tip of the fedora goes to my best critic and best friend: my wife, Barbara Collins, whose love, help, and support makes the work possible.

ABOUT THE AUTHOR

MAX ALLAN COLLINS is the author of over twent
novels in the mystery/suspense field, including *True Detec*
tive, a historical novel featuring Chicago private detectiv
Nathan Heller. The book is the winner of the Private Ey
Writers of America award for Best Hardcover Novel. I
sequel, *True Crime*, was nominated for the same award
One of the top writers in the comics field, Collins script
the *Dick Tracy* newspaper strip and such comic books a
Batman and his own creation *Ms. Tree*. He lives in Iow
with his wife and son.